RAINSHADOW ROAD

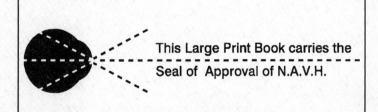

RAINSHADOW ROAD

LISA KLEYPAS

THORNDIKE PRESS

A part of Gale, Cengage Learning

Detroit • New York • San Francisco • New Haven, Conn • Waterville, Maine • London

Thorndike Press® Large Print Core.
The text of this Large Print edition is unabridged.
Other aspects of the book may vary from the original edition.
Set in 16 pt. Plantin.

LIBRARY OF CONGRESS CATALOGING-IN-PUBLICATION DATA

Kleypas, Lisa.
    Rainshadow road / by Lisa Kleypas.
        pages ; cm. — (Thorndike Press large print core)
        ISBN 978-1-4104-4664-0 (hardcover) — ISBN 1-4104-4664-6 (hardcover)
    1. Self-realization in women—Fiction. 2. Large type books. I. Title.
PS3561.L456R35 2012b
813'.54—dc23   2012000223

Published in 2012 by arrangement with St. Martin's Press, LLC.

Printed in the United States of America
1 2 3 4 5 6 7 16 15 14 13 12

To Jennifer Enderlin,

with thanks
for your insight, patience, and
encouragement —
you are a gift I never take for granted.
Love always,
L.K.

ACKNOWLEDGMENTS

As always, I owe endless gratitude to the many people who helped me in this process of getting words from my heart onto the printed page, especially my spectacular agent, Mel Berger, and my editor, Jennifer Enderlin, who deserves every flattering adjective in the dictionary. Huge thanks also to my much-adored friends at St. Martin's Press, including Matthew Shear, Sally Richardson, Lisa Senz, John Murphy, Nancy Trypuc, Sarah Goldstein, Sara Goodman, John Karle, Olga Grlic, Jessica Preeg, Matt Baldacci, Anne Marie Tallberg, Brian Heller, and the entire sales force.

I couldn't make it without the friendship and fantastic work of Cindy Blewett at Truly Texan, Sheila Clover and Michael Miller at Circle of Seven Productions, and Kim Castillo of Author's Best Friend — I am incredibly lucky to have the benefit of so much talent.

Thanks to my lovely author friends Christina Dodd, Teresa Medeiros, Eloisa James, Connie Brockway, and Emily March, who help me spiritually, creatively, professionally, and every other possible "ly."

I am blessed to be friends with some of the nicest and smartest people on the planet: Cristi Swayze, Rich and Amy Kittinger, Tonia Boze, Sue Carlson, Ellyn Ginsburg, and Lynda Lehner.

Thanks to Ireta and Harrell Ellis for their support, love, and great advice.

And most of all, thanks to my husband, Greg (my constant hero and favorite personal photographer), and our two fabulous children, who make every day of my life joyful.

ONE

When Lucy Marinn was seven years old, three things happened: Her little sister Alice got sick, she was assigned her first science fair project, and she found out that magic existed. More specifically, that she had the power to create magic. And for the rest of her life, Lucy would be aware that the distance between ordinary and extraordinary was only a step, a breath, a heartbeat away.

But this was not the kind of knowledge that made one bold and daring. At least not in Lucy's case. It made her cautious. Secretive. Because the revelation of a magical ability, particularly one that you had no control over, meant you were different. And even a child of seven understood that you didn't want to find yourself on the wrong side of the dividing line between different and normal. You wanted to belong. The problem was, no matter how well you kept your secret, the very fact of having one was enough to separate you from everyone else.

She was never certain why the magic came when it did, what succession of events had led to its first appearance, but she thought it had all started on the morning when Alice had woken with a stiff neck, a fever, and a bright red rash. As soon as Lucy's mother saw Alice, she shouted for her father to call the doctor.

Frightened by the turmoil in the house, Lucy sat on a kitchen chair in her nightgown, her heart pounding as she watched her father slam down the telephone receiver with such haste that it bounced off its plastic cradle.

"Find your shoes, Lucy. Hurry." Her father's voice, always so calm, had splintered on the last word. His face was skull-white.

"What's happening?"

"Your mother and I are taking Alice to the hospital."

"Am I going too?"

"You're going to spend the day with Mrs. Geiszler."

At the mention of their neighbor, who always shouted when Lucy rode her bike across her front lawn, she protested, "I don't want to. She's scary."

"Not now, Lucy." He had given her a look

that had caused the words to dry up in Lucy's throat.

They had gone to the car, and her mother had climbed into the backseat, holding Alice as if she were an infant. The sounds Alice had made were so startling that Lucy put her hands over her ears. She shrank herself into as little space as possible, the humid vinyl seat covers sticking to her legs. After her parents dropped her off at Mrs. Geiszler's house, they drove away in such a hurry that the tires of the minivan bruised the driveway with black marks.

Mrs. Geiszler's face was creased like a shutter door as she told Lucy not to touch anything. The house was filled with antiques. The agreeable mustiness of old books and the lemon tang of furniture polish hung in the air. It was as quiet as church, no sounds of television in the background, no music, no voices or telephone ringing.

Sitting very still on the brocade sofa, Lucy stared at a tea set that had been carefully arranged on the coffee table. The tea set was made of a kind of glass Lucy had never seen before. Every cup and saucer glowed with a multicolored luminescence, the glass adorned with thickly painted gold swirls and flowers. Mesmerized by the way the colors seemed to change at different angles, Lucy knelt on the floor, tilting her head from one side to the other.

Mrs. Geiszler stood in the doorway, giving a small laugh that sounded like the crackle of ice cubes when you poured water over them. "That is art glass," she said. "Made in Czechoslovakia. It's been in my family for a hundred years."

"How did they put the rainbows in it?" Lucy asked in a hushed voice.

"They dissolve metal and color into melted glass."

Lucy was astonished by the revelation. "How do you melt glass?"

But Mrs. Geiszler was tired of talking. "Children ask too many questions," she said, and went back to the kitchen.

Soon Lucy had learned the word for what was wrong with her five-year-old sister. Meningitis. It meant that Alice would come back very weak and tired, and Lucy must be a good girl and help take care of her, and not make messes. It also meant that Lucy must not argue with Alice or upset her in any way. "Not now" was the phrase Lucy's parents told her most often.

The long, quiet summer had been a grim departure from the usual routine of play-dates and camps and ramshackle lemonade stands. Alice's illness had turned her into the center of mass around which the rest of the family moved in anxious orbits, like unstable planets. In the weeks after her return from the hospital, piles of new toys and books accumulated in her room. She was allowed to run around the table at mealtimes, and she was never required to say "please" or "thank you." Alice was never satisfied with eating the biggest piece of cake or staying up later than other children. There was no such thing as too much for a girl who already had too much.

The Marinns lived in the Ballard neighborhood of Seattle, originally populated by Scandinavians who had worked in salmon fishing and canning industries. Although the proportion of Scandinavians had diminished as Ballard had grown and developed, abundant signs of the neighborhood's heritage still lingered. Lucy's mother cooked with recipes that had been passed down from her Scandinavian ancestors . . . gravlax, cold-cured salmon flavored with salt, sugar, and dill . . . pork roast rolled with gingered prunes in the center . . . or krumkake, cardamom cookies rolled into perfect cones on the handles of wooden spoons. Lucy loved to help her mother in the kitchen, especially because Alice wasn't interested in cooking and never intruded.

As the summer thinned into a brisk autumn, and school started, the situation at home showed no signs of changing. Alice was well again, and yet the family still seemed to operate on the principles of Alice's illness: Don't upset her. Let her have whatever she wants. When Lucy complained, however, her mother snapped at her in a way she never had before.

"*Shame* on you for being jealous. Your sister almost died. She was in terrible pain. You are very, very lucky not to have gone through what she did."

Guilt radiated through Lucy for days afterward, renewing itself in cycles like a persistent fever. Until her mother had spoken so sharply, Lucy had not been able to identify the nagging feeling that had drawn her insides as tight as violin strings. But it was jealousy. Although she didn't know how to get rid of the feeling, she knew that she must never say a word about it.

In the meantime, all Lucy could do was wait for things to go back to the way they had been. But they never did. And even though her mother said she loved both her daughters equally but in different ways, Lucy thought the way she loved Alice seemed like more.

Lucy adored her mother, who always came up with interesting rainy-day activities, and never minded if Lucy wanted to play dress-up with the high-heeled shoes in her closet. Her mother's playful affection, however, seemed folded around some mysterious sadness. Now and then Lucy would enter a room to find her staring vacantly at some fixed spot on the wall, a lost look on her face.

Early some mornings Lucy would tiptoe to her parents' room and climb into her mother's side of the bed, and they would snuggle until the chill of Lucy's bare feet had dissolved beneath the warm covers. It annoyed her father when he realized that Lucy was in bed with them, and he would grumble that she should go back to her own room. "In a little while," her mother would murmur, her arms wrapped securely around Lucy. "I like to start the day this way." And Lucy would burrow against her more tightly.

There were repercussions, however, when Lucy failed to please her. If a note was sent home because Lucy had been caught talking in class, or gotten a low grade on a math test, or if she hadn't practiced her piano lessons sufficiently, her mother would become cold and tight-lipped. Lucy never understood why it felt as if she had to earn something that was given freely to Alice. After the near-fatal illness, Alice was indulged and spoiled. She had terrible manners, interrupting conversations, playing with her food at dinner, grabbing things out of other people's hands, and all of it was ignored.

One evening when the Marinns had planned to go out and leave their daughters with a babysitter, Alice cried and screamed until they canceled their dinner reservation and stayed home to appease her. They had pizza delivered, and they ate it at the kitchen table, both of them still dressed in their nice clothes. Her mother's jewelry sparkled and scattered glints of reflected light across the ceiling.

Alice took a piece of pizza and wandered to the living room to watch cartoons on television. Lucy picked up her own plate and headed to the living room.

"Lucy," her mother said, "don't leave the table until you're finished eating."

"But Alice's eating in the living room."

"She's too little to know better."

Surprisingly, Lucy's father joined the conversation. "She's only two years younger than Lucy. And as I recall, Lucy was never allowed to wander around during dinner."

"Alice still hasn't gained back the weight

16

she lost from the meningitis," her mother said sharply. "Lucy, come back to the table."

The unfairness of it clamped around Lucy's throat like a vise. She carried her plate back to the table as slowly as possible, wondering if her father would intervene on her behalf. But he had given a shake of his head and had fallen silent again.

"Delicious," Lucy's mother said brightly, biting into her pizza as if were a rare delicacy. "I was actually in the mood for this. I didn't feel like going out. So nice to be cozy at home."

Lucy's father didn't reply. Methodically he finished his pizza, took his empty plate to the sink, and went in search of the phone.

"My teacher said to give this to you," Lucy said, extending a piece of paper to her mother.

"Not now, Lucy. I'm cooking." Cherise Marinn chopped celery on the cutting board, the knife neatly dividing stalks into little *U* shapes. As Lucy waited patiently, her mother glanced at her and sighed. "Tell me what it is, sweetheart."

"Instructions for the second-grade science fair. We have three weeks to do it."

Reaching the end of the celery stalk, Lucy's mother set the knife down and reached for the paper. Her fine brows knit together as she read it. "This looks like a time-consuming project. Are all the students required to participate?"

Lucy nodded.

Her mother shook her head. "I wish these teachers knew how much time they're asking parents to spend on these activities."

"You don't have to do anything, Mommy. I'm supposed to do the work."

"Someone's going to have to take you to the crafts store to get the trifold board and the other supplies. Not to mention supervising your experiments and helping you practice for the oral presentation."

Lucy's father entered the kitchen, looking weary, as usual, after a long day. Phillip Marinn was so busy teaching astronomy at the University of Washington and working as a NASA consultant on the side, that he often seemed to be visiting their home rather than actually living in it. On the evenings when he made it back in time for dinner, he ended up talking with colleagues on the phone while his wife and two daughters ate without him. The names of the girls' friends and teachers and soccer coaches, the minutiae of their schedules, were foreign to him. Which was why Lucy was so surprised by her mother's next words.

"Lucy needs you to help with her science project. I just volunteered to be a room mother for Alice's kindergarten class. I have too much to do." She handed him the piece of paper, and went to scrape the chopped celery into a pot of soup on the stove.

"Good God." He scanned the information with a distracted frown. "I don't have time for this."

"You'll have to make time," her mother said.

"What if I ask one of my students to help her?" he suggested. "I could set it up as an extra-credit activity."

A frown pleated her mother's face, her soft mouth tightening at the corners. "Phillip. The idea of pawning off your child on a college student —"

"It was a joke," he said hastily, although Lucy wasn't entirely sure of that.

"Then you'll agree to do this with Lucy?"

"I don't appear to have a choice."

"It'll be a bonding experience for you two."

He gave Lucy a resigned glance. "Do we need a bonding experience?"

"Yes, Daddy."

"Very well. Have you decided what kind of experiment you want to do?"

"It's going to be a report," Lucy said.

19

"About glass."

"What about doing a space-themed project? We could make a model of the solar system, or describe how stars are formed —"

"No, Daddy. It has to be about glass."

"Why?"

"It just does." Lucy had become fascinated by glass. Every morning at breakfast she marveled at the light-gifted material that formed her juice cup. How perfectly it contained bright fluids, how easily it transmitted heat, coldness, vibration.

Her father took her to the library and checked out grown-up books about glass and glasswork, because he said the children's books on the subject weren't detailed enough. Lucy learned that when a substance was made of molecules that were organized like bricks stacked together, you couldn't see through it. But when a substance was made out of random disorganized molecules, like water or boiled sugar or glass, light found its way through the spaces between them.

"Tell me, Lucy," her father asked as they glued a diagram to the trifold board, "is glass a liquid or a solid?"

"It's a liquid that behaves like a solid."

"You're a very smart girl. Do you think

you'll be a scientist like me when you grow up?"

She shook her head.

"What do you want to be?"

"A glass artist." Lately Lucy had started to dream about making things out of glass. In her sleep she watched light glimmer and refract through candy-colored windows . . . glass swirling and curving like exotic undersea creatures, birds, flowers.

Her father looked perturbed. "Very few people can actually earn a living as an artist. Only the famous ones make any money."

"Then I'll be a famous one," she said cheerfully, coloring the letters on her trifold board.

On the weekend, her father took her to visit a local glassblowing shop, where a red-bearded man showed her the basics of his craft. Mesmerized, Lucy stood as close as her father would allow. After the glassblower melted sand in a high-temperature furnace, he pushed a long metal rod into the furnace and gathered molten glass in a glowing red lump. The air was filled with the scents of hot metal, sweat, scorched ink, and ash from the wads of wet newspaper the studio used to hand-shape the glass.

With each additional gather of glass, the glassblower enlarged the fiery orange mass, turning it constantly, reheating it frequently. He added an overlay of blue frit, or ceramic powder, onto the post and rolled it on a steel table to distribute the color evenly.

Lucy watched with wide-eyed interest. She wanted to learn everything about this mysterious process, every possible way to cut, fuse, color, and shape glass. Nothing had ever seemed so important or necessary to know.

Before they left the shop, her father bought her a blown-glass ornament that looked like a hot-air balloon, painted with shimmering rainbow stripes. It hung on its own little stand made of brass wire. Lucy would always remember it as the best day of her entire childhood.

Later in the week, when Lucy came home from soccer practice, early evening had turned the sky dark purple, with an overlay of clouds like the silvery wax bloom on a plum. Stiff-legged in her armor of plastic shin guards encased in tube socks, Lucy went to her room and saw that the lamp on her nightstand had been turned on. Alice was standing there, holding something.

Lucy scowled. Alice had been told more than once that she wasn't allowed to go into her room without permission. But the fact that Lucy's room was off-limits seemed to have made it the one place Alice most wanted to be. Lucy had suspected that her sister had sneaked in there before, when she'd discovered that her stuffed animals and dolls weren't in their usual places.

At Lucy's wordless exclamation, Alice turned with a start, something dropping from her hands to the floor. The resulting shatter caused them both to jump. A flush of guilt swept over Alice's small face.

Lucy stared dumbly at the glittering mess on the wood floor. It was the blown-glass ornament that her father had bought for her. "Why are you in here?" she demanded with incredulous rage. "This is *my* room. That was *mine.* Get out!"

Alice burst into tears, standing with the broken glass shards around her.

Alerted by the noise, their mother dashed into the room. "Alice!" She rushed forward and plucked her off the floor, away from the glass. "Baby, are you hurt? What happened?"

"Lucy scared me," Alice sobbed.

"She broke my glass ornament," Lucy said furiously. "She came into my room without asking and broke it."

Her mother was holding Alice, smoothing her hair. "The important thing is that no one was hurt."

"The important thing is that she broke something that was mine!"

Her mother looked exasperated and distressed. "She was just curious. It was an accident, Lucy."

Lucy glared at her little sister. "I hate you. Don't ever come in here again, or I'll knock your head off."

The threat elicited a fresh storm of tears from Alice, while their mother's face darkened. "That's enough, Lucy. I expect you to be nice to your sister, especially after she's been so sick."

"She's not sick anymore," Lucy said, but the words were lost in the sound of Alice's vehement sobbing.

"I'm going to take care of your sister," her mother said, "and then I'll come back and clean up that glass. Don't touch any of it, those pieces are razor-sharp. For heaven's sake, Lucy, I'll get you another ornament."

"It won't be the same," Lucy said sullenly, but her mother had already carried Alice out of the room.

Lucy knelt in front of the shattered glass, glinting with the delicate iridescence of soap bubbles on the wood floor. She huddled and sniffled, and stared at the broken ornament until her vision blurred. Emotion filled her until it seemed to rise from her skin and pour into the air . . . fury, grief, and a craving, nagging, desperate wish for love.

In the dim smear of lamplight, little points of light awakened. Swallowing back tears, Lucy wrapped her arms around herself and took a shivering breath. She blinked as the glimmers rose from the floor and swirled around her. Astonished, she wiped her eyes with her fingers and watched the lights circle and dance. Finally she understood what she was seeing.

Fireflies.

Magic meant just for her.

Every shard of glass had transformed into living sparks. Slowly the dancing procession of fireflies made their way to the open window and slipped into the night.

When her mother returned a few minutes later, Lucy had gone to sit on the edge of her bed, staring at the window.

"What happened to the glass?" her mother asked.

"It's gone," Lucy said absently.

It was her secret, this magic. Lucy didn't know where it had come from. She only knew that it would find the spaces it needed, take life in them, like flowers growing in the cracks of broken pavement.

"I told you not to touch it. You could have

cut your fingers."

"I'm sorry, Mommy." Lucy reached for a book on her nightstand. She opened the volume to a random page, staring at it blindly.

She heard her mother sigh. "Lucy, you have to be more patient with your little sister."

"I know."

"She's still fragile after what she went through."

Lucy kept her gaze fixed on the book in her hands, and waited in dogged silence until her mother had left the room.

After a desultory dinner, with only Alice's chatter to relieve the quietness, Lucy helped to clear the table. Her mind was filled with thoughts. It had seemed as if her emotions had been so strong, they had changed the glass into a new shape. She thought the glass might have been trying to tell her something.

She went to her father's home office, where he was in the act of dialing the phone. He didn't like to be disturbed when he was working, but she needed to ask him something. "Daddy," she said hesitantly.

She could tell the interruption had annoyed him by the way his shoulders tensed. But his voice was mild as he set down the phone and said, "Yes, Lucy?"

"What does it mean when you see a fire-fly?"

"You won't see any fireflies in Washington State, I'm afraid. They don't appear this far north."

"But what do they *mean?*"

"Symbolically, you're asking?" He thought for a moment. "The firefly is an unassuming insect in the daytime. If you didn't know what it was, you'd think it was nothing special. But at night, the firefly glows with its own light source. The darkness brings out its most beautiful gift." He smiled at Lucy's rapt expression. "That's an extraordinary talent for an ordinary-looking creature, isn't it?"

From then on, magic had come to Lucy when she most needed it. And sometimes when she least wanted it.

TWO

"I have trust issues," Lucy had once told Kevin, not long after they had met.

He had put his arms around her and whispered, "Not with me, you don't."

After two years of living with Kevin Pearson, Lucy still couldn't believe her luck. He was everything she could have wished for, a man who understood the value of small gestures, such as planting Lucy's favorite flower in the front yard of the house they shared, or calling her in the middle of the day for no reason at all. He was a sociable man, frequently pulling Lucy out of her studio to go to a party or have dinner with friends.

Her obsessive work habits had caused trouble in her previous relationships. Although she made a variety of pieces such as mosaics, lighting fixtures, and even small pieces of furniture, what she loved most was to make stained-glass windows. Lucy had never found a man who had fascinated her half as much as her work did, with the result that she had been a much better artist than a girlfriend. Kevin had broken the pattern. He had taught Lucy about sensuality, and trust, and they had shared moments in which Lucy had felt closer to him than any other person she had ever known. But even now there was still a small but untraversable distance between them, preventing them from knowing the essential truths of each other.

A cool April breeze slid through a half-open window into the converted garage. Lucy's art studio was filled with the tools of her trade: a cutting and layout table with a built-in light box, a soldering station, sheet glass storage racks, a kiln. A cheerful glass mosaic sign hung outside, featuring the silhouette of a woman on an old-fashioned plank swing against a celestial background. Beneath it, the words SWING ON A STAR had been etched in a swirly gilded font.

Sounds drifted in from nearby Friday Harbor: the cheerful squabble of seagulls, the blare of an arriving ferry. Even though San Juan Island was part of Washington State, it seemed like another world entirely. It was protected by the rainshadow of the Olympic Mountains, so that even when

Seattle was shrouded in grayness and drizzle, sunlight fell on the island. The coast was rimmed with beaches, the inland lush with forests of fir and pine. In spring and autumn, puffs of water vapor broke the horizon as pods of orca whales chased after salmon runs.

Carefully Lucy arranged and rearranged pieces before pressing them into a tabletop covered with thin-set bonding mortar. The mosaic mix was a jumble of beach glass, broken china, Murano, and millefiori, all of it arranged around a cut-glass swirl. She was making a birthday gift for Kevin, a table with a swirl design he had admired in one of her sketches.

Intent on her work, Lucy forgot all about lunch. Some time in mid-afternoon, Kevin knocked at the door and came in.

"Hey," Lucy said with a grin, drawing a cloth over her mosaic to keep him from seeing it. "What are you doing here? Want to take me out for a sandwich? I'm starving."

But Kevin didn't answer. His face was stiff, and he had trouble meeting her gaze. "We have to talk," he said.

"About what?"

He let out an unsteady breath. "This isn't working for me."

Understanding from his expression that

something was seriously wrong, Lucy went cold all over. "What . . . what isn't working for you?"

"Us. Our relationship."

A rush of bewildered panic caused her mind to go blank. It took several moments for her to gather her wits. "It's not about you," Kevin was saying. "I mean, you're great. I hope you believe that. But lately it hasn't been enough for me. No . . . 'enough' isn't the right word. Maybe it's that you're *too much* for me. It's like there's not room in this for me, like I'm being crowded. Does any of this make sense?"

Lucy's stunned gaze fell to the shards of scrap glass on the worktable. If she focused on something else, anything but Kevin, maybe he wouldn't go on.

". . . need to be really, really clear about this, so I don't end up being the bad guy. Nobody has to be the bad guy. It's just exhausting, Luce, always having to reassure you that I'm in this relationship just as much as you are. If you could put yourself in my shoes for just a minute, you'd realize why I need to take some time off from this. From us."

"You're not taking time off." Lucy fumbled for a glass cutter and dabbed the tip of it in oil. "You're breaking up with

31

me." She couldn't believe it. Even as she heard herself saying the words, she couldn't believe it. Using an *L*-shaped ruler as a guide, she scored a piece of glass, barely aware of what she was doing.

"See, this is what I'm talking about. That tone in your voice. I know what you're thinking. You've always been worried that I'd break up with you, and now I'm doing it, so you think you were right all along. But that's not what this is." Kevin paused, watching her grip the scored glass with a pair of running pliers. An expert clamp, and the sheet of glass split neatly along the scored line. "I'm not saying it's your fault. What I'm saying is, it's not my fault."

Lucy set the glass and pliers down with excessive care. She had the sensation of falling, even though she was sitting still. Was she a fool, to be so astonished? What signs had she missed? Why had she just been blindsided?

"You said you loved me," she said, and cringed at the pathetic sound of those words.

"I did love you. I still do. That's why this is so tough for me. I'm hurting as much as you are. I hope you get that."

"Is there someone else?"

"If there was, that would have nothing to

do with why I'm taking a break from us."

She heard her own voice, like the edge of something torn. "You're saying 'take a break' like you're going out for coffee and a bagel. But it's not a break. It's permanent."

"I knew you'd be pissed. I knew this would be a lose-lose situation."

"How could it be anything but lose-lose?"

"I'm sorry. I'm sorry. How many times do you want me to say it? I can't be any sorrier than I am right now. I did the best I could, and I'm sorry that wasn't good enough for you. No, I know you never said it wasn't good enough, but I could tell. Because nothing I ever did could make it over your insecurity. And I finally had to face the fact that the relationship wasn't working for me. Which was not fun, believe me. If it makes you feel any better, I feel like shit." Faced with Lucy's uncomprehending stare, Kevin let out a short sigh. "Look, there's something you need to hear from me before you find out from someone else. When I realized our relationship was in crisis, I had to talk about it with someone. I turned to . . . a friend. And the more time we spent together, the closer we got. Neither of us had any control over it. It just happened."

"You started going out with someone else? Before you broke up with me?"

"I'd already broken up with you emotionally. I just hadn't talked to you about it yet. I know, I should have handled it differently. The thing is, I have to go in this new direction. It's the best thing for both of us. But the part that makes it tough for everyone, including me, is that the person I'm with now is . . . close to you."

"Close to me? You mean one of my friends?"

"Actually . . . it's Alice."

All her skin tightened, the way it did when you had just saved yourself from a fall but still felt the sting of adrenaline. Lucy couldn't say a word.

"She didn't mean for it to happen any more than I did," Kevin said.

Lucy blinked and swallowed. "For what to happen? You . . . you're going out with my sister? You're in love with her?"

"I didn't plan on it."

"Have you slept with her?"

His shamed silence was her answer.

"Get out," she said.

"Okay. But I don't want you to blame her for —"

"Get out, get *out!*" Lucy had had enough. She wasn't exactly sure what she was going to do next, but she didn't want Kevin to be there when she did it.

He went to the doorway of the studio. "We'll talk more later when you've had a chance to think about this, okay? Because I want us to stay friends. But the thing is, Luce . . . Alice is going to be moving in pretty soon. So you'll need to find a place."

Lucy was silent. She waited in shattered stillness for minutes after he left.

Bitterly she wondered why she was surprised. The pattern had never changed. Alice had always gotten what she wanted, took whatever she needed, without ever sparing a thought as to the consequences. Every member of the Marinn family put Alice first, including Alice. It would have been easy to hate her, except that at certain times Alice possessed a mixture of vulnerability and melancholy that had seemed like an echo of their mother's quiet sadness. Lucy had always found herself in the position of taking care of Alice; paying for dinner when they went out, loaning her money that was never repaid, letting her borrow clothes and shoes that were never returned.

Alice was smart and articulate, but it had always been difficult for her to finish anything she started. She changed jobs frequently, left projects unfinished, broke off relationships before they went anywhere. She made a dazzling first impression —

35

charismatic and sexy and fun — but she ran through people quickly, apparently unable to last through the mundane day-to-day interactions that cemented a relationship.

For the past year and half, Alice had been a junior scriptwriter for a long-running daytime soap. It was the longest time she had ever stayed in a job. She lived in Seattle, occasionally traveling to New York to meet with the head writers about overall story arcs. Lucy had introduced her to Kevin, and they had hung out on a few occasions, but Alice had never shown any interest in him. Foolishly Lucy had never suspected that the borrowing of her possessions would extend to stealing her boyfriend.

How had Alice and Kevin's relationship started? Who had made the first move? Had Lucy been so needy that she had driven Kevin away? If it wasn't his fault, as he had claimed, then it had to be her fault, didn't it? It had to be someone's fault.

She crinkled her eyes shut against the hot pressure of tears.

How did you think about something that hurt this much? What did you do with memories, feelings, needs, that didn't belong anywhere?

Lurching to her feet, Lucy went to her vintage three-speed bike, which was propped near the doorway. It was a turquoise vintage Schwinn, with a flowered basket on the handlebars. She reached for the helmet that hung on a hook beside the door and took the bike outside.

Mist had settled on the cool spring afternoon, stands of Douglas fir puncturing a layer of clouds as light as soap foam. Gooseflesh rose on her bare arms as a breeze pressed a damp chill into her T-shirt. Lucy rode with no direction or destination, until her legs burned and her chest ached. She stopped at a roadside turnout, recognizing a trail that led to a bay on the west side of the island. Walking the bike along the rough trail, she came to a line of steep cliffs made of weathered red basalt and pods of pure limestone. Ravens and seagulls picked over the leavings of low tide on the beach below.

The island's native population, a tribe of the Coast Salish, had once harvested clams, oysters, and salmon in their reef nets. They had believed that the abundance of food in the strait had been a gift from a woman who had long ago married the sea. She had gone swimming one day, and the sea had assumed the form of a handsome young man who had fallen in love with her. After her father had reluctantly given his permission for them to marry, the woman had disappeared with her lover into the sea. Ever since then the sea had offered, in gratitude, rich harvests for the islanders.

Lucy had always liked the story, intrigued by the idea of such encompassing love that you didn't mind losing yourself in it. Giving up everything for it. But it was a romantic notion that existed only in art, literature, or music. It had nothing to do with real life.

At least not hers.

After lowering the kickstand on her bike, Lucy took off her helmet and made her way down to the underslung beach. The terrain was pebbled and rough, patches of gray sand bristling with driftwood. She walked slowly, trying to figure out what to do. Kevin wanted her to leave the house. She had lost her home, her boyfriend, and her sister in one afternoon.

The clouds lowered, smothering the vestigial layer of daylight. In the distance a thunderhead sent rain to the ocean in showers that moved like gauze veils over a window. A raven gained loft over the water, its black wing tips separated into feathery fingers as it rode an updraft and headed inland. The storm was heading this way — she should leave and take shelter. Except that she couldn't seem to think of anywhere to go.

Through a salty blur, she saw a green glimmer among the pebbles. She bent to pick it up. Bottles thrown into the ocean from offshore boats were sometimes churned up and washed to the shoreline, tumbled by waves and sand into frosted pebbles.

Closing her hand around the piece of sea glass, she looked out at the water lapping against the shore in rough blankets. The ocean was a bruised gray, the color of regret and resentment and the deepest kind of loneliness. The worst part about having been deceived the way she had been was it made you lose faith in yourself. When your judgment was that wrong about something, you could never be fully certain of anything ever again.

Her fist was burning, a knot of fire. Feeling an odd squirming tickle against her palm, she opened her fingers reflexively. The sea glass was gone. In its place a butterfly rested on her palm, unfolding iridescent blue wings. It stayed only a moment before shivering into flight, an unearthly blue gleam as it flew away to seek shelter.

A grim smile tugged at Lucy's mouth.

She had never let anyone know what she could do with glass. Sometimes when she experienced powerful emotions, a piece of glass she had touched would change into living creatures, or at least remarkably convincing illusions, always small, always transitory. Lucy had struggled to understand how and why it happened, until she had read a quote by Einstein — that one had to live as though everything was a miracle, or as if nothing was a miracle. And then she had understood that whether she called her gift a phenomenon of molecular physics, or magic, both definitions were true, and the words didn't matter anyway.

Lucy's mirthless smile faded as she watched the butterfly disappear.

A butterfly symbolized acceptance of each new phase in life. To keep faith as everything around you changed.

Not this time, she thought, hating her ability, the isolation it imposed.

In the periphery of her vision, she saw a bulldog making his way along the edge of the water. He was followed by a dark-haired stranger, whose alert gaze was fastened on Lucy.

The sight of him kindled instant unease. He had the strapping build of a man who earned his living outdoors. And something about him conveyed a sense of having been acquainted with life's rougher edges. In other circumstances Lucy might have reacted differently, but she didn't care to find herself alone on a beach with him.

She headed to the trail that led back up to the roadside turnout. A glance over her shoulder revealed that he was following her. That jolted her nerves into high gear. As she quickened her pace, the toe of her sneaker caught on the wind-scuffed basalt. Her weight pitched forward and she hit the ground, taking the impact on her hands.

Stunned, Lucy tried to collect herself. By the time she had struggled to her feet, the man had reached her. She spun to face him with a gasp, her disheveled brown hair partially obscuring her vision.

"Take it easy, will you?" he said curtly.

Lucy pushed the hair out of her eyes and regarded him warily. His eyes were a vivid shade of blue-green in his tanned face. He was striking, sexy, with a quality of rough-and-tumble attractiveness. Although he looked no more than thirty, his face was seasoned with the maturity of a man who'd done his share of living.

"You were following me," Lucy said.

"I was not following you. This happens to be the only path back to the road, and I'd like to get back to my truck before the storm hits. So if you wouldn't mind, either step it up or get out of the way."

Lucy stood to the side and made a sardonic gesture for him to precede her. "Don't let me hold you back."

The stranger's gaze went to her hand, where smears of blood had collected in the creases of her fingers. An edge of rock had cut into the top of her palm when she had fallen. He frowned. "I've got a first-aid kit in my truck."

"It's nothing," Lucy said, although the cut was throbbing heavily. She blotted the welling blood on her jeans. "I'm fine."

"Put pressure on it with your other hand," the man said. His mouth tightened as he surveyed her. "I'll walk up the trail with you."

"Why?"

"In case you fall again."

"I'm not going to fall."

"It's steep ground. And from what I've seen so far, you're not exactly sure-footed."

Lucy let out an incredulous laugh. "You are the most . . . I . . . I don't even know you."

"Sam Nolan. I live at False Bay." He paused as an ominous peal of thunder rent the sky. "Let's get moving."

"Your people skills could use some work," Lucy said. But she offered no objection as

he accompanied her along the rough terrain.

"Keep up, Renfield," Sam said to the
bulldog, who followed with apoplectic
snorts and wheezes.

"Do you live on the island full-time?"
Lucy asked.

"Yes. Born and raised here. You?"

"I've been here a couple of years." Darkly
she added, "But I may be moving soon."

"Changing jobs?"

"No." Although Lucy was usually circum-
spect about her private life, some reckless
impulse caused her to add, "My boyfriend
just broke up with me."

Sam gave her a quick sideways glance.
"Today?"

"About an hour ago."

"Sure it's over? Maybe it was just an argu-
ment."

"I'm sure," Lucy said. "He's been cheating on me."

"Then good riddance."

"You're not going to defend him?" Lucy
asked cynically.

"Why would I defend a guy like that?"

"Because he's a man, and apparently men
can't help cheating. It's the way you're built.
A biological imperative."

"Like hell it is. A man doesn't cheat. If

43

you want to go after someone else, you break up first. No exceptions." They continued along the path. Heavy raindrops tapped the ground with increasing profusion. "Almost there," Sam said. "Is your hand still bleeding?"

Cautiously Lucy released the pressure she had been applying with her fingers, and glanced at the oozing cut. "It's slowed."

"If it doesn't stop soon, you may need a stitch or two." That caused her to stumble, and he reached for her elbow to steady her. Seeing that she had blanched, he asked, "You've never had stitches?"

"No, and I'd rather not start now. I have trypanophobia."

"What's that? Fear of needles?"

"Uh-huh. You think that's silly, don't you?"

He shook his head, a faint smile touching his lips. "I have a worse phobia."

"What is it?"

"It's strictly need-to-know."

"Spiders?" she guessed. "Fear of heights? Fear of clowns?"

His smile widened to a brief, dazzling flash. "Not even close."

They reached the turnout, and his hand dropped from her elbow. He went to the battered blue pickup, opened the door, and began to rummage inside. The bulldog lumbered to the side of the truck and sat, watching the proceedings through a mass of folds and furrows on his face.

Lucy waited nearby, watching Sam discreetly. His body was strong and lean beneath the worn bleached cotton of his T-shirt, jeans hanging slightly loose from his hips. There was a particular look about men from this region, a kind of bone-deep toughness. The Pacific Northwest had been populated by explorers, pioneers, and soldiers who had never known when a supply ship was coming. They had survived on what they could get from the ocean and mountains. Only a particular amalgam of hardness and humor could enable a man to survive starvation, cold, disease, enemy attacks, and periods of near-fatal boredom. You could still see it in their descendants, men who lived by nature's rules first and society's rules second.

"You have to tell me," Lucy said. "You can't just say you have a worse phobia than mine and then leave me hanging."

He pulled out a white plastic kit with a red cross on it. Taking an antiseptic wipe from the kit, he used his teeth to tear the packet open. "Give me your hand," he said. She hesitated before complying. The gentle grip of his hand was electrifying, eliciting a sharp awareness of the heat and strength of the male body so close to hers. Lucy's breath caught as she stared into those intense blue eyes. Some men just had it, that something extra that could knock you flat if you let it.

"This is going to sting," he said as he began to clean the cut with gentle strokes.

The breath hissed between her teeth as the antiseptic burned.

Lucy waited quietly, wondering why a stranger would go to this amount of trouble for her. As his head bent over her hand, she stared at the thick locks of his hair, a shade of brown so rich and dark that it appeared almost black.

"You're not in bad shape, considering," she heard him murmur.

"Are you talking about my hand or my breakup?"

"Breakup. Most women would be crying right now."

"I'm still in shock. The next stage is crying and sending angry text messages to everyone I know. After that is the stage when I'll want to rehash the relationship until all my friends start avoiding me." Lucy knew she was chattering, but she couldn't seem to stop herself. "In the final stage, I'll get a short haircut that doesn't flatter me, and buy a lot of expensive shoes I'll never wear."

"It's a lot simpler for guys," Sam said. "We just drink a lot of beer, go a few days without shaving, and buy an appliance."

"You mean . . . like a toaster?"

"No, something that makes noise. Like a leaf-blower or chain saw. It's very healing."

That drew a brief, reluctant smile from her.

She needed to go home and think about the fact that her life was entirely different from how it had been when she woke up that morning. How could she go back to the home that she and Kevin had created together? She couldn't sit at the kitchen table with the wobbly leg that both of them had tried to fix countless times, and listen to the ticking of the vintage black-cat clock with the pendulum tail that Kevin had given her for her twenty-fifth birthday. Their flatware was a jumble of mismatched knives, forks, and spoons from antiques stores. Flatware with wonderful names. They had delighted in finding new treasures — a King Edward fork, a Waltz of Spring spoon. Now every object in that house had just become evidence of another failed relationship. How was she going to face that damning accumulation?

Sam applied an adhesive bandage to her hand. "I don't think you'll have to worry about stitches," he said. "The bleeding's almost stopped." He held her hand just a fraction of a second longer than necessary before letting go. "What's your name?"

Lucy shook her head, the shadow of a smile still lingering. "Not unless you tell me your phobia."

He looked down at her. The rain was falling faster now, a fabric of droplets glittering on his skin, weighting his hair until the thick locks darkened and separated. "Peanut butter," he said.

"Why?" she asked, bemused. "Do you have an allergy?"

Sam shook his head. "It's the feeling of having it stick to the roof of my mouth."

She gave him a skeptical glance. "Is that a real phobia?"

"Absolutely." He tilted his head, studying her with those striking eyes. Waiting for her name, she realized.

"Lucy," she said.

"Lucy." A new softness edged his voice as he asked, "You want to go somewhere and talk? Maybe have coffee?"

Lucy was amazed by the strength of the temptation to say yes. But she knew that if

48

she went anywhere with this big, good-looking stranger, she was going to end up weeping and complaining about her pathetic love life. In response to his kindness, she was going to spare him that. "Thanks, but I really have to go," she said, feeling desperate and defeated.

"Can I drive you home? I could put your bike in the back of the truck."

Her throat closed. She shook her head and turned away.

"I live at the end of Rainshadow Road," Sam said from behind her. "At the vineyard on False Bay. Come for a visit, and I'll open a bottle of wine. We'll talk about anything you want." He paused. "Any time."

Lucy cast a bleak smile over her shoulder. "Thank you. But I can't take you up on that." She went to her bike, raised the kickstand, and swung her leg over.

"Why not?"

"The guy who just broke up with me . . . he was exactly like you, in the beginning. Charming, and nice. They're all like you in the beginning. But I always end up like this. And I can't do it anymore."

She rode away through the rain, the tires digging ruts into the softening ground. And even though she knew he was watching, she didn't let herself look back.

THREE

As Sam drove along Westside Road toward False Bay, the English bulldog nudged against the closed window.

"Forget it," Sam told him. "I don't want rain to get in the truck. And you're so damn top-heavy, you'd fall out."

Settling back into his seat, Renfield gave him a baleful glance.

"If your nose wasn't half buried back in your head, you might be able to help me track her down. What exactly are you good for?" Keeping one hand on the wheel, Sam reached over and scratched the dog's head gently.

He thought of the woman he'd just met, the forlorn gravity of her expression, that beautiful dark hair. Staring into those ocean-green eyes had been like sinking into moonlight. He wasn't sure what to make of her, he only knew that he wanted to see her again.

The rain was heavier now, obliging him to increase the speed of the windshield wipers. So far it had been a wet spring, which meant he would have to keep an eye out for powdery mildew damage in the vineyard. Fortunately they had consistent breezes coming off the bay. Sam had planted his rows parallel to the prevailing winds, to allow the movement of air to run through the aisles and dry the vines more efficiently.

Growing grapes was a science, an art, and for people like Sam, very nearly a religion. He had started as a teen, reading every book about viticulture he could get his hands on, working at garden nurseries and apprenticing at vineyards on San Juan Island and Lopez.

After majoring in viticulture at WSU, Sam had become a cellar rat at a California winery, working as a winemaker's assistant. Eventually he'd sunk most of what he had into buying fifteen acres at False Bay on San Juan Island. He had planted five acres with Syrah, Riesling, and even some temperamental Pinot Noir.

Until Rainshadow Vineyard could ramp up to mature crop levels, Sam needed an income. Someday he would be able to build a production facility to process the grapes from his own vineyard. He was enough of a realist, however, to understand that most dreams required compromises along the way.

He had found sources for bulk wine, took it to a custom crush operation for bottling, and had developed five reds and two whites to sell to retailers and restaurants. And he'd given most of them nautical names, such as "Three Sheets," "Down the Hatch," and "Keelhaul." It was a modest but steady living, with good potential. "I'm going to make a small fortune with this vineyard," he had told his older brother, Mark, who had said, "Too bad you borrowed a big fortune to start it."

Sam pulled up to the huge Victorian farmhouse that had come with the property. A feeling of dilapidated grandeur hung over the place, enticing you to imagine the glory it had once been. A shipwright had built the house more than a hundred years earlier, framing it with an abundance of porches, balconies, and bay windows.

Over the decades, however, a succession of owners and tenants had wrecked the place. Inner walls had been knocked out to make some rooms larger, while other spaces had been divided with flimsy chipboard partitions. Plumbing and electricity had been badly installed and seldom maintained, and as the house had settled, some of the flooring had acquired a slant. Stained glass had been replaced by aluminum-framed windows, and fishscale shingles and corbels had been covered with vinyl siding.

Even in its ruined condition, the house possessed a winsome charm. Unknown stories lingered in abandoned corners and rickety staircases. Memories had seeped into its walls.

With the help of his brothers, Mark and Alex, Sam had made structural repairs, gutted and remodeled a few of the main rooms, and leveled some of the flooring. There was still a long way to go before the restoration was finished. But this place was special. He couldn't get rid of the feeling that it needed him somehow.

To Sam's surprise, Alex seemed to have a similar fondness for the house. "Beautiful old girl," Alex had said the first time Sam had walked him through the place. As a residential developer, he was familiar with every possible complication of building and remodeling. "She'll need a hell of a lot of work. But she's worth it."

"How much money will it take to get the place in decent shape?" Sam had asked. "I just want it shored up enough that it won't collapse on me while I sleep."

The question had brought a glint of amusement to Alex's eyes. "If you flush hundred-dollar bills down the toilet continuously for a week, that amount would just about cover it."

Undeterred, Sam had bought the property and started work on it. And Alex had brought his construction crews to help with the more difficult projects, such as replacing the header beams on the front porch and repairing damaged joists.

"I'm not doing this for you," Alex had replied when Sam had expressed his gratitude. "I'm doing it for Holly."

A year earlier, on a rainy April night in Seattle, their only sister, Victoria, had died in a car wreck, leaving behind a six-year-old daughter. Since Victoria had never given anyone a clue about who the father was, Holly was an orphan. Her closest relations were her three uncles: Mark, Sam, and Alex.

Mark, the oldest, had been appointed as Holly's guardian, and he had asked Sam to help him raise her.

"I don't see how that could work," Sam had told Mark. "I don't know the first damn thing about being a family."

"You think I do? We had the same parents, remember?"

"We have no business trying to raise a kid,

Mark. Do you know how many ways there are to ruin someone's life? Especially a little girl's."

"Shut up, Sam." Now Mark had begun to look worried.

"What about parent-teacher conferences? Taking her to the men's room? How do we do stuff like that?"

"I'll figure that out. Just let us live here."

"What about my sex life?"

Mark had given him an exasperated glance. "Is that really your priority, Sam?"

"I'm shallow. Sue me."

But eventually, of course, Sam had agreed to the arrangement. He owed it to Mark, who was dealing with a tough situation he'd never expected nor asked for. And even more, he owed it to Victoria. He'd never been close to her, never been there for her, so the least he could do was help her orphaned daughter.

What Sam hadn't counted on was that Holly would have stolen his heart with such ease. It had something to do with the artwork and pasta necklaces she brought home from school. And the glimpses of Victoria that he saw in her, the crinkle-nosed grin, her absorbed gaze as she made a box out of Popsicle sticks and glue, or read a book about talking animals. Having a kid in your life changed you before you were even aware of it. It changed your habits and opinions. It changed the things you worried about and hoped for.

And it made you do dumbass things like adopt an ugly bulldog with eczema and hip problems when no one else wanted him.

"Here you go, buddy," Sam said, lifting Renfield from the truck and placing him carefully on the ground. The dog lumbered after him as he walked to the front porch.

Alex huddled in a battered wicker chair, drinking a beer.

"Al," Sam said casually. He kept a close eye on Renfield, who was lumbering up a specially built ramp. Bulldogs and stairs were never a good combination. "What are you doing here?"

Alex was dressed in frayed jeans and an ancient sweatshirt, completely unlike his usual businesslike attire. His unshaven face was cast with the sullen shadow of a man who'd been drinking steadily for most of the afternoon.

An unpleasant chill chased down the back of Sam's neck as he remembered how often their parents had worn that glazed look. It had seemed as if they'd been drinking a different kind of alcohol than everyone else. The liquor that made other people cheerful, relaxed, sexy, had turned Alan and Jessica Nolan into monsters.

Although Alex had never sunk to that level, he was not his best self while drinking. He became the kind of person Sam wouldn't have had anything to do with if they weren't related.

"Took the afternoon off," Alex said, raising the bottle to his lips, draining the rest of the beer.

He was going through a divorce after four years of marriage to a woman he should have known better than to get entangled with in the first place. His wife, Darcy, had managed to chew through a prenup like a beaver through balsa wood, and was now in the process of dismantling the carefully ordered life Alex had worked so hard to build.

"You met with your lawyer?" Sam asked.

"Yesterday."

"How'd it go?"

"Darcy's keeping the house and most of the money. Now the lawyers are negotiating for my kidneys."

"Sorry. I'd hoped it would work out for you." Which wasn't exactly the truth. Sam had never been able to stand Darcy, whose sole ambition in life was to be a trophy wife. Sam would have bet the vineyard that his brother was being traded in for a more affluent husband.

"I knew when I married her that it wasn't going to last," Alex said.

"Then why'd you do it?"

"Tax benefits." Alex glanced quizzically at Renfield, who was butting his head against his leg, and he reached down to scratch the dog's back. "The thing is," he said, turning his attention back to Sam, "we're Nolans. None of us will ever have a marriage that lasts longer than the average house plant."

"I'm never getting married," Sam said.

"Smart," Alex said.

"It has nothing to do with being smart. It's just that I always feel closer to a woman knowing I can walk away from her at any moment."

At the same time, they both detected the smell of something burning, drifting from the open windows. "What the hell is that?" Sam asked.

"Mark is cooking," Alex said.

The front door opened, and Holly rushed outside, giving a little squeal as she saw Sam. He laughed and caught her as she hurled herself at him. When they saw each other at the end of the day, Holly always acted like they had been apart for weeks.

"Uncle Sam!"

"Hey, gingersnap." He gave her a noisy kiss. "How was school?"

"Miss Duncan taught us some French words today. And I told her I already knew some."

"Which ones?"

"*Rouge, blanc, sec,* and *doux*. Miss Duncan asked where I learned those words, so I told her from my uncle, and he's a winemaker. And then she said she didn't know the French word for 'winemaker,' so we looked it up in the dictionary and we couldn't find it."

"That's because there isn't one."

The child looked aghast. "Why not?"

"The closest word they have is *'vigneron,'* which means vine grower. But the French believe that nature is the winemaker, not the guy who tends the vineyard."

Holly touched her nose to his. "When you start making wine from your own grapes, are you going to name one after me?"

"Of course I am. Should it be a red or a white?"

"Pink," Holly said decisively.

Sam pretended to be appalled. "I do not make pink wine."

"Pink and sparkly," Holly insisted, giggling at his expression. Squirming free of Sam's embrace, she crouched down to Renfield, who had padded over to her.

"What is Mark making for dinner?" Sam asked.

"I can't tell," Holly said, scratching Renfield's neck. "It's on fire."

"It's fish taco Friday at the Market Chef," Sam said. "Why don't you run back in and ask him if he wants to go out to eat tonight?"

Holly sent Alex a hopeful glance. "Will you come too?"

Alex shook his head. "I'm not hungry."

The child looked concerned. "Are you still having your divorce?"

"Still having it," Alex said.

"When it's over, are you going to get married again?"

"Only if I manage to forget what it was like to be married the first time."

"Don't listen to Uncle Alex," Sam said hastily. "Marriage is great." He did his best to sound sincere.

"Marriage is like getting a box of raisins on Halloween," Alex said. "Someone tries to convince you it's a treat. But when you open the box, it's still raisins."

"I like raisins," Holly said.

Sam smiled at her. "So do I."

"Did you know that if you leave grapes under the couch for a really long time, they turn into raisins?"

Sam's smile faded, and his brows lowered. "How did you find that out, Holly?"

A brief hesitation. "Never mind," she said brightly, and disappeared into the house with Renfield hustling after her.

Sam considered his brother with a frown. "Alex, do me a favor. Don't share your opinions about marriage with Holly. I'd like to preserve her illusions until at least the age of eight."

"Sure." Alex set the empty beer bottle on the porch railing and stood. "But if I were you, I'd be careful what you tell her about marriage. At worst it's a mindfuck, and at best, it's an outdated institution. The fact is, there probably isn't someone out there who's just right for you, and if you do find that person, it's not likely the feeling will be mutual. So if you're raising Holly to think that life's a fairy tale, you're setting her up for some painful lessons in reality."

Sam watched his brother walk to the BMW parked on the graveled drive. "Dipshit," he muttered affectionately as the car drove off. Setting his back against one of the sturdy porch columns, he looked from the closed front door to the planted fields beyond the house, where a former apple orchard was now crossed with rows of young vines.

He couldn't help agreeing with Alex's view of marriage — it was a losing proposition for a Nolan. Whatever genetic combination was required for a person to maintain a lasting relationship, Nolans didn't have it, with the possible exception of their older brother, Mark. As far as Sam was concerned, however, the risks of marriage far outweighed the potential benefits. He genuinely liked women, enjoyed their company, and he had a hell of a great time in bed with them. The problem was that women tended to attach emotions to the sex act, which always messed up the relationship. And so far even the ones who had claimed to share Sam's desire for a simple, uncomplicated affair eventually got to the point when they wanted commitment. When it became clear that Sam couldn't give them what they wanted, they broke up with him and moved on. And so did Sam.

Luckily he'd never found a woman who had tempted him to give up his freedom. And if he ever did, he knew exactly how to handle it: Run like hell in the opposite direction.

FOUR

As the rain worsened, Lucy headed to the place she always went when she wasn't sure where to go. Her friends Justine and Zoë Hoffman ran a bed-and-breakfast in Friday Harbor, just a two-minute walk from the ferry terminal at the port. The bed-and-breakfast, named Artist's Point, was a converted mansion with wide porches and picture windows with views of Mount Baker's blunt crown in the distance.

Although Justine and Zoë were cousins, they were nothing like each other. Justine was slim and athletic, the kind of person who liked to test herself, see how far she could bike, run, swim. Even when she was sitting still, she gave the impression of being on the move. She was incapable of coyness or dishonesty, and she approached life with a kind of cheerful fortitude that some people found slightly off-putting. When confronted with a problem, Justine didn't like to dither, she took action, sometimes before she had thought everything through.

Zoë, on the other hand, measured her decisions as precisely as the ingredients she used for her recipes. She loved nothing more than to loiter at open markets or produce stands, choosing the most perfect organic fruits and vegetables, buying jars of berry jam, lavender honey, crocks of freshly churned butter from an island dairy. Although she had earned a culinary degree, she also relied on instinct. Zoë loved hardcover books and classic movies, and writing letters by hand. She collected vintage brooches and pinned them on an antique dressmaker's mannequin in her bedroom.

After Zoë had married and divorced a year later, she had let Justine talk her into helping her run the bed-and-breakfast. Zoë had always worked in restaurants and bakeries, and although she had toyed with the idea of starting her own café, she didn't want the responsibility of management and accounting. Working with Justine was a perfect solution.

"I like the business side of it," Justine had told Lucy. "I don't mind cleaning, and I can even fix the plumbing, but I can't cook to save my life. And Zoë's a domestic goddess."

It was true. Zoë loved being in the kitchen, where she effortlessly turned out confections like banana muffins topped with snowy mascarpone cheese frosting, or cinnamon coffee cake baked in an iron skillet with a melting crust of brown sugar. In the afternoons, Zoë set out trays of coffee and sweets in the common areas. Tiered plates were piled with pumpkin cookies sandwiched with cream cheese, chocolate brownies as heavy as paperweights, tarts heaped with shiny glacéed fruit.

Zoë had been asked out by various guys, but so far she had refused them all. She was still getting over her disaster of a marriage. To Zoë's chagrin, she had been the only one surprised by the revelation that her husband, Chris, was gay.

"Everyone knew," Justine had told her bluntly. "I told you before you married him, but you wouldn't listen."

"Chris didn't seem gay to me."

"What about his obsession with Sarah Jessica Parker?"

"Straight men like Sarah Jessica Parker," Zoë said defensively.

"Yes, but how many of them use Dawn by Sarah Jessica Parker as an aftershave?"

"It smelled like citrus," Zoë said.

"And remember when he took you to

Aspen on that ski trip?"

"Straight men ski in Aspen."

"During gay ski week?" Jessica persisted, which Zoë had admitted had probably been a giveaway.

"And remember how Chris always said 'everyone has a little gay in them'?"

"I thought he was being sophisticated."

"He was being gay, Zoë. Do you think any straight guy would say something like that?"

Unfortunately Zoë's father was against divorce for any reason. He had insisted that everything would have worked out if they had gone into counseling, and he'd even suggested that Zoë should have done more to keep Chris interested. And Chris's family had also blamed Zoë, saying that Chris had never been gay until he'd gotten married. For her part, Zoë didn't blame her ex-husband for being gay, only for having made her an unwitting casualty of his sexual self-discovery.

"It's so humiliating," Zoë had confessed to Lucy, "having your husband leave you for another man. It makes you feel like you've let down your entire gender. Like I was the one who finally sent him over to the other team."

Lucy reflected that a feeling of shame was often a result of being cheated on. Even though it wasn't fair, you couldn't help but take it as a sign that you were lacking something.

"What is it?" Justine asked with a frown as she opened the back door to let Lucy in. As usual, Justine was dressed in jeans and a sweatshirt, her hair pulled up in a swingy ponytail. "You look terrible. Here, come to the kitchen."

"I'm all wet," Lucy said. "I'll mess up the floors."

"Take off your shoes and come in."

"I'm sorry. I should have called first." Lucy slipped out of her mud-caked sneakers.

"No problem, we're not busy."

Lucy followed her into the big, warm kitchen. The walls were covered in wallpaper printed with cheerful clusters of cherries. The air was filled with good smells: flour, hot butter, melting chocolate. Zoë was taking a muffin pan from the oven, her hair drawn to the top of her head in a knot of golden curls. She looked like an old-fashioned pinup girl, her figure curvy and small-waisted, her cheeks pink from the heat of the oven.

Zoë smiled. "Lucy. Want to be a taste tester? I just tried a new recipe for chocolate ricotta muffins."

Lucy shook her head dumbly. Somehow the cozy warmth of the kitchen was making her feel even worse. She raised a hand to her throat to soothe away a sharp twinge of misery.

Justine stared at her in concern. "What is it, Luce?"

"Something really bad," Lucy managed to say. "Something awful."

"You and Kevin had a fight?"

"No." Lucy drew in a shivering breath. "He dumped me."

She was immediately guided to a chair by the table. Zoë gave her a wad of paper napkins to blot her wet hair and blow her nose, while Justine poured a shot of whiskey. As Lucy took a sip of smooth liquid fire, Justine poured another shot in a new glass.

"For heaven's sake, Justine, she hasn't even finished the first one," Zoë said.

"This isn't for Lucy, it's for me."

Zoë smiled, shook her head, and brought a plate piled with muffins. She took the chair on Lucy's other side. "Have one," she said. "There's hardly any problem that a warm muffin can't help."

"No, thank you, I can't eat anything."

"It's chocolate," Zoë said, as if that gave it medicinal value.

With an unsteady sigh, Lucy took a muffin and broke it open, letting its damp heat filter through her fingers.

"So what's the deal with Kevin?" Justine asked, biting into a muffin.

"He's been cheating on me," Lucy said dully. "He just told me about it."

"That *jerk,*" Zoë said in astonishment. "That slime, that . . . that . . ."

"I believe 'dickwad' is the word you're looking for," Justine said.

"I wish I could say I was surprised," Zoë said. "But Kevin's always seemed to me like the kind of guy who might cheat."

"Why do you say that?" Justine asked.

"He's a looker, for one thing."

"Just because he's handsome —" Justine began, but Zoë interrupted.

"No, not that kind of looker. I mean he looks at women. I always catch him looking at my chest."

"Everyone looks at your chest, Zoë. People can't help it."

Zoë pointedly ignored her cousin as she continued. "Kevin's not built for a sustained relationship. He's like one of those car-chasing dogs. The dog doesn't really want the car. It's the chasing part he likes."

"So who did he cheat on you with?" Justine asked Lucy.

"My sister, Alice."

The cousins gave her identical wide-eyed stares.

"I can't believe it," Zoë said. "Are you sure Kevin's telling the truth?"

"Why would he lie about something like that?" Justine asked.

Zoë gave Lucy a concerned glance. "Have you called Alice to ask her about it?"

"What if she says it's true?" Lucy asked miserably.

"Then let her have it. Tell her she's a turbo slut, and she deserves to rot in hell."

Lucy lifted her glass of whiskey and drained it. "I hate confrontation."

"Let me call her," Justine offered. "I love confrontation."

"What are you going to do for tonight?" Zoë asked Lucy gently. "Do you need a place to stay?"

"I don't know. I guess I do. Kevin wants me to move out as soon as possible. Alice's coming to live with him."

Justine nearly choked. "She's moving from Seattle? Into *your* house? My God, this is *heinous*."

Lucy took a bite of her muffin, the soft tang of ricotta blending perfectly with the dark complexity of the chocolate. "I'll have to leave the island," she said. "I couldn't handle running into them all the time."

70

"If it were me," Justine said, "I wouldn't leave. I'd stay and make them feel as guilty as hell. I'd be in their faces at every possible opportunity."

"This is where your friends are," Zoë told Lucy. "Stay with us. You have a support system to help you through this."

"I do?"

"Of course you do. Why would you even ask that?"

"Because I've met most of my friends on the island through Kevin. Even you. Do all the friends go back to him now?"

"He'll probably keep some of them," Justine said. "But you get us, and our awesome advice, and a place to stay for as long as you want."

"Do you have an available room?"

"Only one," Zoë said. "The room that's *always* available." She gave Justine a dark glance.

"Which one is that?" Lucy asked.

Justine answered somewhat sheepishly. "The Edvard Munch room."

"The artist who painted *The Scream?*" Lucy asked.

"He painted things other than just *The Scream,*" Justine said. "I mean, yeah, I put that particular print in the room because it's his most famous work, but I also included some pretty ones, like *Four Girls on a Bridge.*"

"Doesn't matter," Zoë said. "All anyone ever notices in that room is *The Scream.* I told you people don't want to go to sleep looking at that."

"I do," Lucy said. "It's the perfect room for a woman going through a breakup."

Justine gave her a fond glance. "You can stay there as long as you want."

"And after she leaves," Zoë said, "we'll redecorate with a new artist."

Justine scowled. "Who do you have in mind?"

"Picasso," Zoë said decisively.

"You have a problem with Munch, but not with a man who painted women with three eyes and square breasts?"

"Everyone who checks in to the bed-and-breakfast asks if they can stay in the Picasso room. I'm tired of telling them we don't have one."

Justine heaved a sigh and turned her attention to Lucy. "After you finish your muffin, I'll drive you over to the house to pick up your stuff."

"We may run into Kevin," Lucy said gloomily.

"She's hoping to run into Kevin," Zoë assured her.

Justine smiled grimly. "Preferably with my car."

A couple of days after settling into the room at Artist's Point, Lucy finally worked up the nerve to call her sister. The situation felt unreal. After all the years of enabling Alice, giving her whatever she wanted or needed, had it now come to this? Had Alice actually felt entitled to take Lucy's boyfriend without worrying about the consequences?

Lucy sat on the bed with the phone in hand. The Munch room was attractive and warm, the walls painted a spicy reddish-brown that contrasted perfectly with the crisp white trim, the bedding a colorful geometric pattern. And the giclée prints, such as *Four Girls on a Bridge,* or *Summer Night at Asgardstrand* were nice. It was only the nightmarish *The Scream,* with its gape-mouthed anguish and palpable suffering, that brought the mood down. Once you caught sight of it, you couldn't focus on anything else.

As Lucy pressed the speed-dial button, she stared at the openmouthed figure clutching his ears, the bloodred sky above him, the blue-black fjord below. She knew exactly how he felt.

Her stomach flipped over as Alice picked up.

"Hello?" Her sister's voice was wary.

"It's me." Lucy took a shallow breath. "Is Kevin there with you?"

"Yes."

Silence.

It was a different kind of silence than they had ever shared before. Choking, chilling. Lucy had practiced many ways to have this conversation, but now that it was here, she couldn't get the words out.

Alice spoke first. "I don't know what I'm supposed to say."

Lucy found refuge in anger, clinging to it like a survivor with a life preserver. *Supposed* to say? "You could tell me why you did it," she said.

"It just happened. Neither of us had any control over it."

"You may not have been able to control your feelings," Lucy said, "but you could have controlled your actions."

"I know. I know everything you're going to say. And I know it doesn't help for me to say I'm sorry, but I am."

"Alice. Every time in your life that you've said 'I'm sorry,' to me, I've always said it was okay. But this is not okay. It will never be okay. How long have you been doing it?"

"You mean how long have we been dating, or —"

"Having sex. When did you start having sex?"

"A few months. Since Christmas."

"Since —" Lucy broke off. There wasn't enough air in the room. She was breathing like a landed fish.

"We haven't gotten together all that often," Alice said quickly. "It was hard to find the time to —"

"To sneak around behind my back?"

"Kevin and I should have handled this differently. But I didn't take anything away from you, Lucy. You and Kevin had grown apart. It was obvious things weren't going well between you."

"It wasn't obvious to me. We'd been together for two years. We shared a house. We had sex just last week. So from my perspective, things were going pretty fucking well."

The word didn't come easily to Lucy — she wasn't one of those people who could swear naturally. But it felt good to say it right now. Appropriate to the occasion. And she could tell from Alice's silence that she hadn't thought Lucy and Kevin were still sleeping together.

"What do you expect is going to happen

now?" Lucy asked. "Am I supposed to forgive you, and forget all about my relationship with Kevin, and make small talk with the two of you during family get-togethers?"

"I know it will take time before that can happen."

"It won't take time. No amount of time would be enough. You've done more than break my heart, Alice. You've broken our family. What's supposed to happen now? Was it really worth it to steal my boyfriend?"

"Kevin and I love each other."

"Kevin only loves himself. And if he cheated on me, don't you think he would do the same to you? Do you think anything good can come of a relationship that started this way?"

"He has a different relationship with me than he did with you."

"Based on what?"

"I don't understand what you're asking."

"I'm asking, what is the difference? Why you and not me?"

"Kevin wants someone he can be himself with. You're so perfect, Lucy. You have standards that no one can live up to. Except, apparently, you."

"I never said I was perfect," Lucy said unsteadily.

"You didn't have to. It's the way you are."

"You're actually trying to blame me for what you did?"

"We joke about what a control freak you are," her sister said ruthlessly. "Kevin said you couldn't handle it if he left a sock on the floor. You're so busy controlling everyone and everything, you never stop to notice what's right in your face. I can't help it if Kevin wanted me more. I don't push him the way you do. And in the future you're going to keep losing boyfriends if you don't change."

"I didn't need your help in losing this one," Lucy said unsteadily, and hung up before her sister could reply.

FIVE

It was exhausting, the exertions your mind went through after a breakup. Past events had to be recalled and parsed, conversations reevaluated. Clues were matched together like socks from the dryer. After all that effort, the wonder was not that you had broken up, the wonder was that you hadn't noticed all the signs.

"Most people don't have the time to put something in context at the moment it's happening to them," Justine said. "Most of us are too busy remembering the dentist appointment and trying to get to work on time, and remembering to clean the fish's bowl before it gets tail rot."

"I can't believe how easily Kevin lied to me," Lucy said. "I thought I knew him so well, and it turns out I didn't know him at all."

"That's how betrayal works. People can't

hurt you unless they get you to trust them first."

"I don't think the goal was to hurt me," Lucy said. "But somewhere along the line Kevin's feelings for me changed, and I didn't notice. Maybe he just fell in love with Alice, and it's as simple as that."

"Doubt it," Justine said. "I think Kevin used Alice as a way to get out of the relationship with you, and now he's stuck with her."

"Even if that's true, I need to understand why he fell out of love with me."

"What you need is a new boyfriend."

Lucy shook her head. "I'm taking a break from men until I can figure out why I keep ending up with the wrong ones."

But her friend was having none of that. "I know a lot of great guys. I can fix you up with someone." Justine was involved in nearly every kind of group or club in Friday Harbor. She volunteered for charity drives and fun runs, and sponsored a local women's self-defense class. Although Justine's involvements with men often lasted no longer than a patdown from a TSA agent, she had the knack of staying friends with the guys she had dated.

"Of course," Justine said reflectively, "you may have to lower your standards just a little."

"My standards aren't high to begin with," Lucy said. "All I want is a man who takes care of himself but isn't a narcissist . . . who works but isn't obsessed with his job, and is confident without being arrogant . . . and isn't still living with his parents when he's in his thirties, and doesn't expect that taking me for a romantic dinner at a local restaurant on the first date is automatically going to lead to the removal of my clothes. Is that so unreasonable?"

"Yes," Justine said. "But if you can forget that laundry list of qualities, you might find a pretty decent guy. Like Duane."

She was referring to her current boyfriend, a biker who dressed in leathers and rode an '81 Harley Shovelhead.

"Did I tell you I'm doing some work for Hog Heaven?" Lucy asked. It was the biker church that Duane attended.

"No, you didn't mention it."

"They commissioned me to replace that big window at the back of the building. I'm using some suggestions from the congregation. The horizontal part of the cross is going to be made with stylized motorcycle handlebars."

"Very cool," Justine said. "I can't believe they could afford you."

"They couldn't," Lucy admitted with a

grin. "But they were such nice guys, I couldn't turn them away. So basically we did a barter deal. I'm doing the glasswork for them, and whenever I need a favor in the future, I'm supposed to call them."

After Lucy had moved out of the house with Kevin and into the room at Artist's Point, she worked in her studio for nearly two days straight. She emerged only to catch a few hours of sleep in her room at the bed-and-breakfast, and returned to the studio before daybreak. As the biker church window took shape, Lucy felt an even deeper connection to her work than usual.

The church congregated in what had formerly been an old movie theater. The room was small and windowless except for the stained-glass panel that had recently been installed in the center of the front wall where a movie screen had once been. The entire building couldn't have been more than twenty feet wide, with rows of six seats on either side of the aisle. "We're aiming for heaven," the pastor had said to her, "because hell won't have us." Lucy had known exactly how to design the window after those words.

She coupled the traditional lead came method — joining pieces of glass in a framework of soldered metal — with a modern technique of gluing a few sections of vibrant flash-glass plates to larger pieces of glass beneath. It had given the window extra depth and dimension. After working a glazing compound into the spaces between the lead and glass, Lucy soldered a matrix of reinforcement bars to the window.

Finishing the project around two in the morning, she stood back from the worktable. She felt a thrill of satisfaction as she looked at the window. It had turned out exactly the way she had envisioned — reverent and beautiful, a little quirky. Exactly like the biker church congregation.

It had felt good to do something productive, and focus on something other than her own problems. Her glass, she thought, skimming her fingertips over a gleaming translucent panel, had never let her down.

Lucy had put off calling her parents about her breakup with Kevin. Not only did she need time to think about what had happened and what to do next, but also she was certain that by now Alice would have called them and put her own spin on the situation. And Lucy wasn't going to waste her emotions or her energy on a useless battle. Her parents would take Alice's side, and Lucy would be expected to keep her mouth shut and fade into the background.

The Marinns had moved to a condo close to Cal Tech, where Phillip was teaching part-time. They flew up to Seattle every two or three months to visit their daughters as well as keep in touch with friends and colleagues. The last time they had visited, they had been displeased to learn that a generous birthday check they had given Lucy had been spent entirely on a new Jet Ski for Kevin.

"I had hoped you'd buy something nice for yourself," her mother had scolded Lucy gently in private. "Or gotten your car fixed up and repainted. Something for your benefit."

"It benefits me if Kevin is happy."

"How soon after you received that check did he mention wanting a Jet Ski?"

Nettled by the question, Lucy had replied casually, "Oh, he didn't mention it. I was the one who came up with the idea."

Which hadn't been true, of course, and her mother hadn't believed it anyway. But it had bothered Lucy to realize that her parents didn't like her boyfriend. Now she wondered what they would make of him dumping one sister in favor of the other. If it was what Alice wanted, if it made her happy, Lucy suspected they would find a way to live with it.

However, when her mother called from Pasadena, her reaction was different from what Lucy had anticipated.

"I just talked to Alice. She told me what happened. I can't believe it."

"I couldn't either, at first," Lucy said. "Then when Kevin asked me to move out, I started believing it."

"Were there any signs? Did you have any idea this was coming?"

"No, I had no clue."

"Alice says that you and Kevin were having problems."

"Apparently," Lucy said, "the problem we were having was Alice."

"I told Alice that your father and I are incredibly disappointed in her, and that we can't support this kind of behavior. For her own sake."

"Really?" Lucy asked after a moment.

"Why do you sound surprised?"

Lucy gave a disconcerted laugh. "Mom, in my entire life, I don't ever remember hearing you or Dad say that you were disappointed in anything Alice did. I thought you and Dad were going to ask me to accept Alice's relationship with Kevin and just get over it."

"You lived with that man for two years. I don't know how you could 'just get over it.' " There was a long pause. "I can't imagine how you got the idea that your father and I would approve of Alice's actions."

Her mother sounded so genuinely bewildered that Lucy couldn't repress an incredulous laugh. "You've always approved of whatever Alice wanted to do, right or wrong."

Her mother was quiet for a moment. "I admit, I've always tended to overindulge your sister," she eventually said. "She's always needed more help than you, Lucy. She's never been as capable as you. And she was never the same after the meningitis. Mood swings and depressions . . ."

"Those could also have been caused by being spoiled rotten."

"Lucy." Her mother's tone was reproachful.

"It's my fault too," Lucy said. "I've enabled Alice as much as everyone else. We've all treated her like she's a dependent child. I'm not ruling out the possibility that she's had to deal with some long-lasting effects from the meningitis. It's just . . . at some point Alice has to be responsible for her own behavior."

"Do you want to come to California for a visit? Get away for a couple of days? Dad

85

and I will buy you a ticket."

Lucy smiled at the obvious effort to change the direction of the conversation. "Thanks. That's really sweet of you. But all I would do is sit around there and mope. I think I'm better off staying here and keeping busy."

"Is there anything you need?"

"No, I'm fine. I'm taking it day by day. I think the tough part is going to be running into Kevin and Alice — I'm not sure how I'm going to handle that yet."

"Hopefully Kevin will have the decency to spend time with her in Seattle, rather than insist that she visit him on the island."

Lucy blinked, perplexed. "They're both going to be here, Mom."

"What do you mean?"

"Didn't Alice tell you? She's moving in with Kevin."

"No, she —" Her mother broke off. "Dear Lord. Into the house you shared with him?"

"Yes."

"What is Alice going to do with her Seattle apartment?"

"I don't know," Lucy said dryly. "Maybe she'll sublet it to me."

"Lucy, that's not at all funny."

"Sorry. It's just . . . Alice has stepped into my life like it's a pair of old shoes. And the crazy thing is, she doesn't seem to feel guilty at all. I actually think she feels *entitled* to my boyfriend. Like I was supposed to hand him over just because she wanted him."

"It's my fault. The way I raised her —"

"Wait," Lucy said, more sharply than she had intended. She took a frayed breath and softened her tone. "For once, Mom, *please,* can something be her fault? Can we just agree that Alice did something wrong, and not find a dozen ways to excuse her for it? Because every time I think of her sleeping in my house, in my bed, with my boyfriend, I really feel like blaming her."

"But Lucy — even though it's probably too soon to bring this up — she is your sister. And one day when she comes to you with a sincere apology, I hope you'll forgive her. Because family is family."

"It is too soon to bring that up. Listen, Mom, I . . . need to go." Lucy knew that her mother was trying to help. But this wasn't the kind of conversation that had ever gone well for them. They could talk about superficial things, but whenever they ventured into deeper territory, her mother seemed compelled to tell her how to think and feel. As a result, Lucy usually confided the personal details of her relationships to her friends rather than her family.

"I know you think I don't understand how you feel, Lucy," her mother said. "But I do."

"You do?" As Lucy waited for her mother to continue, her gaze fell on a print of Munch's painting *The Dance of Life.* The work depicted several couples dancing on a summer night. But two women stood alone in the picture. The one on the left was dressed in white, looking innocent and hopeful. The older woman on the right, however, was dressed in black, the uncompromising angles of her body conveying the bitterness of a love affair gone wrong.

"Before I was married," her mother said, "I was involved with a man — I loved him very much — and one day he broke the news to me that he was in love with my best friend."

Her mother had never divulged anything of the kind to her before. Lucy gripped the phone, unable to make a sound.

"It was beyond painful. I had . . . well, I suppose you would call it a nervous breakdown. I've never forgotten that feeling of not being able to get out of bed. That feeling of your soul being too heavy for you to move."

"I'm sorry," Lucy said in a hushed voice. "It's hard to think of you going through something like that. It must have been terrible."

"The most difficult part was that I lost my boyfriend and my best friend at the same time. I think they both regretted the pain they had caused me, but they loved each other so much that nothing else mattered. They got married. Later my former friend asked for my forgiveness, and I gave it to her."

"Did you mean it?" Lucy couldn't help asking.

That provoked a rueful laugh. "I said the words. That was the most I could manage. And I was glad I had done that, because about a year after the wedding, she died of Lou Gehrig's."

"What about the guy? Did you ever get back in touch with him?"

"You could say that." Her mother's voice turned gently arid. "I eventually married him, and we had two daughters."

Lucy's eyes widened at the revelation. She had never known that her father had been married before. That he had loved and lost another woman. Was that the reason for his eternal remoteness?

So many secrets, hidden in a family's history. Inside a parent's heart.

"Why are you telling me now?" she finally

managed to ask.

"I married Phillip because I still loved him, even though I knew that he didn't care for me in the same way. He came back to me because he was grieving, and lonely, and he needed someone. But that's not the same as being in love."

"He does love you," Lucy protested.

"In his way. And it's been a good marriage. But I've always had to live with the knowledge that I was his second choice. And I would never want that for you. I want you to find a man who thinks you're the sun and the moon."

"I don't think that guy is out there."

"He is. And Lucy, even though you said yes to the wrong man, I hope that won't cause you to say no to the right one."

Six

After two months of living at Artist's Point, Lucy had narrowed down a list of potential apartments, but there were issues with each of them. One was out in the middle of nowhere, another was too expensive, another was depressingly dark, and so forth. She would have to make a decision soon, but Justine and Zoë had encouraged her to take as much time as she needed.

It had done Lucy a world of good to stay with the Hoffmans. Their company had been the perfect antidote for her post-breakup blues. Any time she felt gloomy or lonely, she could keep company with Zoë in the kitchen, or go for a run with Justine. It was nearly impossible to stay depressed around Justine, with her raffish sense of fun and boundless energy.

"I've got the perfect guy for you," Justine announced one afternoon, as she, Zoë, and Lucy prepared the inn for a monthly event at the bed-and-breakfast — a silent reading party. It had originally been Zoë's idea. People could bring their favorite books, or choose from the selection at the bed-and-breakfast. They would settle into the deep sofas or chairs in the big downstairs common room, and have wine and cheese while reading to themselves. Justine had initially scoffed at the idea — "Why would people go somewhere to read when they could do that at home?" — but Zoë had persevered. And it had become a huge success, with long lines forming at the front door, even in bad weather.

"I'd suggest him for you, Lucy," Justine continued, "but Zoë's gone longer without a guy. It's like triage — I have to assign priority to those in the worst condition."

Zoë shook her head as she set a tray of cheese on a huge antique sideboard in the common room. "I don't need triage. I'll meet someone eventually, when the time is right. Why can't you just let these things happen naturally?"

"Letting things happen naturally takes too long," Justine said. "And you need to start going out again. I've seen the signs."

"Like what?" Zoë asked.

"For one thing, you spend too much time with Byron. He is so spoiled."

Much of Zoë's spare time was spent indulging her Persian cat, who had a mahogany-paneled litter box, a selection of rhinestone collars, and a blue velvet cat bed. Byron was regularly bathed and groomed, and ate his designer cat food from china saucers.

"That cat lives better than I do," Justine continued.

"He certainly has better jewelry," Lucy said.

Zoë frowned. "I'll take a cat's company over a man's any day."

Justine gave her a sardonic look. "Have you ever been on a date with a guy who coughed up a hairball?"

"No. But unlike a man, Byron is always on time for dinner, and he never complains about my shopping."

"Despite your weakness for neutered males," Justine said, "I think you'd get along great with Sam. You like cooking, he makes wine . . . it's a natural."

Zoë looked dubious. "This is the Sam Nolan who was so geeky in elementary school?"

Lucy had nearly dropped a stack of books as she heard his name. Fumbling a little, she piled the heavy volumes on a coffee table in front of a flower-upholstered sofa.

"He wasn't that bad," Justine protested.

"Please. He was always walking around playing with a Rubik's Cube. Like Gollum petting his ring."

Justine began to laugh. "God, I remember that."

"And he was so skinny, we used to have to hold him down during a strong breeze. Did he actually grow up to be cute?"

"He grew up to be *hot*," Justine said emphatically.

"In your opinion," Zoë said. "But you and I have different taste in men."

Justine gave her a perplexed glance. "You think Duane's cute, don't you?"

Zoë's soft shoulders hitched in an uncomfortable shrug. "I can't tell. He's all covered up."

"What do you mean?"

"I can't see his face because his sideburns are the size of my cast-iron skillets. And he has all those tattoos."

"He only has three," Justine protested.

"He has way more than that," Zoë said. "I could read him like a Kindle."

"Well, I like tattoos. But to put your fears to rest, Sam doesn't have any. No piercings either." As Zoë opened her mouth, Justine added, "And no sideburns." She made a sound of exasperation. "I'll get photographic proof."

"Justine's right," Lucy said to Zoë. "I've met him, and he is hot."

Their gazes flew to her.

"You met Sam and you never mentioned it?" Justine asked.

"Well, it was only one time, and it was very brief. I had no idea you knew him."

"I've been friends with Sam forever."

"Why hasn't he ever dropped by here?" Zoë asked.

"Sam's been crazy-busy for a couple of years, ever since he started the vineyard. He's got a crew, but he does a lot of the work himself." Justine's attention returned to Lucy. "Tell me how you met him."

Lucy set out wineglasses on a sideboard as she replied. "I was out riding my bike, and I sort of . . . stopped for a minute. We had a quick conversation. It wasn't a big deal."

"Justine, why aren't you going out with him?" Zoë asked.

"I did in middle school, after your family moved to Everett. It was one of those summer flings. Once school started, it sort of evaporated. Sam and I have been friends ever since." Justine paused. "The thing about Sam is, he's not a long-term guy. He's not looking to get serious with anyone. He's a free spirit. Very upfront about never wanting to get married." A strategic pause. "Just ask Denise Rausman."

Lucy recognized the name of a stunning blond television reporter who had recently been voted as Seattle's Hottest News Babe. "He went out with *her?*"

"Yes, she has a vacation house near Roche Harbor, and she and Sam had quite a thing going for almost a year. She was *wild* about him. But she couldn't get him to commit, and she finally gave up. And then there was Laura Delfrancia."

"Who's she?" Zoë asked.

"The head of Pacific Mountain Capital . . . she invests in all these early-stage companies in hi-tech and clean-energy fields. She's classy and *loaded,* and she couldn't persuade Sam to get serious with her either."

"It's hard to imagine that kind of woman chasing after Sam Nolan," Zoë said. "He had a lot of geekitude to overcome."

"In defense of geeks," Justine said, "they're great in bed. They fantasize a lot, so they're really creative. And they love to play with gadgets." As the other two started laughing, Justine handed them glasses of wine. "Here. Whatever else you may say about Sam, he makes fantastic wine."

"This is one of his?" Lucy asked, swirling the rich garnet vintage in her glass.

"It's called 'Keelhaul,' " Justine said. "A Shiraz-Cab."

Lucy took a sip. The wine was amazingly smooth, the fruit strong but silky, the finish mocha-inflected. "This is good," she said. "It would be worth going out with him to get bottles of this for free."

"Did you give Sam your number?" Justine asked.

Lucy shook her head. "Kevin had just dumped me."

"No problem. I can set you up with Sam now. As long as Zoë has no objections."

"None," Zoë said distinctly. "I'm not interested."

Justine let out an exasperated laugh. "Your loss, Lucy's gain."

"I'm not interested either," Lucy said. "It's only been two months since my breakup. And the rule is that you have to wait for exactly half the time of the relationship . . . which for me would be about a year."

"That's not the rule," Justine exclaimed. "You only have to wait one month for each year of the relationship."

"I think all these rules are ridiculous," Zoë

said. "Lucy, you should let your instincts guide you. You'll know when you're ready again."

"I don't trust my instincts where men are concerned," Lucy said. "It's like this article I read the other day about the decline of the firefly population. One of the reasons they're disappearing is because of modern artificial lighting. Fireflies can't find the signals of their mates, because they're so distracted by porch lights, streetlamps, il-luminated sign letters . . ."

"Poor things," Zoë said.

"Exactly," Lucy said. "You think you've found the perfect mate and you head for him, blinking as fast as you can, and then you find out he's a Bic lighter. I just can't handle that again."

Justine shook her head slowly as she looked at the two of them. "Life is a ban-quet, and you are both wandering around with chronic indigestion."

After helping the Hoffmans to set up for the reading party, Lucy went up to her room. Sitting cross-legged on the bed with her laptop, she checked her e-mail, and found a message from a former professor and mentor, Dr. Alan Spellman. He had recently been appointed as the arts and industry coordinator at the world-renowned

Mitchell Art Center in New York.

Dear Lucy,
Remember the Artist in Residence program I mentioned last time we talked? A full year, all expenses paid, working with artists from all around the world. You would be perfect for it. I believe you have a unique sense of glass as a medium, whereas too many modern artists overlook its illusory possibilities. This grant would give you the freedom to experiment in ways that would be difficult — if not impossible — for you in your current circumstances.
Let me know if you decide to give it a shot. The application form is attached. I've already put in a word for you, and they're excited about the chance to make something happen.

Best,
Alan Spellman

The chance of a lifetime — a year in New York to study and experiment with glass.
Clicking on a link at the bottom of the e-mail, Lucy glanced over the application requirements — a one-page proposal, a cover letter, and twenty digital images of her work. For one tantalizing moment, she

let herself think about it.

A new place . . . a new beginning.

But the likelihood of being chosen over all the other applicants was so slight that she wondered why she was even bothering.

Who are you, to think you have a chance at this? she asked herself.

But then another thought occurred to her . . . *Who are you, to not at least try?*

SEVEN

"I need to talk to you, Lucy," her mother had said on the answering machine. *"Call me when you get a minute in private. Please don't put this off, it's important."*

Despite the urgency in her mother's voice, Lucy hadn't yet returned the call. She had no doubt that the message had something to do with Alice, and she wanted just one day of not thinking or talking about her younger sister. Instead she had spent the afternoon packing her latest finished pieces and taking them to a couple of shops in Friday Harbor.

"Wonderful," Susan Seburg, a shop manager and a friend, exclaimed as she viewed the selection of glass mosaic pieces that Lucy had brought. It was a series of women's shoes: pumps, high-heeled sandals, wedges, and even a pair of sneakers. They were all made of glass, tile, crystals, and beads. "Oh, I wish I could actually wear them! You know someone's going to come in and buy the entire set at once. Lately I can't keep your work on the shelves — it sells as soon as I set it out."

"That's good to hear," Lucy said.

"There's something so charming and . . . I don't know, special . . . about your recent stuff. A couple of customers are thinking of asking you to do something on commission."

"That's great. I can always use the work."

"Yes, it's good to stay busy." Setting down the accent lamp, Susan gave her a compassionate look. "I imagine it helps to keep your mind off what's happening." Seeing Lucy's blank expression, she clarified, "With Kevin Pearson and your sister."

Lucy dropped her gaze to her phone schedule planner. "You mean the two of them living together?"

"That, and the wedding."

"Wedding?" Lucy repeated faintly. It seemed as if a sheet of ice had instantly formed beneath her feet. Any direction she tried to go in, she was guaranteed to slip and fall.

Susan's face changed. "You didn't know? Shit. I'm sorry, Lucy, I would never have wanted to be the one to tell you."

"They're engaged?" Lucy couldn't believe

it. How had Alice managed to convince Kevin to make such a commitment? *"I don't mind the idea of getting married, someday,"* he had once told Lucy, *"but it's not something I'd ever rush into. I mean, I'm willing to stay with someone, by choice, for a long time. But how exactly is that different from marriage?"*

"It's a different level," Lucy had said.

"Maybe. Or maybe it's just some goal that other people have set for us. Do we really need to buy into that?"

Apparently now he was buying into it. Because of Alice. Did this mean he truly loved her?

It wasn't that Lucy was jealous. Kevin had cheated on her, and would likely cheat in his future relationships. But the news made her wonder what was wrong with her. Maybe Alice had been right — Lucy was a control freak. Maybe she would drive away any man who was foolish enough to love her.

"I'm sorry," Susan said again. "Your sister's been driving around the island with a wedding planner. They're checking out locations."

The phone was trembling in her hand. Lucy put it into her bag and attempted a smile that came out as a grimace. "Well," she said, "now I know why my mother left a message for me this morning."

"All the color's gone out of your face. Come to the back with me — I've got soft drinks, or I could make some coffee —"

"No. Thanks, Susan, but I'm going to call it a day." The mass of emotion had begun to separate into layers. Sadness, bewilderment, anger.

"Is there something I can do?" she heard Susan ask.

Lucy shook her head instantly. "I'm fine. I'm really fine." Readjusting the strap of her bag over her shoulder, she headed to the front door of the shop. She paused as Susan spoke again.

"I don't know a lot about Kevin, and I know practically nothing about your sister. But from everything I've seen and heard so far . . . they deserve each other. And that's not a compliment to either of them."

Lucy's fingertips found the glass panel of the door, and for a moment there was relief in the contact, the reassuring cool smoothness of it. She sent Susan a brittle smile. "It's okay. Life goes on."

Going to her car, Lucy sat and put her key in the ignition. When she turned it, nothing happened. An incredulous laugh broke from her. "You've got to be kidding me," she said, and tried it again. *Click-click-*

click-click. The engine refused to turn over. Since the lights were still working, it couldn't be the battery.

Getting back to the inn wouldn't be a problem, since it was relatively close. But the idea of having to hassle with mechanics, and pay for budget-blowing repair work, was too much. Lucy leaned her head on the steering wheel. This was the sort of thing that Kevin had always handled for her. "One of the perks," he'd quipped, after making certain the oil was changed and the wiper blades replaced.

Without a doubt, Lucy reflected bleakly, the worst part of being a single woman was having to take care of your own car. She wanted a drink, a shot of something strong and anesthetizing.

Climbing out of the lifeless car, she walked to a bar near the harbor, where people could watch the boats and see the loading and unloading of ferries. The bar had once been a saloon in the eighteen hundreds, established to serve prospectors on their way to British Columbia during the Fraser Gold Rush. By the time the prospectors had gone, the saloon had acquired a new clientele of soldiers, pioneers, and Hudson Bay employees. Over the decades, it had turned into a venerable old bar.

A series of musical notes spilled from her bag as the cell phone rang. Fumbling among the assortment of objects — lip gloss, loose change, a pack of gum — Lucy managed to pull the phone from her bag. Recognizing Justine's number, she answered wanly. "Hi."

"Where are you?" her friend asked without preamble.

"Walking in town."

"Susan Seburg just called me. I can't believe it."

"I can't either," Lucy said. "Kevin's going to be my brother-in-law."

"Susan feels like shit for being the one to tell you."

"She shouldn't. I was going to find out about it sooner or later. My mom left a message this morning — I'm sure it had to do with the engagement."

"Are you okay?"

"No. But I'm going out for a drink, and then I'll be okay. You can meet me if you want."

"Come home and I'll whip up some margaritas."

"Thanks," Lucy said, "but it's too quiet at the inn. I want to be at a bar with people. A lot of noisy people with problems."

"Okay," Justine said, "so where —"

The phone beeped, cutting her friend off.

Lucy looked down at the tiny screen, which featured a blinking red battery symbol. She had just run out of juice.

"Figures," she muttered. Dropping the spent phone back into her bag, she went into the shadowy interior of the bar. The place had a distinctive old-building smell, sweet and musty and dark.

Since it was still early evening, the after-work crowd hadn't yet appeared. Lucy went to the end of the bar where the shadows were darkest, and studied the drink menu. Lucy ordered a lemon drop, made with vodka, muddled lemons, and triple sec, served in a sugar-rimmed glass. It went down her throat with a pleasant chill.

"Like a kiss from an iceberg, isn't it?" the bartender, a blond woman named Marty, asked with a grin.

Draining the glass, Lucy nodded and set it aside. "Another one, please."

"That's pretty fast. You want some munchies? Nachos or jalapeño poppers, maybe?"

"No, just another drink."

Marty gave her a dubious look. "I hope you're not driving after this."

Lucy laughed bitterly. "Nope. My car just broke down."

"One of those days, huh?"

"One of those years," Lucy said.

The bartender took her time about getting her the next drink. Turning on the bar stool, Lucy glanced at the other patrons at the bar, some lined up at the other end, others gathered at tables. At one table, a half-dozen bikers knocked back beers and made raucous conversation.

Too late, Lucy realized they were from the biker church, and that Justine's boyfriend, Duane, was among them. Before she could look away, he glanced in her direction.

From across the room, Duane motioned for her to join them.

She shook her head and gave him a little wave before turning back to the bar.

But the big, kindhearted biker lumbered over to her and clapped an amiable hand between her shoulder blades.

"Lucy-goosey," he said, "how's it going?"

"Just stopped for a quick one," Lucy replied with a halfhearted smile. "How are you, Duane?"

"Can't complain. Come sit with me and the guys. We're all from Hog Heaven."

"Thanks, Duane. I appreciate the invitation. But I really, really need to be alone right now."

"What's wrong?" At her hesitation, he said, "Anything bothers you, we'll take care of it, remember?"

As Lucy stared up into the broad face swathed in oversized sideburns, her smile became genuine. "Yes, I remember. You guys are my guardian angels."

"So tell me your problem."

"Two problems," she said. "First, my car is dead. Or at least it's in a coma."

"Is it the battery?"

"I don't think so. I don't know."

"We'll take care of it," Duane said readily. "What's the other problem?"

"My heart feels like something that should be scooped up with a folded newspaper and dropped in the trash can."

The biker gave her a sympathetic glance. "Justine told me about your boyfriend. Want me and the boys to take him down for you?"

Lucy managed a little chuckle. "I wouldn't want to encourage you to commit a mortal sin."

"Oh, we sin all the time," he said cheerfully. "That's why we started a church. And it sounds like your ex could use a little righteous ass-kicking." A grin connected his extended sideburns as he quoted, " 'For thou shalt heap coals of fire upon his head, and the Lord shall reward thee.' "

"I'll settle for the car being fixed," Lucy said. At Duane's prompting, she told him where her car was, and gave him the keys.

"We'll have it back to Artist's Point in a day or two," Duane said, "all fixed and ready to go."

"Thanks, Duane. I can't tell you how much I appreciate it."

"You sure you won't have a drink with us?"

"Thank you, but I'm really sure."

"Okay. But me and the boys are going to keep an eye on you." He gestured to the corner of the bar, where a small live band was setting up. "It's going to get crowded in here soon."

"What's going on?" Lucy asked.

"It's Pig War day."

Her eyes widened. "That's today?"

"June fifteenth, same as every year." He patted her shoulder before returning to his friends.

"I've got to get out of here," Lucy muttered, picking up her second drink and taking a swallow. She was *not* in the mood for a Pig War party.

The tradition had resulted from an event in 1859, when a pig belonging to the British-owned Hudson Bay trading post had wandered into the potato field of Lyman Cutler, an American farmer. Upon finding the large pig rooting in his field and consuming his crop, the farmer shot the pig. That incident had launched a thirteen-year war between the British and the Americans, both of them establishing military camps on the island. The war finally ended through arbitration, with possession of the island being awarded to America. Throughout the long standoff between American and British military units, the only casualty had been the pig. Approximately a century and a half later, the start of the Pig War was celebrated with barbecued pork, music, and enough beer to support a flotilla of tall-masted ships.

By the time Lucy had finished her drink, the band was playing, platters of free pork ribs were being served at the bar, and every inch of the place was packed with boisterous people. She gestured for the tab, and the bartender nodded.

"Can I buy you another?" a guy on the stool beside her asked.

"Thanks, but I'm done," Lucy said.

"How about one of these?" He tried to pass her a platter of pork ribs.

"I'm not hungry."

"They're free," the guy said.

As Lucy frowned at him, she recognized him as one of Kevin's landscaping employees — she couldn't quite remember his name. Paul something. With his glazed eyes and his sour breath, he appeared to have started his celebrating much earlier in the day. "Oh," he said uncomfortably as he realized who she was. "You're Pearson's girlfriend."

"Not anymore," Lucy said.

"That's right, you're the old one."

"The *old one?*" Lucy repeated in outrage.

"I meant old girlfriend . . . uh . . . have a beer. On me." He grabbed a large plastic cup from a tray on the bar.

"Thank you, but no." She shrank back as he shoved the sloshing mug toward her.

"It's free. Take it."

"I don't want a beer." She pushed the cup away as he tried to give it to her. He was jostled by someone in the crowd behind him. As if in slow motion, the entire cup of beer hit Lucy's chest and poured over her. She gasped in shock as the icy liquid soaked through her shirt and bra.

There was a brief, stunned moment as the people around them registered what had happened. A multitude of gazes turned in Lucy's direction, some sympathetic, some cool with distaste. No doubt more than a few assumed that Lucy had spilled the beer on herself.

Humiliated and furious, Lucy pulled at her beer-drenched shirt, which was plastered all over her.

Taking one look at Lucy, the bartender passed an entire roll of paper towels over the counter. Lucy began to blot her shirt.

Meanwhile Duane and the other bikers had reached them. Duane's massive hand grasped the back of Paul's collar and nearly lifted him off his feet. "You dumped beer on our Lucy?" Duane demanded. "You're going to pay, dumbass."

The bartender said urgently, "Do *not* start a fight in here!"

"I didn't do anything," Paul sputtered. "She was reaching for the beer, and it slipped out of my hand."

"I wasn't reaching for anything," Lucy said indignantly.

Someone pushed through the crowd, and a gentle hand settled on her back. Stiffening, Lucy began to snap at him, but the words died away as she looked up into a pair of blue-green eyes.

Sam Nolan.

Of all people to see her in these circumstances, did it really have to be him?

"Lucy," he said quietly, his gaze taking swift inventory. "Did anyone hurt you?" He cast a bladelike glance at Paul, who cringed.

"No," Lucy muttered, crossing her arms over her chest. The fabric of her shirt was clammy and nearly transparent. "I'm just . . . wet. And cold."

"Let's get you out of here." Reaching for her bag on the counter, Sam handed it to her and said over her head, "How much is the tab, Marty?"

"Her drinks are on the house," the bartender said.

"Thanks." Sam glanced at the bikers. "Don't maim the kid, Duane. He's too hammered to know what's going on."

"No maiming," Duane said. "I'm just going to drop him into the harbor. Maybe push him under a couple of times. Give him a mild case of hypothermia. That's all."

"I don't feel good," Paul whimpered.

Lucy almost began to feel sorry for him. "Just let him go, Duane."

"I'll think about it." Duane's eyes narrowed as Sam began to guide Lucy through the crowd. "Nolan. Watch it with her, or you're next in line."

Sam gave him a sardonic smile. "Who made you prom chaperone, Duane?"

"She's Justine's friend," Duane said. "Which means I'll have to kick your ass if you try anything with her."

"You couldn't kick my ass," Sam said, and grinned as he added, "Justine, on the other hand . . ." He accompanied Lucy as she plowed through the clusters of people.

Emerging from the building, Lucy stopped on the sidewalk and turned to face Sam. He was as vital and good-looking as she had remembered. "You can go back in," she said abruptly. "I don't need any help."

Sam shook his head. "I was leaving anyway. Too crowded."

"Why were you there in the first place?"

"I went to have a drink with my brother Alex. His divorce was final today. But he left as soon as he realized there was going to be a Pig War party."

"I should have done the same thing." A soft breeze hit the soaked front of Lucy's shirt and caused her to shiver. "Ugh. I've got to go home and change."

"Where's home?"

"Artist's Point."

"Justine Hoffman's place. I'll walk you there."

"Thanks, but I'd rather go by myself. It's not far."

"You can't walk through Friday Harbor like that. The souvenir shop next door is still open. Let me buy you a T-shirt."

"I'll buy my own shirt." Lucy knew that she sounded ungrateful and rude, but she was too miserable to care. She went into the shop, while Sam followed.

"My goodness," the elderly blue-haired woman behind the counter exclaimed when she saw Lucy. "Did we have an accident?"

"Some drunk jerk spilled a beer on me," Lucy said.

"Oh, dear." The woman's face brightened as she saw the man behind her. "Sam Nolan. It wasn't you, was it?"

"You know me better than that, Mrs. O'Hehir," he chided with a grin. "I always hold my liquor. Is there a place in here where my friend can change into a new shirt?"

"Right in the back," she said, indicating a door behind her. She gave Lucy a sympathetic glance. "What kind of shirt are you looking for, dear?"

"Just a regular T-shirt."

"I'll find something," Sam told Lucy. "Why don't you go back there and start washing up while I look around?"

Lucy hesitated before nodding. "Don't pick out anything weird," she said. "Nothing with skulls, stupid sayings, or dirty language."

"Your lack of trust wounds me," Sam said.

"I don't know you well enough to trust you."

"Mrs. O'Hehir will vouch for me." Sam went up to the elderly woman, braced his

116

hands on the counter, and leaned toward her conspiratorially. "Come on, tell her what a good guy I am. An angel. A sunbeam."

The woman said to Lucy, "He's a wolf in sheep's clothing."

"What Mrs. O'Hehir was trying to say," Sam informed her, "is that I'm a sheep in wolf's clothing."

Lucy bit back a smile, her mood lightening as the diminutive woman gave her a meaningful glance and shook her head slowly. "I'm sure she knew exactly what she was saying."

She went into the closet-sized bathroom, pulled off the wet shirt and dropped it into the wastebasket. Since her bra was also soaked, she tossed that as well. It was an old bra, the elastic shot, the straps raggedy. Using hot water and paper towels, she began to wash her arms and chest.

"How did you end up with a biker entourage?" she heard Sam ask from the other side of the door.

"They commissioned me to do a stained-glass window for their church. And now they've sort of . . . well, taken me under their wing, I guess."

"Is that what you do for a living? You're a glass artist?"

"Yes."

"Sounds interesting."

"It can be, at times." Lucy threw away a wad of damp paper towels.

"I found a shirt. Ready for me to hand it to you?"

Lucy went to the door and opened it a couple of inches, taking care to keep herself well concealed. Sam reached in to give her a dark brown T-shirt. After the door closed, Lucy held up the shirt to view it critically. The front was decorated with a diagram of pink chemical symbols.

"What is this?"

His voice filtered through the closed door. "It's a diagram of a theobromine molecule."

"What's theobromine?" she asked blankly.

"The chemical in chocolate that makes you happy. Want me to find something else?"

In spite of the rotten day she'd had, Lucy couldn't help but be amused. "No, I'll take this one. I like chocolate." The stretchy knit fabric was soft and comfortable as it settled over her damp torso. Opening the door, Lucy came out of the bathroom.

Sam was waiting for her, his gaze sweeping over her. "Looks great."

"I look like a geek," Lucy said. "I smell like a brewery. And I need a bra."

"My dream date."

Sternly suppressing a grin, Lucy went to

the counter. "How much is it?" she asked.

Mrs. O'Hehir gestured to Sam. "He already paid."

"Consider it a birthday present," Sam said as he saw Lucy's expression. "When's your birthday?"

"November."

"A really early birthday present."

"Thank you, but I can't —"

"No strings attached." Sam paused. "Well, maybe one string."

"What is it?"

"You could tell me your full name."

"Lucy Marinn."

He reached out to shake hands, and she hesitated before complying. His grip was warm, the fingers slightly roughened with calluses. A workingman's hand. Heat chased up her arm, as if her skin was coming alive, and she pulled back instantly.

"Let me walk you home," Sam said.

Lucy shook her head. "You should go find your brother and keep him company. If his divorce was final today, he's probably depressed."

"He'll still be depressed tomorrow. I'll see him then."

Mrs. O'Hehir, who had been listening from behind the counter, said, "Tell Alex he's better off without her. And tell him to marry a nice island girl the next time."

"I think by now all the nice island girls know better," Sam said, and followed Lucy from the shop. "Look," he said when they were outside, "I don't want to be a pest, but I have to make sure you get home safely. If you'd prefer, I'll follow at a distance."

"How much of a distance?" she asked.

"The average restraining order, give or take a hundred yards."

A reluctant laugh escaped her. "That won't be necessary. You can walk with me."

Obligingly Sam fell into step beside her.

As they proceeded to Artist's Point, Lucy noticed the beginnings of a spectacular sunset, the sky glazed with orange and pink, the clouds gilded at the edges. It was a sight that, under different circumstances, she would have enjoyed.

"So what stage are you in now?" Sam asked.

"Stage? . . . Oh, you mean my post-breakup schedule. I guess I'm near the end of stage one."

"Sarah MacLachlan and angry text messages."

"Yes."

"Don't get the haircut," he said.

"What?"

"The next stage. Haircut and new shoes.

Don't change your hair, it's beautiful."

"Thank you." Self-consciously Lucy tucked a long, dark lock behind her ear. "Actually, the haircut is stage three."

They paused at a street corner, waiting for the light to change.

"At the moment," Sam remarked, "we happen to be standing in front of a wine bar that serves the best mahi in the Pacific Northwest. What do you think about stopping for dinner?"

Lucy glanced through the window of the wine bar, where people sat in the glow of candlelight and seemed to be having a perfectly wonderful time. She returned her attention to Sam Nolan, who was watching her intently. Something was hidden beneath his nonchalance, not unlike the effect in a chiaroscuro painting. *Clair-obscur,* the French called it. Clear-obscure. She had the feeling that Sam Nolan wasn't quite the uncomplicated character Justine had made him out to be.

"Thank you," she said, "but that wouldn't lead to any place I want to go."

"It doesn't have to lead anywhere. It could just be dinner." At her hesitation, Sam added, "If you say no, I'll end up microwaving something out of a box at home. Can you really live with yourself, letting that happen to me?"

"Yes."

"Yes, you'll have dinner with me?"

"Yes, I can live with the idea of you eating out of a box."

"Heartless," he accused softly, but there was a glint of amusement in the vivid depths of his eyes.

They continued to the inn.

"How long are you going to stay at Artist's Point?" Sam asked.

"Not much longer, I hope. I've been looking for an apartment." Lucy gave a self-deprecating laugh. "Unfortunately the apartments I can afford aren't nearly as appealing as the ones I can't afford."

"What's on your wish list?"

"One bedroom is all I need. Something quiet but not too isolated. And I would love a water view if possible. In the meantime, I'm staying at Justine's place." She paused. "I guess you and I have a friend in common."

"Did Justine say we're friends?"

"Aren't you?"

"That depends on what she said about me."

"She said that you were a great guy and I should go out with you."

"In that case, we're friends."

"She went on to say that you were the perfect transitional guy, because you're fun and you like to avoid commitment."

"And what did you tell her?"

"I said I wasn't interested. I'm tired of making stupid mistakes."

"Going out with me would be a very smart mistake," Sam assured her, and she laughed.

"Why is that?"

"I never get jealous, and I don't make promises that I would end up breaking. With me, you get what you see."

"Not a bad sales pitch," Lucy said. "But I'm still not interested."

"The sales pitch comes with a free test-drive," he said.

Lucy smiled and shook her head.

They approached Artist's Point and stopped at the front steps.

Turning to face him, Lucy said, "Thanks for the new shirt. And for helping me out of the bar. You were . . . a nice ending to a rough day."

"No problem." Sam paused. "About that apartment you're looking for — I may have an idea. My brother Mark has been renting out his place — a condo on the waterfront — ever since he and Holly moved in with me."

"Who's Holly?"

"My niece. She's seven years old. My sister Victoria died last year, and Mark was named as Holly's guardian. I'm helping him out for a little while."

Lucy stared at him closely, interested by the revelation. "Helping to raise her," she clarified.

Sam responded with a single nod.

"And you let them move into your house," Lucy said rather than asked.

Sam shrugged uncomfortably. "It's a big house." His face turned unreadable, his voice deliberately casual. "So about the condo . . . the current resident is gone, and as far as I know, Mark's still trying to sublet it. You want me to check it out for you? Maybe take you for a walk-through?"

"I . . . maybe." Lucy realized that she was being hypercautious. A waterfront condo wasn't easy to find, and it would be worth taking a look at. "I'm sure it's out of my price range. How much is he asking?"

"I'll find out and let you know." Sam pulled out his cell phone and looked at her expectantly. "What's your number?" He grinned as she hesitated. "I swear I'm not a stalker. I take rejection well."

He had a kind of easygoing charm that she couldn't seem to resist. Lucy gave him her number, and looked up into his blue-green eyes, and felt an unwilling smile tug at her lips. It was a pity, really, that she couldn't let loose enough to have some fun with him.

Except that Lucy was a woman who knew better. She was tired of wanting and hoping and losing. Later, months from now, more likely years, the need for companionship would reawaken, and she would risk getting involved with someone again. Not now, however. And never with this man, who would keep the relationship strictly superficial.

"Thank you," Lucy said, watching as Sam slid the phone into his back pocket. She extended her hand in an awkward, business-like gesture. "I'll look forward to hearing from you if the condo's available."

Sam shook her hand gravely, his eyes dancing.

The warmth of his hand, the secure way his fingers folded around hers, felt unspeakably good. It had been so long since she had been touched or held in any way. Lucy prolonged the moment a little longer than necessary, even as a flush of mortified color went from her toes to her scalp.

Sam studied her, his expression turning inscrutable. He used his grip on her hand to ease her closer, his head bending over hers. "About that test-drive . . ." he murmured.

Lucy couldn't catch up with her own thoughts. Her heart had begun to thump. She stared blindly at the sunset melting into cool blue darkness. Sam surprised her by easing her against his shoulder, his hand gliding over her spine in a soothing motion. Their bodies touched at intervals, the pressure of him warm and hard and knee-weakening.

Disoriented, Lucy didn't make a sound as one of his hands came to the side of her face, holding her steady as his mouth descended. He was gentle, easing her into the kiss. She opened for him instinctively, the wrong instincts winning out over the right ones.

The kiss beguiled her, just for a moment, into thinking she had nothing left to lose. *This is crazy,* she thought, but his tongue touched hers, and her hand slid up and groped for the back of his neck. Sensation flowed into the spaces between her heartbeats.

Sam was the one to end the kiss. He kept his arms around Lucy until she could find her balance. Bewildered and disarmed, Lucy finally managed to pull away from him. She headed up the front steps.

"I'll call you soon," she heard him say.

Pausing, Lucy glanced at him over her shoulder. "It wouldn't be a good idea," she said in a low voice.

They both knew she wasn't referring to the condo.

"No one's going to rush you into anything," he said. "You call the shots, Lucy."

A little huff of laughter escaped her. "If you have to tell someone they call the shots, they're not really calling the shots." And she went up the rest of the stairs without looking back.

EIGHT

"It's too soon," Kevin had protested, when Alice brought up the idea of marriage. "You just moved in."

She had given him a long, hard look. "What kind of time line are we looking at?"

"Time line," he repeated dazedly.

"Six months? A year? I'm not going to wait forever, Kevin. A lot of guys are married at your age. What's the problem? You said you're in love with me."

"I am, but —"

"What else is there to know about me? What's the holdup? I have no problem with leaving, if you feel like this relationship isn't the right fit."

"I never said that."

But Alice had decided that something big needed to happen for her, especially in light of having just lost her scriptwriting job. A call had come from her agent, who had just talked to the head writer of *What the Heart*

Knows. The show had been canceled. The ratings had been so poor that they weren't even going to finish out the story lines. It had already been replaced with a couple of game shows. The distributor was trying to shop the show to a cable network, but in the meantime Alice would have to sit tight and live off her limited savings.

Marrying Kevin would solve three problems. It would entitle her to his financial support, and it would prove to Lucy that Kevin loved Alice the most. It would also force her parents to accept the union. Alice and her mother would plan the wedding together, and everyone would get swept up in the excitement. It would make the family whole again. And Lucy would have to swallow her hurt pride and get over it.

As soon as she had gotten the engagement diamond on her finger, Alice called her parents triumphantly. She was stunned to discover that instead of offering congratulations, they were harshly critical.

"Have you set a date?" her mother had asked.

"Not yet. I thought you and I would go over some ideas together and —"

"There's no need to involve me in your plans," her mother said. "Dad and I will attend the wedding, if you want us to. But planning and paying for it is your responsibility."

"*What?* I'm your first daughter to get married — and you're not going to give me a wedding?"

"We'll be more than happy to pay for a wedding when our family is healed. But as things stand now, you've gained your happiness at the expense of your sister's. And in consideration for her feelings, that means we can't support your relationship with Kevin. That also means that we're not going to be supplementing your monthly income any longer."

"I feel like I'm being disowned," Alice cried in astonished fury. "I can't believe how unfair this is!"

"You've created a situation that's unfair to everyone, Alice. Including yourself. There are so many events ahead of us . . . holidays, births, illnesses . . . things we need to go through as a family. And that won't be possible until you've worked things out with Lucy."

Outraged, Alice had repeated the conversation to Kevin, who had shrugged and said they should probably put off the wedding.

"Until Lucy gets over losing you? She'll stay single for the next fifty years, just to be a bitch."

"You can't make her start going out again," Kevin said.

Alice was deep in thought. "As soon as Lucy gets a new guy, she can't be the victim anymore. My parents will have to admit that she's gone on with her life. And then they'll have to give me a wedding, and things will go back to the way they've always been."

"Where are you going to get this guy for her?"

"You know a lot of people on the island. Who do you suggest?"

He gave her a startled glance. "This is getting weird, Alice. I'm not going to fix up my ex-girlfriend with one of my buddies."

"Not a close friend. Just a normal, decent-looking guy who would appeal to her."

"Even if I can come up with someone, how are you going to . . ." Kevin's voice trailed away as he read her stubborn expression. "I don't know. Maybe one of the Nolans. I heard Alex is getting a divorce."

"No divorced guys. Lucy won't go for that."

"The middle brother, Sam, is single. He has a vineyard."

"Perfect. How do we get them together?"

"You want me to introduce them?"

"No, it has to be secret. Lucy would never agree to go out with someone that either of

131

us had suggested."

Kevin considered how to get two people to go out together without revealing that you were the one behind it. "Alice, do we really have to —"

"Yes."

"I guess Sam owes me one," Kevin said reflectively. "I did some ground work for him a couple years back, and I didn't charge him anything."

"Good. Call in the favor, then. Get Sam Nolan to take Lucy out."

Holly giggled as Sam hoisted her spindly body to carry her through the vineyard on his shoulders. "I'm tall!" she cried. "Look at me!"

She weighed no more than dandelion fluff, her small arms loosely wrapped around his forehead.

"I told you to wash your hands after breakfast," Sam said.

"How did you know I didn't?"

"Because they're sticky, and they're in my hair."

A giggle floated over his head. They had made s'mores pancakes, their own invention, which Mark almost certainly wouldn't have allowed had he been there. But Mark had spent the night at his fiancée Maggie's house, and when he was gone, Sam tended to loosen up on the rules.

Anchoring Holly's ankles with his hands, Sam called out to the vineyard crew, who were starting up the Caval tractor. The vehicle was fitted with a huge spool of netting that would cover four or five rows of vines at a time.

Holly wrapped her arms more tightly around Sam's head, nearly blinding him. "How much are you going to pay me for helping you this morning?"

Sam grinned, loving the slight weight of her on his shoulders, her sugar-scented breath, her endless quick-spun energy. Before Holly had come into his life, little girls had been alien creatures to him, with their love of pink and purple, of glitter glue, stuffed animals, and fairy tales.

In the spirit of gender equality, the two bachelor uncles had taught Holly how to fish, throw a ball, and hammer nails. But her love of bows and baubles and fluffy things remained intractable. Her favorite hat, which she was wearing at the moment, was a pink baseball cap with a silver tiara embroidered on the front.

Recently Sam had bought some new clothes for Holly and put the old ones that no longer fit into a bag for Goodwill. It had occurred to him that Holly's past with her mother was eroding. The clothes, the old toys, even the old phrases and habits, were all gradually, inevitably, being replaced. So he had set a few things aside to be kept in a box in the attic. And he was jotting down his own memories of Vick, funny or sweet stories, to share with Holly someday.

Sometimes Sam wished he could talk to Vick about her daughter, to tell her how damn cute and smart Holly was. To tell her the ways Holly was changing, and the way she was changing everything around her. Sam now understood things about his sister that he had never thought about when she'd been alive — how tough it must have been as a single parent, how troublesome it was to leave the house whenever you wanted to go on an errand. Because when you had to take Holly somewhere with you, it never took less than fifteen minutes to find her shoes.

But there were rewards Sam had never expected. He'd been the one to teach Holly how to tie her shoelaces. All Holly's shoes had Velcro fastenings, and when they'd bought her ones with laces, she hadn't known how to tie them. Since she had been six years old, Sam had figured it was high time for her to learn. He had shown her how to make bunny-ear loops and twist them together.

What Sam hadn't expected was the feeling that had come over him as he had watched Holly's little brow furrow in concentration as she worked at the laces. A fatherly feeling, he guessed. Damned if he hadn't gotten misty-eyed over a little girl tying her shoes. He wished he could have told his sister about it. And about how sorry he was for having had so little to do with her or her baby when he'd had the chance.

But that was the Nolan way.

Holly's light-up sneakers thumped gently against his chest. "How much are you going to pay me?" she persisted.

"You and are I both working free today," Sam told her.

"It's against the law for me to work for free."

"Holly, Holly . . . you aren't going to turn me in for breaking a couple of measly little child labor laws, are you?"

"Yep," she said cheerfully.

"How about a dollar?"

"Five dollars."

"How about a dollar and a ride into Friday Harbor for ice cream this afternoon?"

"Deal!"

It was Sunday morning, the vineyard still dressed with mist, the bay a quiet silver. However, the atmosphere was disrupted by the rumble of the Caval as it started up and began to prowl slowly between the rows.

"Why are we going to put netting over the vineyard?" Holly asked.

"To keep birds away from the fruit."

"Why didn't we have to do it before now?"

"The grapes were still in the beginning part, when the flowers were turning into grape berries. Now we're in the next stage, which is versaison."

"What does that mean?"

"The grapes get bigger and they start to accumulate sugar, so they get sweeter and sweeter as they mature. Like me."

They stopped, and Sam set Holly down with care. "Why do we call it versaison instead of just calling it grape-growing?" she asked.

"Because the French got to name it before we did. Which is a good thing, since they make everything sound prettier."

It would take about two to three days to tent the entire vineyard, which would keep it safe from predators but also allow for easy access when the crew went with lopping shears to drop the fruit that was too green.

After the first few panels of netting were

laid out, Sam hoisted Holly onto his shoulders again, and one of the crew showed her how to thread twine through the edge of the netting with a short wooden dowel.

Holly's small hands were deft as she stitched the panels together. Her pink hat glittered in the morning sun as she looked up at her handiwork. "I'm sewing up the sky," she said, and Sam grinned.

When it was time for lunch, the crew took a break, and Sam sent Holly inside the house to wash up. He took a solitary stroll through the vineyard, listening to the whisper of leaves, occasionally pausing to rest his fingers against a trunk or cane. He could feel the subtle vibration of health in the vines, the water rising from tap roots, the leaves eating up sunlight, grapes beginning to soften and turn heavy with sugar.

As his hand hovered near the cane growth at the top of the plant, the leaves moved toward him visibly.

Sam's affinity for growing things had revealed itself in childhood when he'd worked in a neighbor's garden.

Fred and Mary Harbison had been an elderly childless couple that had lived in the neighborhood. When Sam was about ten, he had been playing with a boomerang he'd gotten as a birthday present, and it had gone through their living room window.

Fred had hobbled outside. His form had been as tall and gnarled as a Garry Oak tree, but there was an innate kindness in his stern, homely face. "Don't run off," he had said, as Sam had prepared to bolt. And Sam had stayed, staring at him with wary fascination.

"You can have your toy back," Fred had informed him, "soon as you do some chores to help pay for that window. To start with, Mrs. Harbison needs some weeding done in her garden."

Sam had instantly liked Mary, who was as short and round as her husband was tall and gangly. After she had shown him which sprouting green plants were weeds, and which were the flowers, Sam had set to work.

As he had knelt and pulled weeds and dug holes for bulbs and seedlings, he had felt as if the plants were communicating with him, telling him in their wordless way what they needed. Without even asking for permission, Sam had gotten a small spade from the Harbisons' toolshed and had replanted primulas where they would get more sun, and had put the larkspur and Shasta daisy seedlings in different parts of the garden than Mary had told him to.

After that Sam had gone to the Harbisons' house nearly every day after school, even after Fred had given back the boomerang. While Sam did his homework at their kitchen table, Mary always gave him a glass of cold milk and a stack of white salted crackers. She had let him pore through her books on gardening, and had provided whatever he told her the soil needed . . . kelp and seed meal, crushed eggshells, lime and dolomite, even fish heads left over from the market. As a result of Sam's labors, the garden had burst with flowers and lavish colors, until people stopped their cars on the road to admire it.

"Why, Sam," Mary had said in pleasure, her face soft and wrinkly-smiled in a way he had loved, "you have a green thumb."

But Sam had known it was more than that. Somehow he and the garden had become attuned to each other. And he had become aware, as few people were, that the entire world was sentient and alive. He knew instinctively which seeds to plant when the moon waned, and which to plant when it rose. He knew without being told how much water and sun the plants needed, what to add to the soil, how to get rid of fungus with a soap-and-water spray, how to control the aphid population by planting marigolds.

Sam had started a vegetable garden for Mary in back of the house, and it had produced fat, flavorful produce and all kinds of herbs. He had intuited that the squash liked to be planted next to the cucumbers, and that the beans liked the celery but didn't want to be near the onions, and at all costs never plant the cauliflower next to the tomatoes. As Sam tended the plants, bees never stung him and flies never bothered him, and the trees extended their branches as far as they could to keep him shaded.

It was Mary who had encouraged Sam to dream of owning a vineyard one day. "Wine isn't about drinking," she had told him. "Wine is about living and loving."

Deep in thought, Sam went to the corner of the vineyard, to check on a vine unlike all the others. It was large and gnarled, alive but not flourishing. No fruit, only tightly closed buds. Despite Sam's best efforts, he hadn't yet discovered how to make it thrive. And there was no silent communication, no sense of what it needed . . . just blankness.

When Sam had first bought the property at Rainshadow Road and walked the perimeters, he had found the vine growing wild on an easement. It looked like the kind of

European vinifera vine that had been brought to the New World by colonists . . . but it couldn't have been. All the vinifera had been wiped out by unfamiliar insects, disease, and weather. The French had developed hybrids with native species that produced fruit without needing to be grafted onto disease-resistant rootstock. Maybe this vine was one of those antique hybrids. But it didn't resemble anything Sam had encountered or read about before. So far no one else had been able to identify it, not even a specialist who'd been studying the photos and samples that Sam had sent.

"How can I help?" Sam murmured, passing his hand gently across the large, flat leaves. "What's your secret?"

Usually he could feel the energy in the soil and roots, as well as the signals of what was needed; a change in temperature, humidity, light, or nutrients. But the vine remained silent, in trauma, impervious to Sam's presence.

Leaving the vineyard, Sam headed to the kitchen to make lunch. He pulled a jug of milk and a wedge of cheese from the fridge. While he was in the middle of assembling grilled cheese sandwiches, the doorbell rang.

The visitor was Kevin Pearson, whom Sam hadn't seen in a couple of years. They weren't friends, but they had both grown up on the island, which had made it impossible to avoid each other. Kevin had always been good-looking and popular, a jock who had developed earlier than everyone else and had gotten the best girls.

Sam, by contrast, had had all the physical substance of a string bean, and had walked around with his nose in the latest issue of *Popular Science* or a Tolkien novel. He had grown up being his father's least favorite son, the geeky middle one who preferred to study bivalves, mud shrimp, and polychaetes left behind in tidal pools at False Bay. He'd been competent at sports, but he had never enjoyed them the way Mark had, or approached them with the vicious energy that Alex had.

The strongest memory Sam had of Kevin Pearson was back in seventh grade, when they'd been assigned as a team to do a report on someone in the medical or scientific field. It had entailed doing an interview with a local pharmacist, making a trifold poster board, and writing a paper on the history of pharmacology. In the face of Kevin's procrastination and laziness, Sam had ended up doing everything himself. They had gotten an A, which Kevin had shared equally. But when Sam had protested that it wasn't fair for Kevin to get half the credit for work he hadn't done, Kevin had given him a contemptuous look.

"The reason I didn't is because my dad wouldn't let me," Kevin had told him. "He said your parents are drunks."

And Sam hadn't been able to argue or deny it.

"You could have invited me to your house," Sam had pointed out sullenly. "We could have done the poster board there."

"Don't you get it? You wouldn't make it past the front door. No one wants their kids to be friends with a Nolan."

Sam hadn't been able to think of a reason why anyone should want to be friends with a Nolan. His parents, Jessica and Alan, had fought with no boundaries, no sense of decency, screaming in front of their children or neighbors, in front of *anyone.* They didn't hesitate to broadcast secrets about money, sex, private matters. As they tore at each other and diminished themselves in the process, their children learned something about family life: They wanted nothing to do with it.

Not long after the science project with Kevin, when Sam had been about thirteen, his father had drowned in a boating accident. The family had fallen apart after that, no regular hours for eating or sleeping, no rules of any kind. It had surprised no one that Jessica drank herself to death in the five years following her husband's death. And there had been no small amount of guilt in the fact that somewhere in the mass of grief, the Nolan offspring had found it a relief that she was gone. No more phone calls in the middle of the night to come pick up a mother who was too drunk to drive after making an exhibition of herself at the bar. No more humiliating jokes or comments from outsiders, no more crises popping up out of nowhere.

Years later, when Sam had bought the land at False Bay for the vineyard, he'd needed to rent some heavy-duty landscaping equipment, and he discovered that Kevin had started his own business. They'd talked over beers, exchanged a few jokes, even reminisced a little. As a favor, Kevin had done some work for Sam at a fraction of his usual price.

Unable to fathom why Kevin could be at his front door now, Sam reached out to shake hands. "Pearson. It's been a while."

"Good to see you, Nolan."

They took measure of each other in a brief glance. Sam was privately struck by the thought that Kevin Pearson, whose family had never allowed a no-account Nolan to cross their threshold, was now visiting his home. The former schoolyard bully could no longer kick Sam's ass or taunt him with his social inferiority. In all measurable ways, they were equals.

Sliding his hands into the pockets of his khaki shorts, Kevin walked in and cast a bemused smile around the entrance hall. "Place is coming along."

"Keeps me busy," Sam said amiably.

"I heard about you and Mark taking care of your niece." Kevin hesitated. "Sorry about Vickie. She was a great gal."

Even if she was a Nolan, Sam thought, but he only said, "Holly and I are about to have lunch. You want some food?"

"No, thanks, I can't stay for long."

"Want to hang out in the kitchen while I make sandwiches?"

"Sure." Kevin followed Sam. "I'm here to ask a favor," he said, "although you may end up thanking me for it."

Sam took a frying pan from the cabinet, heated it on the stove, and drizzled some olive oil into it. Having long ago realized that Holly wasn't going to thrive on a bachelor's diet of pizza and beer, Sam had learned to cook. Although he still had plenty to learn, he'd reached a level of basic competence that had so far kept them all from starving.

While Sam poured the tomato soup into a microwavable dish, he asked, "So what's the favor?"

"A couple of months ago, I broke up with my girlfriend. And it's turned out to be a little more complicated than I expected."

"She stalking you or something?"

"No, nothing like that. In fact, she hardly goes out at all."

The cheese sandwiches sizzled gently as Sam lowered them into the hot pan. "That's normal after a breakup."

"Yes. But she needs to get on with her life. I was trying to think of someone for her to meet — someone she could have some fun with. And from what I've heard, you're not going out with anyone right now . . . are you?"

Sam's eyes widened incredulously as he realized what Kevin was getting at. And then he began to laugh. "I'm not interested in your leftovers. And I'm sure as hell not going to be thanking you for them."

"It's not like that," Kevin protested. "She's great. She's hot. Well . . . not hot, actually, but pretty. And sweet. Supersweet."

"If she's so great, why'd you break up with her?"

"Well, I sort of have a thing going with her younger sister."

Sam just looked at him.

Kevin's expression turned defensive. "Dude, the heart wants what it wants."

"Right. But I'm not dealing with your toxic waste."

"Toxic waste?" Kevin repeated quizzically.

"Any woman would have major issues after something like that. She's probably radioactive." Sam flipped the sandwiches deftly.

"She's fine. She's ready to move on. She just doesn't know it yet."

"Why don't we let her decide when she's ready? Why are you so interested in finding a new guy for her?"

"The situation has caused some problems in the family. I just got engaged to Alice."

"That's the younger sister? Congratulations."

"Thanks. Anyway . . . Alice's parents are pissed off about the situation. They're not going to pay for the wedding, or help with the planning, or any of that crap. And she wants the family to come together. But the kumbaya moment won't happen until her sister gets over me and starts going out with someone."

"Good luck with that."

"You owe me, Nolan."

With a scowl, Sam put the soup into the microwave and started it. "Damn it," he muttered. "I knew that was coming."

"All that dirt work and haul-off I did for you, for practically nothing. Not to mention helping you transplant that wild grapevine."

It was true. The vine would have fallen victim to a road project if it hadn't been transplanted. Not only had Kevin done a good job with the painstaking and difficult process, he had charged Sam a fraction of what anyone else would have.

So yes. He owed Kevin.

"How many times do you want me to take her out?" Sam asked tersely.

"Just a couple of times. Maybe once for drinks, and then for dinner."

Sam put the steaming sandwiches onto plates, and cut Holly's into four precise triangles. "After I take this woman out — if I can even get her to agree to go somewhere with me — the score is even, Pearson. No more favors. We're done."

"Absolutely," Kevin said at once.

"How do you want to introduce us?"

"Well, the thing is . . ." Kevin looked uncomfortable. "You'll have to find a way to meet her on your own. Because if she knew I had anything to do with this, she

148

wouldn't go for it."

Sam stared at him disbelief. "So you want me to track down your bitter, man-hating ex-girlfriend, and talk her into going out with me?"

"Yeah, that's basically it."

"Forget it. I'd rather pay you for the dirt work."

"Don't want your money. I want you to take my ex out. Once for drinks, once for dinner."

"I feel like a manwhore," Sam said sourly.

"You don't have to sleep with her. In fact —"

"What's a manwhore, Uncle Sam?" came Holly's voice as she wandered into the kitchen. She went to Sam and linked her arms around his waist, smiling up at him.

"Man*horse*," he said hastily, reversing the pink ballcap on her head so the bill hung in the back. "It's what a guy smells like after he's gotten sweaty working outside. But don't use that word, or Uncle Mark will rip my lips off." He bent obligingly as she reached up to pull his head down.

"Who is that?" she whispered.

"He's an old friend of mine," Sam said. He gave her a plate with a sandwich on it, sat her at the table, and went to ladle out some soup. Giving Kevin a narrow-eyed

149

glance, he asked, "You got a picture of her?"

Taking a phone from his back pocket, Kevin scrolled through some photos. "Here's one. I'll send it to your cell."

Sam took the phone from him and looked down at the woman in the photo. His breath caught as he recognized her.

"She's an artist," he heard Kevin say. "Her name is Lucy Marinn. She's staying at Artist's Point, has her own studio in town. She does stained-glass stuff . . . windows, lampshades, some mosaic stuff . . . she is cute, see?"

The situation was interesting, to say the least. Sam considered mentioning that he'd already met Lucy, that he'd walked to Artist's Point with her the previous night. But he decided to keep it to himself for the time being.

In the taut silence that followed, Holly said from the table, "Uncle Sam, what about my soup?"

"Here you go, gingersnap." Sam set the bowl before her, and tucked a length of paper towel at her neck.

With that concluded, he turned to face Kevin.

"So you'll do it?" Kevin asked.

"Yeah, I'll do it." Sam gestured casually to the doorway. "I'll see you out."

"If you like Lucy," Kevin said, "you should see her sister. Younger and hotter." As if to reassure himself that he, Kevin, had still gotten the best of the bargain.

"Great," Sam said. "I want this one."

"Okay." Kevin looked more puzzled than relieved. "I have to say, I didn't expect you'd go along with it this easy."

"No problem. But there's one thing I don't get."

"Yeah?"

"What's the real reason you broke up with Lucy? And don't give me crap about wanting someone younger or hotter, because what this woman doesn't have, you don't need. So what is it?"

Kevin wore the bemused expression people sometimes had when they tripped on their own feet and turned around to check out some invisible obstacle on the sidewalk. "I just found out everything there was to know about her, and . . . it got boring. It was time to move on." He frowned as he saw Sam's faint smile. "Why is that funny?"

"It's not." Sam wasn't about to explain that his amusement stemmed from the uncomfortable awareness that he was no better than Kevin when it came to women. In fact, he hadn't been able to manage

151

anything close to a long-term relationship, nor would he want to.

"How will I know what happens?" Kevin asked, as Sam shepherded him through the front hallway and opened the front door.

"You'll find out eventually." Sam saw no need to tell him that he was going to call Lucy that night.

"I'd rather know up front. Text me when you go out with her."

Leaning one shoulder on the doorjamb, Sam gave him a mocking glance. "No texts, no e-mails, no PowerPoint presentation. I'll take your ex out, Pearson. But when I do, and what happens afterward, is my business."

NINE

In the morning, Lucy checked her voice mail and listened to a message that Sam Nolan had left the previous evening.

"The condo's still available. It's got a great view of the port, and it's only a two-minute walk from Artist's Point. Give me a call if you want to check it out."

It took almost until lunchtime for Lucy to work up the nerve to call him back. She had never been inclined to dither over what she wanted. But ever since the breakup with Kevin, she was questioning things she didn't usually question . . . especially herself.

Over the past two years she had become entirely too wrapped up in her relationship with Kevin. She had let friendships drift, and she had set aside her own opinions and desires. Was it possible that she'd tried to make up for that by nagging and controlling Kevin? She wasn't sure how to set herself on the right course, how to find herself again. But one thing was clear: There was no point in fooling around with Sam Nolan, who was a dead-end street where serious relationships were concerned.

"Does every relationship have to be serious?" Justine had asked, when Lucy had said as much the previous night.

"Why bother if it's not going to go anywhere?"

"I've learned some great things from relationships that didn't go anywhere. What's more important, the destination or the journey?"

"I know I'm supposed to say the journey," Lucy said glumly. "But right about now, I'm ready for the destination."

Justine had laughed. "Think of Sam as one of those roadside attractions that turns out to be unexpectedly fun," she said.

Lucy had given her a skeptical glance. "Like the world's largest ball of twine? Or Carhenge?"

Although the questions had been sarcastic, Justine responded with unbounded enthusiasm. "*Exactly*. Or maybe one of those traveling carnivals with the fun twirly thrill rides."

"I hate fun twirly thrill rides," Lucy said. "You feel like you're going somewhere, but when it's over, you find yourself in the same place you started. Not to mention dizzy and sick to your stomach."

At Lucy's invitation, Sam dropped by her glass studio in the afternoon. He was dressed in worn jeans and a black polo shirt, his eyes a startling turquoise against his tan. As she welcomed him inside, a jumpy feeling awakened in the pit of her stomach.

"Nice place," Sam commented, glancing at their surroundings.

"It used to be a garage, but the owner converted it," Lucy said. She showed him her soldering and light tables, and stacks of trays filled with cut glass that was ready to be built into windows. One section of shelves was laden with cans of waterproofing compound and whiting powder, along with disciplined rows of tools and brushes. The largest section of the studio, however, was taken up with floor-to-ceiling vertical racks of glass. "I collect every kind of glass I find," Lucy said. "Sometimes I'll salvage some antique glass that I might be able to use in historic restoration projects."

"What is this?" Sam went to a treasure trove of blue-green glass misted with silver. "It's beautiful."

She joined him, reaching out to run her fingers over a sheet of glass. "Oh, that was the score of the *year,* let me tell you. It was going to be used for some massive public

155

art installation in Tacoma, but the funding fell through, so all this gorgeous experimental glass was sitting in some guy's barn for more than twenty years. Then he wanted to get rid of it, and a mutual friend told me about it. I got the whole lot for practically nothing."

"What are you going to do with it?" Sam asked, smiling at her enthusiasm.

"I don't know yet. Something special. Look at how the color is flashed into the glass — all those blues and greens." Before she thought better of it, she glanced up at him and added, "Like your eyes."

His brows lifted.

"I wasn't flirting," Lucy said hastily.

"Too late. I already took it that way." Sam wandered to the big electric kiln in the corner. "Some oven. How hot does it get?"

"It can go up to fifteen hundred degrees Fahrenheit. I use it to fuse or texture glass. Sometimes I'll cast pieces of glass inside a mold."

"No glassblowing, though?"

Lucy shook her head. "That would require the kind of substantial furnace that you would have to keep hot all the time. And although I did some glassblowing in the past, it's not my forte. I like working on windows more than anything."

"Why?"

"It's . . . creating art with light. A way of sharing how you look at the world. Emotion made visible."

Sam nodded toward a set of speakers on the worktable. "Do you usually play music while you work?"

"Most of the time. If I'm doing some intricate glass cutting, I need it to be quiet. But other times, I'll put on whatever I'm in the mood for."

Sam continued to explore, browsing among jars of colored glass canes and rods. "When did you first get interested in glass?"

"Second grade. My father took me to visit a glassblowing studio. From then on, I was obsessed. When I'm away from my work too long, I start to crave it. It's sort of like meditation — it keeps me centered."

Sam went to her table and looked down at a sketch she had made. "Is glass feminine or masculine?"

Lucy gave a surprised laugh, having never been asked such a question before. She considered it carefully. You had to let glass do what it would, partner it rather than control it, handle it with gentleness and strength. "Feminine," she said. "What about wine? Is it feminine or masculine?"

"The French word for wine — *vin* — is

masculine. But to me, it depends on the wine. Of course" — Sam flashed a grin at her — "there are objections to using sexist language in the wine world. Like describing a Chardonnay as feminine if it's light and delicate, or saying a big Cabernet is masculine. But sometimes there's no other way to describe it." He resumed his study of the sketch. "Do you ever have problems letting one of your pieces go?"

"I have problems letting everything go," Lucy said with a self-deprecating laugh. "But I'm getting better at it."

Eventually they left the studio and headed to the condo, walking along the streets of Friday Harbor. Old-fashioned ice-cream parlors and coffee shops were tucked between glossy art galleries and trendy restaurants. The occasional blast from an approaching ferry did nothing to disrupt the humid, lazy atmosphere. Rich smells of sunblock and fried seafood overlaid the mixture of seawater and marine diesel.

The condo was part of a multiuse development on West Street, with a terraced pedestrian walk down to Front Street. A rooftop deck and huge windows contributed to the sleek and modern design. Lucy didn't even try to conceal her awe as they entered the residence. It was furnished with a few contemporary pieces, the rooms trimmed with natural wood and sky-and-earth colors.

"What do you think?" Sam asked, watching as Lucy tested the view from every window in the main room.

"I love it," she said wistfully. "But there's no way I can afford it."

"How do you know? We haven't talked numbers yet."

"Because this is nicer than any apartment I've ever lived in, and I couldn't even afford those places."

"Mark's pretty eager to get someone in here. And this place wouldn't work for just anyone."

"Who wouldn't love it?"

"People who don't like stairs. People who want a lot more privacy than all these windows would allow."

"I think it's perfect."

"Then we'll figure something out."

"What does that mean?" Lucy asked, instantly wary.

"It means I'll make sure the rent is a number you can live with."

She shook her head. "I don't want to be obligated to you."

"You wouldn't be."

"Of course I would, if I let you start doing favors for me. Especially financial favors."

Sam's brows lowered. "You think I would try to take advantage of you?" He approached her, and Lucy backed away reflexively until she felt the edge of the granite countertop against her back. "You expect me to show up someday twirling a mustache and wearing a black top hat, demanding sex instead of rent money?"

"Of course I don't expect that." Lucy fidgeted as he put his hands on either side of her, his palms braced on the counter. "It's just . . . this isn't a situation I feel comfortable with."

Sam leaned over her without quite touching her. He was close enough that she found herself staring at his smooth tanned throat.

"Lucy," he said, "you're acting like I'm trying to push you into something. I'm not. If it turns out you're interested in something more than friendship, I'll be as happy as a damn bird with a French fry. But in the meantime, I'd appreciate it if you wouldn't put me in the same category as assholes like Kevin Pearson."

Lucy blinked in astonishment. Each breath started knocking into the next, like a line of dominoes. "H-how did you know his name?"

"He came to the vineyard yesterday and

160

said he had a favor to ask me. It was about you."

"He . . . about . . . you know Kevin?"

"Of course I know him. I did his science homework all through seventh grade to keep him from beating the crap out of me in the school parking lot."

"I . . . what did he tell you? What did he want?"

"He said he's marrying your sister. He also said your parents aren't going to cough up any money for the wedding until Alice works things out with you."

"I hadn't heard about that last part. Alice must be freaking out. My parents have been giving her money for years."

Pushing away from her, Sam went to a tall stool and sat negligently. "Apparently Kevin and Alice think the solution is to set you up with someone. They want some guy to romance you until you're so full of endorphins, you won't have a problem with them getting married anymore."

"And you're supposed to be that guy?" she asked incredulously. "Mr. Endorphins?"

"Speaking."

A suffocating blanket of outrage settled over her. "What am I supposed to do now?"

Sam responded with a lazy shrug. "Do what you want to do."

"Even if I wanted to, there's no way I would go out with you now. They would laugh at me behind my back and talk about how gullible I was."

"But you'd be laughing at them," Sam pointed out.

"I don't care. I'd rather avoid the whole thing."

"Fine," he said. "I'll tell them you wouldn't go for it, that I'm not your type. But don't be surprised if they try to set you up with someone else."

Lucy couldn't hold back a disbelieving laugh. "This is the most ridiculous thing I've ever . . . Why can't they just leave me alone?"

"Apparently," Sam said, "your parents will only approve of Alice's wedding — and start giving her money again — when one condition has been met."

"What condition is that?"

"Your happiness."

"My God," Lucy exclaimed in exasperation, "my family is so *bizarre.*"

"Believe me, they have nothing on the Nolans."

She barely heard him. "*Now* they care about my happiness?" she demanded. "A thousand times in the past they could have taken my side but didn't, and now all of a sudden, they want me to be happy? Screw them! And screw you too."

"Hey, don't shoot the messenger."

"Oh, that's right," Lucy said, glaring at him. "You're not the problem, you're the solution. You're my one-stop shop for endorphins. Well, I'm ready. Give it to me."

Sam blinked. "Give what to you?"

"Endorphins. If everyone wants me to be happy, I'm all for it. So give me a shot of your best, grade-A, mood-enhancing endorphins."

He gave her a dubious glance. "Maybe we should have lunch first."

"No," Lucy said, fuming, "let's get it over with. Where's the bedroom?"

Sam looked torn between amusement and concern. "If it's revenge sex you're after, I'd be perfectly happy to help out. But first would you mind telling me exactly who you're mad at?"

"Everyone. Including myself."

"Well, sleeping with me is not going to solve anyone's problems." Sam paused. "Except maybe mine. But that's beside the point." Approaching her, he took her by the shoulders and gave her a little coaxing shake. "Deep breath. Come on. Let it out."

Lucy obeyed. She took another breath, and another, until the red haze faded from before her eyes. Her shoulders slumped in defeat.

"Let's go to lunch," Sam said. "We'll open a bottle of wine and talk. If you still want endorphins after that, I'll see what I can do about it."

TEN

They left the condo, crossed Front Street, and went to Downrigger's, a popular seafood restaurant. On a warm summer day, there was no better place in Friday Harbor to have lunch than the outside deck facing Shaw Island. Sam ordered a bottle of white wine and an appetizer of Alaskan sea scallops wrapped in bacon, charbroiled, and served on corn relish. The melting sweetness of the scallops was perfectly balanced by the salty bacon and the smoky-sweet corn.

Sipping from a glass of chilled Chardonnay, soothed by Sam's easy charm, Lucy felt herself begin to relax. She told Sam about Alice's childhood meningitis and its aftereffects, about how off balance the family dynamic had been afterward.

"I was always jealous of Alice," Lucy said. "But eventually I realized there was no reason for me to feel that way. Because she grew up expecting everything to be given to her, and that's a terrible way to go through life. She never finishes anything she starts. I think my mom is beginning to regret having spoiled her so much, but it's too late. Alice's never going to change."

"It's never too late to change."

"You wouldn't say that if you'd met Alice. It goes down to the bone. I honestly can't figure out what Kevin sees in her."

Sam's eyes were obscured by a pair of aviator sunglasses. "What did you see in Kevin?"

Lucy chewed slowly on her lower lip. "He was really thoughtful in the beginning," she eventually said. "Affectionate. Dependable."

"What about the sex?"

Lucy flushed and darted a glance at their surroundings to see if anyone had overheard. "What does that have to do with anything?"

Sam shrugged slightly. "Sex is the canary in the coal mine." At Lucy's blank look, he continued. "Miners used to bring a canary in a cage underground. If there was a carbon dioxide leak in the mine, the canary would drop dead first, and they would know to get out of there. So . . . how was it?"

"I don't want to talk about it," Lucy said primly.

His smile was edged with friendly mockery. "Never mind. I already know the answer."

Her eyes turned huge. "Kevin told you about our sex life?"

Sam squinted his eyes with the effort to remember. "Something about Crisco, jumper cables, a snorkel mask —"

"It was *entirely normal,*" Lucy whispered sharply, now crimson. "Plain old regular, boring, vanilla sex."

"That was my second guess," he said gravely.

She scowled. "If you're going to make fun of me all during lunch —"

"I'm not making fun of you. I'm teasing you. There's a difference."

"I don't like being teased."

"Fair enough," Sam said, his voice softening. "I won't do it anymore."

After the waitress came to take their entree orders, Lucy contemplated Sam with cautious interest. He was a bundle of contradictions . . . a reputed womanizer who seemed to have spent a lot more time working in his vineyard than chasing females . . . a man who maintained the pretense of being carefree while at the same sharing the responsibility of raising a child.

"I'm surprised I haven't met you before,"

167

she said. "Especially since we both know Justine."

"I haven't been all that social since I started the vineyard. It's a lot of work, especially at the beginning. Not the kind of job you set aside on weekends. And for the past year, Holly's needed all the attention Mark and I could spare."

"You've both sacrificed a lot for her, haven't you?"

"It wasn't a sacrifice. Holly is the best thing that ever happened to me. With kids, you get a lot more than you give." Sam paused reflectively. "I also got a brother out of the deal."

"You and Mark weren't close before?"

Sam shook his head. "But in the past year we've gotten to know each other. We've had to depend on each other. And it turns out I like the guy."

"I'm getting the impression," she said hesitantly, "that you might have come from . . . a troubled family?"

"It wasn't a family. It looked like one on the outside, but it was no more a family than the carcasses hanging in a meat locker are a herd of cows."

"I'm sorry," Lucy said gently. "Was there a problem with one of your parents?"

Sam hesitated for such a long moment

that Lucy thought he might not reply. "There's always a town drunk in a small community," he finally said. "With my parents, you got two for the price of one." His mouth took on a faint, wry curve. "A pair of married alcoholics will support each other all the way to hell."

"Did either of them ever try to get help?"

He shook his head. "Even if one of them had, it's almost impossible to get sober when you live with another alcoholic."

The conversation had acquired a sense of carefulness, boundaries being tested, tricky territory.

"They were always that way?" Lucy asked.

"For as long as I can remember. As the kids got old enough to leave in turn, we got the hell out of there. Until only Alex was left. And now . . ."

"He's an alcoholic?"

"I'm not sure where to draw that line. But if he hasn't crossed it yet, he will soon."

No wonder he was afraid of commitment, Lucy thought. No wonder he had a problem with relationships that went beyond the physical. Having one parent as an alcoholic was enough to ruin a family. The children would always have to be on guard, dealing with constant manipulation and abuse. But when both of them were drinkers . . . there was no safe place. No one you could trust.

"With your parents' issues," Lucy asked, "did you worry about getting into the wine business?"

"Not at all. Just because my parents were drunks doesn't mean I can't love wine. Besides, I'm not as much of a winemaker as I am a grape grower. A farmer."

Lucy was privately amused. With his laid-back sexiness, wearing those dark aviator sunglasses, Sam couldn't have looked less like a farmer. "What do you like most about being a grape grower?"

"It's a mixture of science, hard work . . . and a touch of magic."

"Magic," Lucy repeated, staring at him closely.

"Sure. A vintner can grow the same kind of grapes in the same patch of soil, but it turns out differently every year. The flavor of the grapes tells you about the soil composition, how long the sun shone, how cool the nighttime breezes were, how much rain fell. It's the unique expression of a place and a season. *Terroir,* the French call it."

Conversation was momentarily interrupted as the waitress brought their entrees and refilled their water glasses. As lunch continued at a leisurely pace, Lucy found herself relaxing and enjoying herself even more than she would have expected. Sam had a way of focusing on a person that was immensely flattering, especially to a woman with a bruised ego. He was smart, self-deprecating, and so charming that she could easily have been lulled into a false sense of security.

But she could not let herself forget that he was the kind of guy who would find his way past your guard, take what he wanted, and convince you that it was what you wanted as well. He would run you in circles, put mileage on you, and then go on to his next conquest without a backward glance. And you wouldn't be able to complain, because he hadn't put up a pretense of being anything other than what he was.

Eventually the waitress brought the check, and Sam put his hand over Lucy's as she began to reach for her bag. "Don't even think about it," he told her, and gave the waitress his credit card.

"Friends can go Dutch," Lucy protested.

"It's a small price to pay for the pleasure of your company."

"Thank you," she said sincerely. "I've had a wonderful time. In fact, I'm in such a good mood, I don't think anything could spoil it."

"Don't jinx yourself." He knocked on the table.

She laughed. "Are you superstitious?"

"Of course. I'm an islander. I was raised on superstition."

"Such as?" Lucy asked, entertained.

"The wishing stones on South Beach. You know about those, right? No? People are always looking for them. Smooth stones circled by white bands. If you find one, you make a wish and throw it into the sea."

"Have you done that?"

"Once or twice."

"Did your wishes come true?"

"Not yet. But wishes don't have expiration dates."

"I'm not superstitious," Lucy said. "But I do believe in magic."

"So do I. It's called science."

"I believe in real magic," Lucy insisted.

"Like what?"

Before Lucy could answer, she caught a glimpse of a couple entering the outside seating area. All the color drained from her face. *"Shit,"* she whispered, the glow of well-being fading rapidly. A sick feeling rushed over her. "You were right. I jinxed myself."

Following her gaze, Sam saw Kevin and Alice. He frowned and reached for her nerveless hand. "Look at me, Lucy."

She dragged her gaze to his and managed a bleak smile. "There's no way we can avoid them, is there?"

"No." His grip was firm and reassuring. "There's no need to be scared."

"I'm not scared. I'm just not ready to deal with this yet."

"How do you want to play it?"

Fixing him with a desperate stare, Lucy made a spontaneous decision. "Kiss me," she said urgently.

Sam's eyes flickered with mild surprise. "Right now?"

"Yes."

"What kind of kiss?"

"What do you mean, what kind of kiss? Just a regular kiss."

"A friendly kiss, or a romantic kiss? Are we supposed to be going out together, or —"

"Oh, *for heaven's sake*," she exclaimed, and pulled his head down to hers.

ELEVEN

Sam responded without hesitation as he felt Lucy's small hand grip the back of his neck. He had wanted her all during lunch, fascinated by her prickly vulnerability, the way her smiles never quite reached her eyes. He couldn't stop thinking about the way she had glowed when she'd talked about her work, her fingers unconsciously stroking a sheet of glass as if it was a lover's skin.

He wanted to take Lucy to bed and keep her there, until all the wary tension was gone and she was soft and satiated in his arms. Needing to taste her, Sam increased the pressure of the kiss and touched the tip of his tongue to hers. The glassy softness aroused him instantly, filling him with hard-charging heat. Her body was fine-boned but strong, not quite yielding to his. That hint of resistant tautness made him long to grip her, force her close until she was molded against him.

Realizing the public display of affection was going to spiral out of control — at least on his part — he broke off the kiss and lifted his head just enough to look into her dazed green eyes. Her porcelain skin was infused with color. Her breath struck his lips in hot surges, teasing his senses.

Lucy's gaze shifted. "They've seen us," she whispered.

Still absorbed in thoughts of what he wanted to do with her, Sam felt a surge of annoyance. He didn't want to deal with that pair of idiots, didn't want to talk, didn't want to do anything but take his woman to bed.

A warning chill raced through him. *His* woman . . . ? He'd never thought such a thing in his life. He was not the possessive type. The need to claim one particular woman, to insist on exclusive rights to her, was just not in him. And it never would be.

So why the hell had he made such a slip?

He slung an arm around Lucy's shoulders and turned to face Kevin and Alice, who wore near-comical expressions of dismay.

"Nolan," Kevin said, not quite able to look at Lucy.

"Pearson."

Awkwardly Kevin made an introduction. "Sam Nolan, this is my . . . friend, Alice."

Alice reached out a slender arm, and Sam shook her hand amid a clatter of stacked bracelets. She was as fine-boned as Lucy, with the same rich dark hair. But she was matchstick-thin and angular, teetering on high-heeled cork wedges, her cheekbones as prominent as guardrails. A heavy application of makeup had left her raccoon-eyed and disconcertingly shimmery. Although Sam was predisposed not to like Alice, he felt a touch of sympathy. She gave him the impression of a woman who was trying a little too hard — a woman whose insecurity was revealed by her zealous efforts to conceal it.

"I'm his fiancée," Alice said in a brittle tone.

"Congratulations," Lucy said. Although she was trying her best to look inscrutable, hurt, anger, and vulnerability chased over her features in quicksilver progression.

Alice looked at her. "I wasn't sure how to tell you."

"I've already talked to Mom about it," Lucy replied. "Have you set a date yet?"

"We're looking at the end of summer."

Sam decided that was enough conversation. Time to end it before any fireworks started. "Good luck," he said briskly, urging Lucy with him. "We have to be going."

"Have a nice lunch," Lucy added in a monotone.

Sam kept Lucy's hand in his as they left the restaurant. A weird, distant expression had appeared on her face. He felt somehow that if he let go of Lucy she might wander off somewhere in a daze, like an abandoned shopping cart rolling through a grocery store parking lot.

They crossed the street and headed in the direction of the art studio.

"Why did I say that?" Lucy asked abruptly.

"What?"

" 'Have a nice lunch.' I didn't mean it at all. I hope they have a terrible lunch. I hope they choke on it."

"Believe me," Sam said dryly, "no one thought you meant it."

"Alice looked skinny. Not happy. What did you think of her?"

"I think you're worth a hundred of her." Sam switched places to walk on the curb side.

"Then why did Kevin —" She broke off with an impatient shake of her head.

It took Sam a moment to answer. Not because he had to think of a reason — he already knew why. But Lucy had the damnedest effect on him, provoking odd rushes of tenderness and liking and a nameless sort of *something* . . . he didn't know what it was, but he didn't like it.

"Kevin went for your sister because he feels superior to her," he said.

"How do you know that?"

"Because he's the type who needs a dependent woman. He has to be the one in control. He was attracted to you for obvious reasons, but it was never going to work out long-term."

Lucy nodded, as if that had confirmed something she'd already thought. "But why rush into marriage? When I talked to Mom, she said that Alice had lost her job recently. So maybe Alice doesn't know what else to do. But that doesn't explain why Kevin's going along with it."

"Would you take him back?"

"Never." A desolate note entered her voice. "But I thought he was happy with me, when he obviously wasn't. Not great for the ego."

Sam stopped at the street corner and turned her to face him. He would have loved nothing more than to take her back to the condo and show her a few of his ideas about how to restore her wounded ego. As he looked down into her small, sensitive face, it occurred to him that this was something new in his experience . . . an attraction that seemed to gather momentum from the weight of each second he spent with her.

But how much would he have hurt her, when it was over? With amused self-derision, Sam realized that his instinct to seduce her was equally matched by the desire to warn her away from him.

Smiling slightly, he lifted his hand to trace the delicate edge of her jawline. "You take life seriously, don't you?"

A frown tugged between her brows. "How else am I supposed to take it?"

Sam grinned. Using both hands, he turned her face up and brushed a slow, soft kiss against her lips. Her skin was hot, the throb of her pulse a swift, strong tattoo against his fingers. The contact, limited though it was, aroused him more than it should have, faster than he could have anticipated. Lifting his head, he struggled to moderate his breathing, to will away the gathering ache of desire.

"If you're ever interested in a meaningless physical relationship that's heading absolutely nowhere," he told her, "I hope you'll let me know."

They walked in silence until they reached Lucy's art studio.

Lucy paused at the threshold. "I'm interested in the condo, Sam," she said carefully.

"But not if it's going to lead to a difficult situation."

"It won't," Sam said, having just come to the conclusion that as much as he wanted to have a fling with Lucy Marinn, there was no way it could end well. He offered her a friendly smile and a brief, platonic hug. "I'll get the information from Mark, and call you."

"Okay." Drawing back, Lucy gave him an uncertain smile. "Thanks for lunch. And even more for getting me through the first encounter with Kevin and Alice."

"I didn't do anything," he said. "You would have gotten through just fine on your own."

"I know. But it was easier with you there."

"Good," he said, and smiled at her before leaving.

"It's crooked," Holly announced in the morning, entering the kitchen.

Sam looked up from pouring a bowl of cereal. "What's crooked?"

The child turned around to show him the back of her head. She had asked Sam to arrange her hair in two ponytails, a painstaking process that began with drawing a perfectly straight part down the back. The ponytails could not be too low, too high, too loose, or too tight. Usually Mark was recruited to do Holly's hair, since he had the knack for doing it the way she liked. But Mark had spent the night at Maggie's house, and was uncharacteristically late getting back that morning.

Sam examined the part at the back of Holly's head. "It's as straight as a cat's tail."

She gave him a mildly exasperated glance. "Cats' tails aren't straight."

"They are when you pull them," he said, and gently tugged one of her ponytails. He set the bowl of cereal on the table. "You're going to be late for school if I have to redo it."

Holly heaved a sigh. "I guess I'll have to go around like *this* all day." She tilted her head at a compensating angle.

Sam laughed, nearly choking on a swallow of coffee. "If you hurry through breakfast, we might have time to fix it."

"Fix what?" came Mark's voice as he entered the kitchen. He went to Holly and knelt by her chair. "Good morning, sweetheart."

Her arms went around his neck. "Good morning, Uncle Mark." She kissed him and pressed a grin against his shoulder. "Will you fix my hair?"

Mark gave her a sympathetic glance. "Did

Sam do it crooked again? I'll take care of it. But first eat your cereal while it's still crunchy."

"How's it going?" Sam asked, while Mark emptied the coffeepot and strainer basket. "Everything okay?"

Mark nodded, looking weary and perturbed. "Great dinner with Maggie last night — everything's fine — we're just trying to figure out some tricky scheduling." He paused, his dark brows drawing together. "We're trying to set the wedding date. Maybe move it up a little. I'll tell you more later."

"Why the rush?" Sam asked. "It's not like there's a time limit on your engagement."

Mark filled the tank of the coffee machine. He slid Sam a guarded glance. "There is, actually."

"I don't get it. Why . . ." Then it hit him. Sam's eyes widened. "We're talking about a nine-month time limit?" he asked gingerly.

A slight nod.

"Is Maggie going to have a baby?" Holly asked around a mouthful of cereal.

Mark turned away and swore quietly, while Sam gave Holly an incredulous glance. "How did you know what I was asking?"

"I watch the Discovery Channel."

"Thanks, Sam," Mark growled.

Sam grinned and gave him a back-slapping bear hug. "Congratulations."

Holly leaped from her chair and bounced up and down. "Can I help take care of the baby? Can I help name it? Can I have a day off of school when it's born? When's the baby coming?"

"Yes, yes, yes, and we don't know yet," Mark said. "Sweetheart, is there any way we can keep this private for a little while? We're not at the point where Maggie wants to start telling people yet."

"Sure," Holly said brightly. "I can keep a secret."

Mark and Sam exchanged a rueful glance, knowing that everyone at the elementary school would know by day's end.

After Mark had dropped Holly at school, he came back to find Sam staining the newly installed wainscoting in the living room. The smell of the stain, a dark walnut color, packed a hefty punch even though Sam had opened the windows to provide good ventilation.

"Don't come in unless you want a buzz," Sam said.

"In that case, I'm definitely helping you."

Sam smiled quizzically as Mark entered the room. "The news was a shock, huh? You two weren't planning on this?"

"No." Sighing, Mark sat beside him and picked up a paintbrush.

"This wainscoting's a son of a bitch to stain," Sam said. "You have to get it into all the grooves. So how did you react when Maggie told you?"

"One hundred and ten percent positive, of course. I told her it was the best news ever, and I loved her, and everything's going to be great."

"So what's the problem?" Sam asked.

"I'm scared shitless."

Sam laughed quietly. "That's normal, I guess."

"My biggest worry is Holly. I don't want her to feel shoved aside. I wanted some time to focus on her, for me and Maggie to do things with just her."

"I think Holly needs just the opposite," Sam said. "I mean, hell, Mark, she's had the two of us — and sometimes Alex — focused entirely on her for a year. The poor kid could probably use a break. With a baby coming into the picture, Holly will have some company. She'll love it."

A doubtful glance. "You think so?"

"How could she not? A mom, a dad, and a baby brother or sister — a perfect family."

Mark worked the stain into the wainscoting. A couple of minutes passed before he could bring himself to admit what was really bothering him. "I hope to God I can be good enough for them, Sam."

Sam understood. When you came from a family as dysfunctional as theirs, you had no idea how to do things. There was no template, no trove of memories to call on when you needed to know how to handle something. You wanted a guarantee that you wouldn't somehow end up like one or the other of your parents. But there were no guarantees. There was only the hope that if you did everything the opposite of how you were raised, maybe things would turn out okay.

"You're already good enough," Sam said.

"I'm not ready to be a father. I'm worried as hell that I'm going to drop the ball."

"Don't worry about dropping the ball. It's dropping the baby that causes problems."

Mark scowled. "I'm trying to tell you that I think I'm more screwed up than I seem."

"I've never doubted that," Sam said, and grinned at his expression. Sobering, he continued, "You, Alex, and I are all screwed up by virtue of being Nolans. But you're the one most likely to turn out okay. I can picture you being a pretty decent father. Which is a miracle, and a hell of a lot more than I could say about Alex or me."

"I had it better than you and Alex," Mark said after a moment. "Mom and Dad weren't as bad early on in their marriage. It was only after Alex was born that they became raging alcoholics. So I had the benefit of . . . well, it wasn't exactly family life . . . but it was as close as the Nolans ever got. You had no one."

"I had the Harbisons," Sam pointed out.

Mark paused in the middle of dipping a paintbrush. "I'd forgotten about them."

"I'd be as bad off as Alex," Sam said, "maybe even worse, if it weren't for them. Fred had no kids of his own, but he knew a lot more about being a dad than ours. Which leads back to what I was saying . . . you're going to do fine."

"How do you know?"

"Remember when we first got Holly and she was bouncing off the walls at ten p.m., and the pediatrician had to explain to us what 'overtired' meant?"

"Yeah. What does that have to do with it?"

"Only that we knew nothing about raising kids, not even the most basic stuff. But in spite of that, Holly's doing great. You've been more than good enough. So you'll just have to keep figuring it out as you go along, which as far as I can tell is what most parents do. And if you're going to err on the side of anything, err on the side of love. Because that's the point of all of this, isn't it? You're getting another person in your life to love."

"Jesus, you get sentimental when you're high on paint fumes." But Mark's face had relaxed, and he smiled. "Thanks."

"Don't mention it."

"So considering all this advice you're giving me . . . are you going to change your mind at some point?"

"About getting married? Hell, no. I like women too much to do that to one of them. I'm not cut out for it any more than Alex is."

"Hey . . . have you seen Alex recently?"

"A few nights ago," Sam said. "Just for a minute."

"How's he doing?"

"He's overtired."

A grim smile touched Mark's face. "Lately every time I see Alex, he's at least halfway tanked."

"I think that's the only way he can face life." Sam paused. "He's hard up for cash now. Darcy cleaned him out."

"It's what the idiot deserves, for marrying her in the first place."

"True."

They stained wood in silence for a couple

of minutes. "What can we do?" Mark eventually asked.

"Wait until he hits bottom."

"What if Alex doesn't survive hitting bottom? Neither of our parents did."

Unable to tolerate the fumes anymore, Sam replaced the top on the can of stain and went to the open window. He took a few deep, cleansing breaths of fresh air. "I guess we could try some kind of intervention," he said doubtfully.

"If it gives us the chance to kick his ass around for a few minutes, let's do it."

Sam cast a brief smile over his shoulder and looked out at the vineyard, the green canopy reaching skyward. "Wouldn't work with Al," he heard himself say. The air was filled with the scent of growing vines, of sun-braised house shingles and plump blackberries, and the salty, fecund smell of False Bay.

When things had gotten especially bad in the past year, Alex would come over to work on the house or just sit on the porch. Sometimes Sam had persuaded him to walk through the vineyard or down to the bay with him. But Sam had had the feeling that the scenery was all shadows to Alex . . . he was moving through life without experiencing it.

Of all the Nolan offspring, Alex had had it the worst. With each year their parents' neglect had metastasized until there had been nothing left for the youngest son. Now, long after Jessica and Alan were gone, Alex was like a drowning man — you could see him submerged just below the surface. But there was only so far you could go in the effort to help Alex. Get too near someone who was drowning, and in their desperate struggle, they would claw, grasp, and drag you down with them. And Sam wasn't at all certain that he was in any shape to save anyone — at this point it was still unclear whether he could even save himself.

Lucy awakened in the morning in a welter of confusion. She'd been plagued by dreams that had left her with impressions of sliding, twisting, pleasure-tensed bodies . . . of herself, caught beneath the heavy welcome weight of a man. She had been dreaming of Sam, she acknowledged with mortified annoyance. Maybe it was a good sign — it certainly signaled that she had moved on from Kevin. On the other hand, it was idiotic. Sam was a guy for whom any relationship was a guaranteed dead-end street.

What she needed, Lucy decided, was exercise and fresh air. She left the inn, walked to her studio, and retrieved her bike and helmet. It was a beautiful day, sunny and breezy, perfect for visiting a local lavender farm and buying some handmade soap and bath oil.

She rode at a leisurely pace along Roche Harbor Road. Although it was the island's busiest thoroughfare, it had a good wide shoulder for cyclists, and it offered charming views of orchards, pastures, ponds, and densely wooded forest. The pleasant monotony of the ride helped to settle her thoughts.

She considered how it had felt to see Kevin and Alice yesterday. It had been a welcome discovery to realize that she felt nothing for him anymore. The real problem, the source of continuing grief, was her relationship with Alice. Lucy recognized that some form of forgiveness was necessary for her own sake. Otherwise the pain of betrayal would follow Lucy like the closer-than-they-appear objects in a rearview mirror. But what if Alice never expressed any regret whatsoever? How did you forgive someone who wasn't at all sorry for what they had done?

Hearing a car approach, Lucy took care to ride on the outmost edge of the shoulder to give the driver the widest possible berth.

But in the next few seconds she felt that the car was coming on too fast, the sound of it was directly behind her. She glanced over her shoulder. The car, a boatlike sedan, had drifted out of the traffic lane and was swerving toward her. There was a blinding moment, in which she felt the draft of the car just before its impact against the back of her bike. The scene scattered like an overturned display of greeting cards. She was in the air, suspended and topsy-turvy among pieces of sky, slivers of forest and asphalt and metal, and then the ground zoomed up to her at light speed.

When she opened her eyes, her first thought was that it was morning, time to wake up. But she wasn't in bed. She was sprawled in a patch of shivering weeds. A pair of strangers crouched over her, a man and a woman.

"Don't move her," the woman cautioned, a cell phone up to her ear.

"I'm just going to take off her helmet," the man said.

"I don't think you should do that. There might be a spinal cord injury or something."

The man looked down at Lucy in concern as she began to move. "Wait, take it easy. What's your name?"

"Lucy," she gasped, fumbling with the

chinstrap of her helmet.

"Here, let me help you take that off."

"Hal, I told you —" the woman began.

"I think it's all right. She's moving her arms and legs." He unbuckled the helmet and eased it off Lucy's head. "No, don't try to sit up yet. You got banged up real good."

Staying still, Lucy tried to evaluate the catalog of hurts in her body. The right side was scraped and burning, and there was a dull pain in her shoulder, and she had a killer of a headache. The worst by far, however, was her right leg and foot, which felt like they had been set on fire.

The woman leaned over her. "An ambulance is coming. Is there someone I can call for you?"

Her teeth were chattering. The more she tried to make the tremors stop, the worse they became. She was cold, icy trickles of sweat collecting beneath her clothes. Salty metallic smells of dust and blood were thick in her nose.

"Slow down, slow down," the man said, while Lucy panted for air in shallow breaths. "Eyes are dilated."

"Shock." The woman's voice seemed to be coming from a great distance, followed by a peppering of static.

A name came to Lucy. Justine. The effort

to collect syllables was like collecting leaves in a storm. She heard shuddering sounds coming from her lips. Was the name clear enough?

"Okay," the man said in a soothing tone. "Don't try to talk."

There were more sounds, vehicles pulling to the side of the road, the flash of lights, the red gleam of an EMS quick-response vehicle. Voices. Questions. The faltering awareness of unfamiliar hands on her body, an oxygen mask strapped over her mouth and nose, the sting of an IV needle. And then everything slipped away, and she went spinning out into nothingness.

TWELVE

Consciousness came back to Lucy in a puzzle that had to be assembled before she could make sense of anything. Smells of latex, tape, isopropyl alchohol. Sounds of voices, the rattling wheels of a cart or gurney, a telephone ringing, the composed blips of a vital signs monitor. She was disconcerted by the discovery that she was talking like an actress whose lines had been badly dubbed in a movie, syllables not quite matching up.

She was dressed in a thin cotton hospital gown that she had no memory of changing into. An IV needle had been inserted at the top of her hand and taped into place. Every time an ER tech or nurse came into the little curtained-off area, the rollers on the ceiling runners made a whisking sound, like eggs being beaten in a metal bowl.

Her right leg and ankle had been immobilized in a splint. Vague recollections of examinations and X-rays came to her. Even though she knew how lucky she was, how much worse the accident could have been, depression rolled over her in a smothering blanket. As she turned her head to the side, the pillow beneath her head gave a plasticky crackle. A tear runneled down her cheek, absorbed by the pillowcase.

"Here." The nurse handed her a tissue. "That's normal after an accident," she said as Lucy blotted her eyes. "You'll probably be doing that on and off for the next few days."

"Thank you." Lucy gripped the tissue in her palm. "Can you tell me what's wrong with my leg?"

"The doctor's reviewing the X-rays right now. He'll be in to talk to you soon." The woman smiled, her face kind. "In the meantime, you've got a visitor." She whisked the curtain aside and stopped short as she confronted someone. "Oh! You were supposed to wait in that room."

"I need to see her right now," came Justine's brisk voice.

A feeble grin came to Lucy's face.

Justine swept in like a fresh breeze, her dark ponytail swinging, her presence vital in the cold sterility of the hospital surroundings. The relief of having her friend there brought a sting of tears to Lucy's eyes.

"Lucy . . . sweetie . . ." Justine came to her, carefully straightening the loop of the IV tubing. "My God. I'm afraid to hug you. How bad is it? Anything broken?"

"The doctor's coming in soon." She reached for Justine's hand, words coming out in a tumble. "I was riding my bike and I got sideswiped. The car was swerving like it was a drunk driver. I think it was a woman. I don't know why she didn't stop. I don't know where my bike is, or my bag or phone —"

"Slow down." Justine gripped her hand. "It wasn't a drunk driver, it was an old lady. She thought she'd hit a branch, but she stopped a little ways up the road and came back. She was so upset when she realized what had happened, the couple who found you thought she was having a heart attack."

"Poor woman," Lucy murmured.

"Your bag and phone are here. The bike's toast."

"It's a vintage Schwinn," Lucy said mournfully. "From the sixties. All the original parts."

"A bike can be replaced. You can't."

"You were sweet to come here," Lucy said. "I know how busy you are."

"Are you kidding? Nothing's more important than you or Zoë. She wanted to come too, but someone had to stay at the inn." Justine paused. "Before I forget, Duane wanted me to tell you that they've figured out the problem with your car. It has cylinder compression problems."

"What does that mean?"

"It could involve a faulty intake valve or piston rings, cylinder head gaskets . . . Duane's taking it to the shop to make sure it's fixed right. No idea how long it might take."

Lucy shook her head, exhausted and disoriented. "With my leg all messed up, I probably won't be able to drive for a while anyway."

"You have a legion of bikers who'll take you anywhere you want to go." Justine paused. "As long as you don't mind getting there on a Harley."

Lucy managed a faint smile.

The doctor, a black-haired man with tired eyes and a pleasant smile, came in.

"I'm Dr. Nagano," he said, approaching Lucy. "Remember me?"

"Sort of," Lucy said sheepishly. "You asked me to touch my nose. And you wanted to know my middle name."

"Part of a diagnostic test. You have a slight concussion, which means you'll need to rest for the next few days. And in light of your X-rays, that won't be a problem."

"You mean my leg? Is it broken?"

Dr. Nagano shook his head.

"Oh, good," Lucy said.

"Actually, a clean break would be preferable. A bone heals more easily than a strained ligament."

"That's what I have? A strained ligament?"

"Three of them. Plus a hairline crack in the fibula, which is the smaller of your two calf bones. Needless to say, you're going to be completely off your feet for the next three days."

"I can't even walk from one room to another?"

"That's right. No weight at all on that leg. Keep it elevated and iced. Those ligaments are going to require some time to heal properly. I'll be sending you home with some detailed instructions. In three days, you'll come back for an Aircast brace and crutches."

"For how long?"

"A minimum of three months in the brace."

"God." Lucy closed her eyes.

"Any other injuries?" she heard Justine ask.

"Scrapes and bruises, nothing major. The important thing is to monitor her for any side effects from the concussion . . . headache, nausea, confusion . . . in which case she'll need to come in right away."

"Got it," Justine said.

After the doctor left, Lucy opened her eyes and saw Justine rubbing her forehead as if it was a wadded-up piece of paper she was trying to smooth out.

"Oh," Lucy murmured in dawning dismay. "You and Zoë already have your hands full, don't you?" For the past few days, they had been frantically preparing for a huge wedding and reception that would be held this weekend. "This is the worst possible time for me to do this to you."

"You didn't do it on purpose," Justine said. "And it's not like there's ever a convenient time to get hit by a car."

"I've got to think of what to do . . . where to go . . ."

"Do not worry," Justine said firmly. "From this moment every bit of your energy is going to be spent healing up. *Not* stressing. I'll figure out what to do."

"I'm so sorry," Lucy said with a sniffle. "I'm a pain in the ass."

"Shut. Up." Justine reached for a fresh tissue and clamped it to Lucy's nose as if she was a child. "Friends are the support bras of life. We don't let each other down. Right?"

Lucy nodded.

Justine stood and smiled at her. "I'll be in the waiting room, making a few calls. Don't go anywhere."

From the moment Sam had gotten Justine's call, he'd been seized with grim anxiety. "I'll be there" was all he'd said, and within fifteen minutes, he had reached the clinic.

Entering the building with ground-eating strides, he found Justine in the waiting room.

"Sam," she said, a ghost of a smile crossing her face. "Thanks for coming here. It's a hell of a situation."

"How's Lucy?" he asked curtly.

"A mild concussion, scrapes and cuts, and her leg is totally messed up. Strained ligaments and a fracture."

"Damn it," he said softly. "How did it happen?"

Justine explained in a flurry of words, while he listened without comment. ". . . so she can't move *at all* for a few days," she finished. "And even though Lucy doesn't weigh much, Zoë and I can't carry her around."

"I'll help," Sam said at once.

Justine let out a deep sigh. "Thank God. I adore you. I knew you'd have enough room at your house, and Zoë and I have the wedding from hell at the inn this weekend. We won't have one spare second, and there's just no way we could —"

"Wait," Sam interrupted brusquely. "I can't take Lucy to my house."

Justine clamped her hands on her hips and gave him an exasperated glance. "You just said you'd help."

"Yes, *help*. She can't stay with me."

"Why not?"

The strength of his objection had left Sam temporarily mute. He had never let a woman spend the night at his place. And he *especially* didn't want Lucy in his house. Especially not wounded and needing him. He had gone tense all over, a mist of sweat covering his skin.

"Why can't someone else do it?" he asked tersely. "What about her parents?"

"They live in Pasadena."

"Doesn't she have other friends?"

"Yes, but not on the island. With the exception of Zoë and me, she lost the friends she made with Kevin. They didn't want to piss him off by taking her side." With exaggerated patience, Justine asked, "What exactly is the problem, Sam?"

"I barely know her," he protested.

"You like her. You rushed right over here when I called."

"I don't know Lucy well enough to help her in and out of bed, carry her to the shower, change the bandages, all that stuff."

"What, you're all prudish now? Come off it, Sam. You've been with a lot of women. Nothing you haven't seen before."

"It's not that." Sam paced across the empty waiting room, raking a hand through his hair. How could he explain the profound danger of intimacy with Lucy? That the problem was how much he actually wanted to take care of her? He didn't trust himself with her. He would end up having sex with her, taking advantage of her, hurting her.

He stopped pacing and glowered at Justine. "Look," he said through gritted teeth. "I don't want to get close to her. I don't want her to depend on me."

Justine gave him a narrow-eyed glance that should have slayed him on the spot. "Are you really *that* screwed up, Sam?"

"Of course I am," he snapped. "Have I ever pretended to be normal?"

Justine made a sound of disgust. "You know what? I'm sorry I asked. My mistake."

Sam scowled as she turned away. "What are you going to do?"

"Don't worry about it. Not your problem."

"Who are you calling?" he insisted.

"Duane. He and his friends will take care of her."

Sam's mouth fell open. "You're going to give a wounded woman on medication to *a biker gang?*"

"They're good guys. They have their own church."

Instant fury sent hot blood to his face. "Having your own church doesn't make you a good guy. It only makes you tax-exempt."

"Don't shout at me."

"I'm not shouting."

"I wouldn't call that your inside voice, Sam." Justine lifted her phone and tapped on the small screen.

"No," he growled.

"No, what?"

Sam took a deep breath, yearning to put his fist through a wall. "I'll —" He broke off and cleared his throat roughly, and gave her a wrathful glance. "I'll take her."

"To your house," she clarified.

"Yes," he said through gritted teeth.

"Good. Thank you. My God, all this drama." Shaking her head, Justine went to the vending machine and punched some buttons to get a drink.

■ ■ ■ ■

Lucy blinked in bewilderment as Sam Nolan came through the curtain partitions. "What are you doing here?" she asked faintly.

"Justine called me."

"She shouldn't have. I'm sorry."

His gaze slid over her, not missing a detail. When he spoke, his voice was quiet and gruff. "Are you in pain?"

"It's not bad." Lucy gestured to the IV bag. "They've got me on some kind of narcotic something-or-other." Fretfully she added, "There's a needle in my hand."

"We'll get you out of here soon."

She focused on Sam's T-shirt, dark blue with the printed white outlines of what looked like an old-fashioned telephone booth. "What is the phone booth for?"

"Police box. From *Dr. Who.*" Seeing her incomprehension, he explained, "It's a time-traveling spacecraft."

The shadow of a smile crossed her lips. "Geek," she said, and blew her nose.

Drawing closer, Sam settled his hand on her hip, exploring the outlines of a polyure-thane bandage, adjusting the drape of the hospital blanket over her splinted leg. There was something oddly proprietary about the way he touched her. Lucy stared at him in bewilderment, trying to fathom what was the matter with him. He had the air of a man who was facing an unpleasant duty.

"You look angry," she said.

"I'm not."

"You're clenching your jaw."

"That's the way my jaw always looks."

"Your eyes are glaring."

"It's the hospital lighting."

"Something's going on," she insisted.

Sam took her icy hand in his, careful not to dislodge the pulse oximeter that had been clamped to her forefinger. His thumb rubbed lightly over the backs of her fingers. "For the next few days, you're going to need someone to help you out. This is more than you can handle on your own." A measured pause. "So I'm going to take you to Rainshadow Road with me."

Lucy's eyes widened, and she tugged her hand from his. "No. I . . . *no,* I won't do that. Is that why Justine called you? God. I can't go anywhere with you."

Sam turned quietly ruthless. "Where are you planning to go, Lucy? The inn? Being closed off in a room by yourself with no one to help you? Even if Zoë and Justine didn't have a big event going on this weekend, they'd still have a hard time getting you up and down all those stairs."

Lucy pressed a clammy palm to her head, which had begun to ache fiercely. "I . . . I'll call my parents."

"They're at least a thousand miles away."

She was so worried and depleted that she felt her throat tighten against a new threat of tears. Appalled by her lack of control, she put her hand over her eyes and made a frustrated sound. "You're too busy. The vineyard —"

"My crew will cover for me."

"What about your brother and Holly?"

"They won't mind. It's a big house."

As she began to comprehend the situation, Lucy realized that Sam would be helping her with bathing, eating, dressing — intimacies that would be embarrassing even with someone she had known for a long time. And he didn't look any happier about the situation than she was.

"There's got to be another solution," Lucy said, trying desperately to think. She drew in an extra breath, and another, unable to get enough air into the tightening confines of her lungs.

"Damn it, don't start hyperventilating." Sam's hand settled on her chest, rubbing a slow circle. The familiarity of the gesture caused her to gasp.

"I haven't given you the right —" she began unsteadily.

"For the next few days," Sam said, his lashes lowering to conceal his expression, "you'll have to get used to having my hands on you." The circling motion continued, and Lucy subsided helplessly. To her mortification, a little coughing sob escaped her. She closed her eyes. "You're going to let me take care of you," she heard him say. "Don't waste your breath arguing. The fact is, you're coming home with me."

THIRTEEN

It was early evening by the time Sam's pickup turned onto Rainshadow Road and proceeded along the private drive. He had signed all of Lucy's release forms, collected a sheaf of medical instructions and prescriptions, and had accompanied Lucy as an RN had taken her outside in a wheelchair. Justine had been there too, her manner gratingly cheerful.

"Well, kids," she had chirped, "this is going to turn out fine. Sam, I owe you. Lucy, you'll love Sam's house — it's a great place — and someday, I guarantee we'll all look back on this and —What did you say, Sam?"

"I said, 'Shove it, Justine,' " he muttered, gathering Lucy up from the wheelchair.

Unperturbed, Justine followed as Sam carried Lucy around the truck. "I put together an overnight bag for you, Luce. Zoë or I will drop off more of your stuff tomorrow."

"Thank you." Lucy had wrapped her arms

around Sam's neck as he lifted her with astonishing ease. His shoulders were hard against her palms. The smell of his skin was delicious, clean with a hint of salt, like ocean air, and fresh like garden plants and green leaves.

Sam placed Lucy in the truck, adjusted her seat back, and buckled the seat belt. Every movement was deft and efficient, his manner impersonal. He kept glancing at her, taking measure. Unhappily she wondered what Justine had said to persuade him to take her. *"He doesn't want to do this,"* she had whispered to Justine in the hospital, and Justine had whispered back, *"He does. He's just a little nervous about it."*

But Sam didn't seem all that nervous to Lucy. He seemed quietly pissed off. The drive to the vineyard was silent. Although Sam's truck had excellent suspension, there was an occasional bump in the road that caused Lucy to wince. She was sore and exhausted, and she had never felt like such a burden to anyone.

Eventually they turned onto a private drive that led to a Victorian house adorned with gables, balustrades, a central cupola, and a widow's walk. A lazy sunset turned the white-painted house the color of Creamsicles. The foundation was skirted with a profusion of red shrub roses interspersed with white hydrangeas. Nearby, a stalwart gray barn chaperoned the vineyard rows, which frolicked across the terrain like children being let out for recess.

Lucy stared at the scene with bemused wonder. If San Juan Island was a world apart from the mainland, this was a world inside that one. The house waited with its windows open to catch sea breezes, moonlight, wandering spirits. It seemed to be waiting for her.

Taking in Lucy's reaction with an astute glance, Sam pulled the truck to a stop beside the house. "Yes," he said, as if she had asked a question. "That's how I felt when I first saw it." He got out of the truck and walked around to Lucy's side, reaching in to unbuckle the seat belt. "Put your arms around my neck," he said.

Hesitantly Lucy complied. He lifted her, mindful not to bump her splinted leg. As soon as his arms closed around her, Lucy was aware of a new, baffling feeling, a sense of yielding, something dissolving inside. Her head drooped heavily to his shoulder, and she struggled to lift it again. Sam murmured, "It's okay," and, "It's fine," which made her realize she was trembling.

They ascended the front steps to a wide

covered porch with a light blue ceiling. "Haint blue," Sam said, as he noticed Lucy looking upward. "We tried to match the original color as closely as possible. A lot of people around here used to paint their porch ceilings blue. Some say it's to fake out birds and insects, make them think it's the sky. But others say the real reason is to ward off ghosts."

The rush of words made Lucy realize that Sam actually was a little nervous, just as Justine had said. It was an unusual situation for both of them.

"Does your family know that I'm visiting?" she asked.

He nodded. "I called them from the clinic."

The front door opened, allowing a long rectangle of light to slide across the porch. A dark-haired man stood holding the door, while a blond girl and a bulldog came to the threshold. The man was a slightly older, more heavyset version of Sam, with the same roughcast handsomeness. And he had the same dazzling smile. "Welcome to Rainshadow," he said to Lucy. "I'm Mark."

"I'm sorry to impose. I —"

"Not a problem," Mark said easily. His gaze flicked to Sam. "What can I do?"

"Her bag's still in the car."

"I'll get it." Mark brushed past them.

"Make way, guys," Sam said to the child and the dog, and they scuttled to the side. "I'm going to take Lucy upstairs."

They went into an entrance hall with dark floors and a high coffered ceiling, the walls covered with cream paint and hung with framed botanical prints.

"Maggie's making dinner," Holly said, following them. "Chicken soup and yeast rolls, and banana pudding for dessert. *Real* pudding, not from a box."

"I knew it smelled too good to be Mark's cooking," Sam said.

"Maggie and I changed the sheets on your bed. She said I was a good helper."

"That's my girl. Go wash up for dinner now."

"Can I talk to Lucy?"

"Later, gingersnap. Lucy's exhausted."

"Hi, Holly," Lucy managed to say over his shoulder.

The child beamed at her. "Uncle Sam never invites anyone here for a sleepover. You're his first one!"

"Thanks, Holly," Sam said under his breath as he carried Lucy up the sweeping mahogany staircase.

A breathless laugh shivered in Lucy's throat. "I'm sorry. I know Justine made you

212

do this. I'm —"

"Justine couldn't make me do anything I didn't want to do."

Lucy let her head fall to his shoulder, unable to look at him as she said, "You don't want me here."

Sam chose his words carefully. "I don't want complications. Same as you."

As they reached the landing, Lucy's attention was captured by a huge window that afforded a view of the front drive. It was a striking stained-glass work, a bare tree delicately holding an orange winter moon in its branches.

But when Lucy blinked, the colors and patterns disappeared. The window was bare. It was nothing but clear float glass.

"Wait. What's that?"

Sam turned to see what she was staring at. "The window?"

"It used to be stained glass," Lucy said dazedly.

"It could have been."

"No, it *was*. With a tree and a moon."

"Whatever was in there was knocked out a long time ago. At some point someone tried to make the house into apartments." Sam carried her away from the window. "You should have seen it when I bought it. Shag rug in some rooms. They'd knocked out support walls and put in some flimsy chipboard ones. My brother Alex came in with his crew to rebuild load-bearing walls and put in support beams. Now the place is rock solid."

"It's beautiful. Like something from a fairy tale. I feel like I've been here before, or dreamed about it." Her mind was tired, her thoughts not connecting properly.

They went into a long rectangular bedroom paralleling the bay, the walls paneled with wide beadboard, a fireplace in the corner, abundant windows revealing the shining blue flat of False Bay. The window on either end of the row had been fitted with screens and opened to let in the outside air.

"Here we go." Sam set her on a large bed with a seagrass headboard and quilted blue covers that had already been folded back.

"This is your room? Your bed?"

"Yes."

Lucy tried to sit up. "Sam, no —"

"Be still," he said. "I mean it, Lucy. You're going to hurt yourself. You're taking the bed. I'm going to sleep on a rollaway in another room."

"I'm not going to kick you out of your own room. I'll sleep on the roll-away."

"You're going to sleep where I put you."

Sam tugged the snowy white and blue quilt over her. Bracing one hand on either side of Lucy's body, he stared down at her. Maybe it was the effect of the sunset glow pouring through the windows, but his face seemed to have gentled. He reached down to tuck a loose lock of her hair behind her ear. "Think you could stay awake long enough to have some soup?"

Lucy shook her head.

"Rest, then. I'll check on you in a little while."

Lucy lay quietly after he left. The room was serene and cool, and from the distance she could hear the rhythmic lapping of the tide. Pleasantly indistinct sounds filtered through the floor and walls, voices punctuated by an occasional laugh, the clinking of pots and dishes and flatware. Sounds of family and home, floating on the air like a lullaby.

Sam paused to stare out the window on the second-floor landing. The moon had appeared even before sunset had finished, a massive white-gold circle against the magenta sky. Scientists said that the size of the summer solstice moon was an optical trick, that the human eye was unable to accurately measure distance without the help of visual cues. But some illusions were truer than reality.

Once Sam had read a story about an ancient Chinese poet who had drowned while trying to embrace the reflection of the moon. He had been drinking rice wine along the Yangtze River — too much wine, in light of his ignominious death. But God knew there was no choice in yearning for something or someone you would never be able to have. You didn't even want a choice. That was the fatal temptation of moonlight.

Lucy was in his bed, as fragile as a broken orchid. He was tempted to stay in the hallway just outside the bedroom door and sit on the floor with his back to the wall, waiting for any sign that she needed something. But he made himself go downstairs, where Renfield was trotting back and forth with a discarded sock in his mouth, and Holly was setting the table, and Mark was on the phone talking to someone about scheduling a dentist appointment.

Heading into the kitchen, Sam went to the big freestanding wooden worktable where Maggie stood whisking cream in a bowl.

Maggie Conroy was pretty rather than beautiful, her personality so effervescent that she gave the impression of being taller than she actually was. It was only when you stood right next to her that you realized she couldn't be more than five foot one. "I'm five one and a half," Maggie always insisted, as if that last half inch made a damn bit of difference.

In the past Mark had always gone for trophy chicks, the kind who were great to look at but rarely fun to spend any actual time around. Thank God that when Mark had finally gotten serious with someone, it had been Maggie, whose quirky optimism was exactly what the family had needed.

Wordlessly Sam approached, took the whisk and bowl from her, and continued to whip the cream.

"Thanks," Maggie said, shaking out her cramped hand.

"Why don't you use the mixer?"

"Mark didn't tell you?" Maggie scrunched up her face adorably, and hung her head in shame. "I burned up the mixer motor last week. I promise, I'll replace it."

"Don't worry about it," Sam said, still whisking. "We're used to kitchen disasters around here. Except that Mark and I are usually the cause. How did you burn up the motor?"

"I was trying to make whole wheat pizza dough, and it got too heavy and stiff, and then there was a burning smell and the mixer started smoking."

Sam grinned, using the tip of the whisk to test the whipped cream, which was holding its shape. "Maggie, sweetheart, pizza is not something you cook at home. Pizza is what you get when you don't feel like cooking at home."

"I was trying to make a healthy version."

"Pizza's not supposed to be healthy. It's pizza." He handed the bowl to her, and she proceeded to cover it with plastic wrap and put it into the fridge.

After closing the Sub-Zero, which had been camouflaged with cream-painted cabinet doors to blend in with the rest of the kitchen, Maggie went to the stockpot on the stove and stirred the soup. "How is your friend?" she asked. "Lucy, right?"

"Yeah. She'll be fine."

Maggie sent him a perceptive sideways glance. "How about you?"

"Great," he said, a shade too quickly.

She began to ladle the steaming soup into bowls. "Should I fix a dinner tray for her?"

"No, she's down for the count." Sam went to an already-opened bottle of wine and poured himself a glass.

"So you've brought Lucy here to recuperate," Maggie remarked. "And you're going to take care of her. She must be someone special."

"No big deal." Sam kept his tone scrupulously offhand. "We're friends."

"Just friends?"

"Yeah."

"Is there a chance of anything more developing?"

"No." Again, his response was a little too fast. He scowled as he saw Maggie's knowing smile. "She doesn't want my kind of relationship."

"What kind is that? Sex with random beautiful women with no chance of commitment?"

"Exactly."

"If you find the right woman, you may want to try something a little more long-term."

Sam shook his head. "I don't do long-term." He set the table and went in search of Mark and Holly to tell them that dinner was ready. Finding them in the living room, he paused at the broad threshold, where a superfluous wall had been knocked out to allow for a more open floor plan.

Mark and Holly were seated close together on the sofa, a boatlike antique that Maggie had found and convinced Mark to buy. In its original condition, the sofa had been a monstrosity, all scarred and moth-eaten. But after the carved rosewood had been stripped and refinished, and it had been upholstered in acres of sage-green velvet, the settee possessed a whimsical grandiosity that suited the house.

Holly's legs dangled from the sofa. She swung her feet idly while Mark made notes in the family planner spread out on the coffee table.

". . . so when you're at the dentist's, and he asks how often you floss," Mark said, "what are you going to say?"

"I'll say, 'What's floss?' " Holly giggled as Mark goosed her in the side and kissed the top of her head.

Not for the first time, Sam was struck by the fatherly quality in Mark's attachment to her. In the past, it hadn't been a role that Mark had seemed particularly suited for . . . but he had grown into it with lightning speed when Holly had come into their lives.

Mark leaned over to scribble something in the family planner. "Did Maggie order those ballet shoes for your dance class yet?"

"I don't know."

"Okay, I'll ask her."

"Uncle Mark?"

"Mmmm-hmm?"

"The baby's going to be my cousin, isn't he?"

The pen stopped moving. Mark set it down carefully and looked into the child's solemn face. "Technically, yes. But I imagine . . ." He paused, choosing his words with care. "I imagine it will feel like the baby is your brother or sister. Because you'll be growing up together."

"Some kids in my class think you're my dad. You even look like a dad."

Sam, who had been about to say something from the threshold, closed his mouth. He didn't dare disrupt the moment by leaving or intruding. He could only stand there, frozen in the understanding that something important was happening.

Mark's face was carefully impassive. "What do you tell your friends when they ask if I'm your dad?"

"I just let them think it." Holly paused. "Is that wrong?"

Mark shook his head. " 'Course not." His voice was husky.

"Will I still call you Uncle Mark after the baby comes?"

Reaching down, Mark took one of Holly's hands, absurdly small in comparison to his, and sandwiched it between his palms. "You can call me whatever you want, Holly."

The child leaned closer until her head was on his arm. "I want to call you Dad. I want you to be my dad."

Mark was robbed of speech. It was clearly something he had not expected, or had even allowed himself to consider. His throat worked, and he bent to press his face against her pale, moonlight-blond hair. "I would love that. I . . . yes." He lifted her onto his lap and hugged her, clumsily petting her hair. A few indistinguishable murmurs followed, three syllables repeated over and over.

The muscles of Sam's own throat knotted. He was outside the moment and yet part of it.

"You're squishing me," came Holly's muffled voice after a long minute.

Mark's arms loosened, and she wriggled off his lap.

Renfield had padded into the room, a wadded-up paper napkin hanging from his mouth.

"Renfield," Holly scolded, "don't eat that."

Pleased at having gotten her attention, the dog trotted from the room with the napkin.

"I'll get it away from him," Holly said. She paused to rub noses with Mark. "Dad," she said with an impish grin, and dashed after the dog.

Sam had never seen his brother so utterly humbled. He came into the room as Mark let out a short, winded sigh and wiped his eyes with his fingers.

Seeing him, Mark blinked and began unsteadily, "Sam —"

"I heard," Sam interrupted quietly, and smiled. "It's good, Mark. Holly was right. You do look like a dad."

FOURTEEN

Voices floated into the bedroom.

". . . I want Lucy to use my pink bathroom," Holly insisted. "It's prettier than yours."

"It is," came Sam's reply. "But Lucy needs a walk-in shower stall. She can't climb in and out of the tub."

"Can she still see my bathroom? And my room?"

"Yeah, you can give her the official tour later. For now, put your socks on. You're going to be late for school."

Lucy breathed in an elusive scent from the pillow, like leaves and new rain and newly cut cedar. It was Sam's smell, so appealing that she hunted for it shamelessly, digging her head deep into the warm down.

She had a vague memory of waking in pain in the middle of the night. Of Sam coming to her like a shadow. He had given her pills and a glass of water, sliding his arm behind her back as she took the medicine. She had awakened another time, groggily aware of him replacing the cold gel packs around her leg, and she had told him that it wasn't necessary to keep getting up for her, he should get some rest.

"Quiet," he had murmured, straightening the covers around her. "Everything's okay."

As the morning brightened, Lucy lay quietly and listened to the muffled sounds of voices, breakfast, a phone ringing, a house-wide hunt for a missing homework folder and field-trip permission slip. Eventually a car rolled along the drive.

Footsteps ascended the stairs. There was a tap at the door, and Sam ducked his head in. "How are you doing?" The sound of his morning-roughened baritone chased pleasantly across her ears.

"I'm a little sore."

"Probably a lot sore." Sam came into the room, carrying a breakfast tray. The sight of him scruffy and sexy, wearing only flannel pajama pants and a white tee, drew a rampant flush to the surface of her skin. "It's time for another pill, but you should eat first. How does an egg and toast sound?"

"Great."

"After that you can take a shower."

Lucy's color deepened further, her pulse

turning hectic. She wanted a shower badly, but in light of her physical condition, it was obvious that she was going to need a lot of help. "How exactly would that work?" she managed to ask.

Sam set the tray on the bed and helped Lucy to sit up. He propped an extra pillow behind her as he replied in a matter-of-fact tone. "It's a walk-in shower. You can sit on a plastic stool and wash with a handheld spray. I'll have to help you in and out, but you can do most of it yourself."

"Thank you," she said, relieved. "That sounds good." She picked up a piece of lightly buttered toast and began to spread jam on it. "Why do you have a handheld shower spray?"

One of his brows arched. "Something wrong with that?"

"Not at all. It's just the kind of thing I would expect an old person to have, not a guy your age."

"I have hard-to-reach places," Sam said in a deadpan tone. After he saw the smile tugging at her lips, he said, "Also, we wash Renfield in there."

Sam went to shower and shave while she ate. He returned wearing a pair of raggedy-looking jeans and a T-shirt that proclaimed SCHRÖDINGER'S CAT IS ALIVE.

"What does that mean?" Lucy asked, reading the shirt.

"It's a principle in quantum theory." Sam set a plastic bag of supplies on the floor, and lifted the bed tray away from Lucy's lap. "Schrödinger was a scientist who used the example of a cat placed in a box with a radioactive source and a flask of poison, to demonstrate how an observation affects an outcome."

"What happens to the cat?"

"Do you like cats?"

"Yes."

"Then you don't want me to tell you about the theorem."

She made a face. "Don't you have any optimistic T-shirts?"

"This one is optimistic," Sam said. "I just can't tell you why, or you'll bitch about the cat."

Lucy chuckled. But as Sam approached the bed and reached for the covers, she fell silent and shrank back, her heart lurching into overdrive.

Sam let go of the bed linens at once, his expression carefully neutral. He studied her, his gaze alighting on her tightly crossed arms. "Before we do this," he said quietly, "let's deal with the elephant in the room."

"Who's the elephant?" Lucy asked warily.

"No one's the elephant. The elephant is the fact it's surprisingly awkward to help a woman take a shower when I haven't had sex with her first."

"I'm not going to have sex with you just to make the shower easier," Lucy said.

That drew a brief grin from him. "Don't take it personally, but you're wearing a hospital garment printed with little yellow ducks, and you're also bandaged and bruised. So you're not doing a thing for my libido. You're also on drugs, which leaves you unable to make decisions on your own behalf. All of which means there is absolutely no chance that I'm going to make any moves on you." He paused. "Does that make you feel better?"

"Yes, but . . ." Lucy's cheeks burned. "While you're helping me, you're probably going to get an eyeful."

His face was grave, but amusement lurked in the corners of his mouth. "That's a risk I'm willing to take."

Lucy sighed heavily. "I guess there's no alternative." She pushed back the covers and tried to sit up.

Sam came to her immediately, fitting his arm behind her back. "No, let me do the work. You're going to hurt yourself if you don't take it easy. I'm going to help you to the edge of the bed. All you have to do is sit up and let your legs hang over — yes, like that." His breath stopped abruptly as Lucy grappled with the hem of the hospital garment, which had ridden high on her hip. "Okay." He started breathing again. "We're not supposed to take the splint off. But the nurse said to wrap it in plastic when you shower, to keep it from getting wet." He reached for the bag of supplies and pulled out a bulky roller of nonadhesive clear wrap affixed to a metal handle.

Lucy waited quietly while Sam proceeded to wrap her entire lower leg. His touch was deft and careful, but the occasional brush of his fingertips at her knee or behind her calf sent ticklish sensations along her skin. His head was bent over her, his hair rich and dark. Surreptitiously she leaned forward to catch the scent that rose from the back of his neck, a summery smell, like sun and mown grass.

When the leg was covered to Sam's satisfaction, he looked up from his kneeling position on the floor. "How does it feel? Too tight?"

"It's perfect." Lucy noticed that his color had heightened, the high crests of his cheeks burnished beneath the rosewood tan. And he wasn't breathing well. "You said I wasn't doing anything for your libido."

Sam tried to look penitent. "Sorry. But wrapping you in mover's tape is the most fun I've had since college." As he stood and picked Lucy up, she clung to him automatically, her pulse quickening at the feel of his easy strength.

"Do you need to . . . calm down?" she asked delicately.

Sam shook his head, rueful amusement flickering in his eyes. "Let's just assume this is my default mode during showertime. Don't worry — I still won't make any moves on you."

"I'm not worried. I just don't want you to drop me."

"Sexual arousal doesn't rob me of physical strength," he informed her. "Brainpower, yes. But I don't need that to help you shower."

Lucy smiled uncertainly and held on to his sturdy shoulders as he carried her into the bathroom. "You're in good shape."

"It's the vineyard. Everything's organic, which requires extra handwork — cultivating and hoeing — instead of using pesticides. Saves the expense of a gym membership."

He was nervous again, talking a little too fast. Which Lucy found interesting. So far in her acquaintance with Sam, he had seemed completely self-possessed. She would have thought that he would handle a situation like this with aplomb. Instead, he seemed almost as rattled by their enforced intimacy as she was.

The bathroom had been decorated in a clean and uncluttered style, with ivory tile and mahogany cabinetry, and a big framed mirror over a pedestal sink. After lowering Lucy to the plastic stool in the shower stall, Sam showed her how to turn the shower control handles. "Once I clear out of here," he said, giving her the handheld sprayer, "just toss the robe and gown out of the stall and turn on the water. Take as long as you want. I'll be waiting on the other side of the door. If you have any problem, you need anything, just give a shout."

"Thanks."

The accumulated soreness from the accident caused Lucy to grimace and groan as she maneuvered on the stool and tossed the robe to the floor beyond the shower. She turned on the water, adjusted the heat, and directed the spray over her body. "Ow," she said, as her cuts and scrapes started to sting. "Ow, *ow* . . ."

"How's it going?" she heard Sam ask from the other side of the door.

"It hurts and feels good at the same time."

"Need help?"

"No, thanks."

It required a great deal of maneuvering to soap and rinse herself. Eventually Lucy discovered that the project of washing her hair was too much to contend with. "Sam," she said in frustration.

"Yeah?"

"I do need help."

"With what?"

"My hair. I can't wash it by myself. Would you mind coming in here?"

There was a long hesitation. "You can't do it by yourself?"

"No. I can't reach the shampoo bottle, and my right arm is aching, and it's hard to wash all this hair with only one hand." As she spoke, Lucy turned off the water and dropped the sprayer to the floor. Painfully she pulled the towel around herself.

"Okay," she heard him say. "I'm coming in."

As Sam entered the bathroom, he looked like a man who had just been called for jury duty. Stepping into the open shower stall, he picked up the sprayer. He fumbled with it, adjusting the pressure and temperature. Lucy couldn't help noticing that his breathing had changed again, and she said, "With the echo in here, you sound like Darth Vader."

"I can't help it," he said edgily. "With you sitting there all pink and steamy —"

"I'm sorry." She looked up at him contritely. "I hope that being in default mode doesn't hurt."

"Not at the moment." Sam's hand slipped around the back of her head, cradling the shape of her skull. As she looked up into his blue-green eyes, he said, "It only hurts when I can't do anything about it."

The way he was holding her head, the rough-soft sound of his voice, caused a curl of responsive pleasure deep in her stomach. "You're flirting with me," she said.

"I take it back," he said instantly.

"Too late." She smiled as she closed her eyes and let him wash her hair.

It was heaven, sitting there while Sam worked the shampoo through her hair, his strong fingers rubbing her scalp. He took his time, careful not to let water or suds get into her eyes. The rosemary-mint scent of the shampoo filled the steamy air . . . that was what she'd smelled on him earlier, she realized. She breathed deeply and tilted her head back, relaxing.

Eventually Sam turned off the water and hung the sprayer in the wall holder. Lucy squeezed out the excess water from her hair with her hand. Her gaze traveled over Sam's clothes, damp and water-blotched, his jeans sodden at the hems. "I got you wet," she said apologetically.

Sam stared down at her, his gaze lingering at the place where the damp towel drooped low over her breasts. "I'll live."

"I have nothing to wear now."

He continued to stare at her. "I'm so sorry to hear that."

"Do you have anything I could borrow?" At his lack of response, Lucy waved her hand between them. "Sam. Come away from the dark side."

Sam blinked, the glazed blankness leaving his eyes. "I could dig up a clean T-shirt."

With Sam's help, Lucy wrapped her hair in a turban. He kept her steady, lightly gripping her hips as she balanced on one foot and brushed her teeth at the sink. When she was finished, he carried her to the bed, handed her a T-shirt, and turned his back tactfully as she put it on. The turban became dislodged, its weight tugging at her hair. Lucy pulled it away and finger-combed the damp tangled locks.

"What is this?" she asked, glancing at the squares and letters covering the front of the shirt.

"The periodic table of the elements." Sam sank to his haunches to remove the covering from her splint.

"Oh, good. I'd hate to be out somewhere and not know the chemical symbol for rhodium."

"Rh," Sam said, using a small pair of scissors to snip through layers of wet plastic.

Lucy smiled. "How did you know that?"

"It's located on your left breast." Sam tossed the discarded plastic tape to the floor and examined the splint. "If you feel up to it, I'll bring you downstairs for a change of scenery. We've got a big sofa, a flat-panel TV, and Renfield to keep you company."

As she watched the daylight playing over his hair, Lucy was unnerved by the feeling that had swept over her, something beyond gratitude or mere physical attraction. Her pulse jumped in several places at once, and she found herself wanting, needing, impossible things.

"Thank you," she said. "For taking care of me."

"No trouble."

Slowly Lucy reached for his head, letting her fingers delve into the satisfying heavy locks of his hair. It felt unspeakably good to touch him. She wanted to explore him, learn every texture of him.

She thought that Sam would object. Instead he went still, his head bent. Stroking her way down to the solid nape of his neck, she heard his breath fracture.

"It is trouble," Lucy said gently. "Isn't it?"

Sam looked up at her then, his lashes half lowered over unearthly blue, his features taut. He didn't answer. He didn't have to. The truth was suspended in their shared gaze, between them, filling their lungs with every breath.

Definitely trouble. The kind that had nothing to do with splints or bandages or sickroom care.

Sam shook his head as if to clear it, and reached for the covers. "I'll let you rest for a few minutes, while I —"

In a headlong moment, Lucy curled her arm around his neck and brought her mouth to his. It was crazy, reckless, and she didn't care. Sam took all of a half second to respond, his mouth fastening to hers, a faint groan coming from his throat.

He had kissed her before, but this was something different. This was a waking dream of kissing, a feeling of tumbling with nothing to catch her. Her eyes closed against the view through the windows, the blue ocean, the white sun. Sam's arms went around her back, supporting her, while his lips caught hers at varying angles and absorbed the small sounds that climbed in her throat. She went weak, molding to his chest, unable to get close enough. Dragging his mouth from hers, Sam kissed her neck, using his tongue and the edges of his teeth as he worked his way to her shoulder. "I don't want to hurt you," he said against her skin. "Lucy, I'm not —"

She searched blindly for his mouth, rubbing her parted lips across his shaven jaw until Sam shuddered and kissed her again. His mouth became roughly coaxing, searching deeper until Lucy gripped the back of his shirt in shaking handfuls.

One of his hands pushed beneath the hem of her shirt, his fingers cool and textured against the burning skin of her side. Her breasts ached beneath the loose garment, the tips tightening in anticipation of his touch. She groped for his hand, urging it upward. "Please —"

"No. God, Lucy —" He broke off with a quiet curse and tugged the shirt back into place. Forcing himself to let go of her, he scrubbed both his hands over his face as if awakening from a deep sleep. As Lucy reached for him again, he caught her wrists reflexively and kept them manacled in his hands.

Sam kept his face averted, his throat rippling with hard swallows. "Do something," he muttered. "Or I'll . . ."

Lucy's eyes went round as she realized he was fighting for control. "What . . . do you want me to do?"

When Sam could bring himself to answer, a wry note had entered his voice. "Some distraction would be nice."

Lucy looked down at the periodic table that covered the front of her shirt. "Where is glass?" she asked, trying to read the chemical elements upside down.

"Not on the periodic table. Glass is a compound. It's mostly silica, which is . . . crap, I can't think straight. It's SiO_2. Here . . ." He touched the Si, which happened to be located high on the right side of her chest. "And here." The pad of his thumb brushed the O on her left side, close to the tip of her breast.

"Glass also has sodium carbonate," she said.

"I think that's . . ." Sam paused, struggling to concentrate. ". . . Na_2CO_3." He studied the front of the shirt and shook his head. "I can't show you sodium carbonate. Dangerous territory."

"What about calcium oxide?"

His gaze scanned the shirt until he found

it. He shook his head. "I'd have you on your back in about five seconds."

They both started at the harsh metallic ring of the doorbell, a Victorian hand-turn style.

Sam left the bed with a groan, moving slowly. "When I said I wasn't going to make any moves on you —" He opened the door and stood at the threshold, pulling in a couple of deep breaths. "I was planning for it to be a reciprocal arrangement. From now on, hands off. Got it?"

"Yes, but how are you going to take care of me if —"

"Not my hands," Sam said. "Yours."

The doorbell rang a couple more times while Sam made his way downstairs. Heat and arousal played all through him, making it impossible to think straight. He wanted Lucy, wanted to take her slowly and stare into her eyes as he moved inside her, and make it last for *hours.*

By the time Sam reached the front door, his temperature had cooled sufficiently to allow for clear thinking. He was confronted by his brother Alex, who looked more irate and underfed than usual, his frame raw-boned beneath loose-fitting clothes. Clearly Alex was not blossoming in the aftermath of divorce.

"Why do you have the fucking doors locked?" Alex demanded.

"Hey, Al," Sam said curtly, "it's good to see you too. Where's the key I gave you?"

"It's on my other key chain. You knew I was coming over this morning — if you want free work done on your house, the least you can do is leave the door unlocked."

"I've had a couple other things on my mind besides waiting for you to show up."

Alex brushed by him, carrying a vintage metal toolbox. As usual, he headed straight for the kitchen, where he would pour himself a scalding cup of black coffee, down it without ceremony, and go to whatever part of the house he happened to be working on. So far he had refused to take any money for his labors, despite the fact that he could have gotten a fortune doing the same work for someone else. Alex was a developer, but he had started as a carpenter, and the quality of his craftsmanship was impeccable.

Alex had spent hours on the house, skinning walls, repairing cracks in plaster, restoring wood molding, hardware, flooring. Sometimes he redid work that Mark or Sam had already finished, because no one could ever match his exacting standards. Exactly why Alex was so willing to expend so much of his energy on the house was something of a mystery to the other Nolans.

"I think it's his idea of a relaxing hobby," Mark had said.

"I'm all for it," Sam had replied, "if only because he doesn't drink while he works. This house may be the only thing keeping his liver from turning into Jell-O."

Now, as he watched his younger brother cross through the hallway, Sam thought that the signs of stress and drinking were catching up with him. Alex's ex-wife, Darcy, had never been what anyone would call a nurturing kind of woman, but at least she'd gotten him to take her out to eat a few nights a week. Sam wondered when Alex had last eaten a full meal.

"Al, why don't you let me fry you a couple of eggs before you start working?"

"Not hungry. Just want coffee."

"Okay." Sam followed him. "By the way . . . I'd appreciate it if you'd keep the noise level down today. I've got a friend staying here, and she needs rest."

"Tell her to take her hangover somewhere else. I have some trim work to do."

"Do it later," Sam said. "And it's not a hangover. She was in an accident yesterday."

Before Alex could reply, the doorbell rang again.

241

"That's probably one of her friends," Sam muttered. "Try not to be a dick, Alex."

Alex shot him a speaking glance and headed to the kitchen.

Shaking his head, Sam returned to the front door. The visitor turned out to be a curvy little blonde dressed in capris and flats, and a sleeveless button-down shirt knotted at the waist. With her buxom build, her big blue eyes, and her chin-length golden curls, she looked like an old-fashioned movie starlet, or maybe a Busby Berkeley showgirl.

"I'm Zoë Hoffman," she said brightly. "I've brought some of Lucy's things. Is it an okay time to visit? I could come back later —"

"Now's a great time." Sam smiled at her. "Come on in."

Zoë carried a huge pan of muffins that sent out a warm sugared fragrance. As she came inside, she tripped over the threshold and Sam automatically reached out to steady her.

"I'm a klutz," she announced cheerfully, a buttermilk-blond curl dangling over one eye.

"Thank God you didn't lose your balance completely," Sam said. "I'd hate to have to choose between saving you or the muffins."

She handed him the muffin pan and followed him to the kitchen. "How is Lucy?"

"Better than I would have expected. She had a pretty good night, but she's sore today. Still on pain meds."

"You're so nice to take care of her like this. Justine and I both appreciate it."

Zoë carried her va-va-voom figure in an innately apologetic manner, shoulders down and slightly forward. She was perplexingly shy for a woman with such flagrant beauty at her disposal. Maybe that was the problem — Sam guessed that she'd had more than her share of heavy-handed overtures from the wrong kind of men.

They entered the spacious kitchen, with its enameled stove set in a cream-tiled alcove, glass-fronted cabinets, and black walnut flooring. Zoë's marveling gaze swept from the high trussed ceilings to the huge soapstone farmhouse sink. But her eyes widened and her expression went blank as Alex turned from the coffeemaker to face them. Sam wondered what she would make of his brother, who resembled Satan with a hangover.

"Hello," Zoë said in a subdued voice after Sam had introduced them. Alex responded with a surly nod. Neither of them made a move to shake hands. Zoë turned to Sam. "Do you happen to have a cake plate I could set these muffins on?"

"It's in one of those cabinets near the Sub-Zero. Alex, would you help her out while I go upstairs to get Lucy?" Sam glanced at Zoë. "I'll find out if she wants to sit in the living room down here, or visit with you upstairs."

"Of course," Zoë said, and went to the cabinets.

Alex strode to the doorway just as Sam reached it. He lowered his voice. "I've got stuff to do. I don't have time to spend chitchatting with Betty Boop."

From the way Zoë's shoulders stiffened, Sam saw that she'd overheard the remark. "Al," he said softly, "just help her find the damn plate."

Zoë found the glass-domed plate in one of the cabinets, but it was too high for her to reach. She contemplated it with a frown, pushing back the curl that insisted on hanging over one eye. She was aware of Alex Nolan approaching her from behind, and a hot-and-cold chill went down her spine. "It's up there," she said, moving to the side.

He retrieved it easily, and set the plate and dome on the granite countertop. He was tall but rawboned, as if he hadn't had a good meal in weeks. The suggestion of cruelty on his face did nothing to detract from his profligate handsomeness. Or maybe it wasn't cruelty, but bitterness. It was a face that many women would find attractive, but it made Zoë nervous.

Of course, most men made her nervous.

Zoë thought that with the task done, Alex would leave the kitchen. She certainly hoped he would. Instead he stayed there with one hand braced on the countertop, his expensive watch gleaming in the light from the multipaned windows.

Trying to ignore him, Zoë set the glass plate beside the muffin pan. Carefully she extracted each muffin and set it on the plate. The scent of hot berries, white sugar, buttery streusel, rose in a melting-sweet updraft. She heard Alex draw in a deep breath, and another.

Darting a cautious glance at him, she noticed the dark half-moon indentations beneath a pair of vivid blue-green eyes. He looked like a man who hadn't slept in months. "You can go now," Zoë said. "You don't have to stay and chitchat."

Alex didn't bother to apologize for his earlier rudeness. "What did you put in those?" He sounded accusatory, suspicious.

Zoë was so taken aback that she could hardly speak. "Blueberries. Help yourself, if you'd like one."

He shook his head and reached for his coffee.

She couldn't help but notice the tremor in his hand, the dark brew shivering in the porcelain cup. Instantly Zoë lowered her gaze. What would cause a man's hand to shake like that? A nervous condition? Alcohol abuse? Somehow the sign of weakness in such a physically imposing person was infinitely more affecting than it would have been in someone of smaller stature.

Despite his irritable behavior, Zoë's compassionate nature asserted itself. She had never been able to pass by a crying child, a hurt animal, a person who looked lonely or hungry, without trying to do something about it. Particularly a hungry person, because if there was one thing Zoë liked better than anything in the world, it was feeding people. She loved the obvious pleasure that people took in tasting something delicious, something carefully made and nourishing.

Wordlessly Zoë set a muffin on Alex's saucer while the cup was still in his hand. She didn't look at him, only continued to arrange the plate. Although it seemed very likely that he would throw the offering at her, or say something derogatory, he was silent.

Out of the periphery of her vision, she saw him pick up the muffin.

He left with a gruff murmur that she gathered was meant to be a good-bye.

Alex went out to the front porch, taking care to leave the front door unlocked. The muffin was cradled in his hand, the unbleached parchment liner slick with the residue of butter, the dome cobblestoned with streusel.

He sat on a cushioned wicker chair, hunching over the food as if someone were likely to rush forward and snatch it from him.

Lately he'd had a tough time eating. No appetite, no ability to be tempted, and when he did manage to take a bite and chew something, his throat clenched until it was difficult to swallow. He was always cold, desperate for the temporary heat of liquor, always needing more than his body would tolerate. Now that the divorce had gone through, there were plenty of women offering any kind of consolation he might want, and he couldn't work up any interest in them.

He thought of the little blonde in the kitchen, almost comically beautiful, with her big eyes and perfect bow-shaped mouth . . . and beneath the tidily buttoned clothes, the voluptuous curves that approximated an amusement park ride. Not at all his taste.

As soon as he took a bite of the muffin, a saliva-spiking mixture of tartness and sweetness nearly overwhelmed him. The texture of it was dense and yet cakelike. He consumed it slowly, his entire being absorbed in the experience. It was the first time he'd been able to taste something, really experience a flavor, in months.

He finished it bite by disciplined bite, while a sense of relief flowed through him. The grooves of tension on his face eased. He would swear on his life that Zoë had put something in the muffins, something illegal, and he didn't give a damn. It gave him a clean, good feeling . . . a feeling of sinking into a warm bath after a raw day. His hands had stopped shaking.

He sat still for a minute, testing the sensation, sensing that it would hold at least for a little while. Heading back into the house, he picked up his toolbox and slunk up the stairs toward the attic with catlike quietness. He was intent on keeping the good feeling, determined not to let anyone or anything interfere with it.

On the way up he passed by Sam, who was carrying a slender young brunette with big green eyes. She was swathed in a robe, one of her legs wrapped in a bulky splint. "Alex," Sam said without stopping, "this is Lucy."

"Hi," Alex muttered, also not stopping, and he continued to the third-floor attic.

"Are you okay here?" Zoë asked Lucy, after Sam had left them alone to talk.

Lucy smiled. "I really am. As you can see . . ." She gestured to the gargantuan green velvet sofa, ice packs that Sam had settled around her leg, the cream-colored throw blanket tucked at her sides, and the tumbler of water he had set beside her. "I'm being very well taken care of."

"Sam seems nice," Zoë said, her blue eyes twinkling. "As nice as Justine said. I think he likes you."

"Sam likes women," Lucy replied wryly. "And yes, he's a great guy." She paused before adding diffidently, "You should go out with him."

"Me?" Zoë shook her head and gave her a quizzical glance. "There's something going on between you two."

"There's not. There won't be. Sam's very honest, Zoë, and he's made it clear that he will never make a permanent commitment to a woman. And although it's tempting to just let go and have fun with him . . ." Lucy hesitated and lowered her voice to a whisper. "He's the worst kind of heartbreaker, Zoë. The kind that's so appealing, you try to convince yourself that you could change him. And after everything I've been through . . . I'm not strong enough to be hurt again quite so soon."

"I understand." Zoë's smile was warm and compassionate. "I think it's very wise of you, Lucy. Sometimes giving up something you want is the very kindest thing you can do for yourself."

FIFTEEN

After Zoë's visit, Lucy relaxed on the sofa with her cell phone and an electronic reading tablet. Sam had packed fresh ice bags around her leg and brought her a tumbler of cold water before heading outside to confer with his vineyard crew. They were busy removing leaves to expose developing grape clusters to the sun, and hand-tilling the ground with spades.

"I'll be out there for forty-five minutes to an hour," Sam said. "My phone's on. Call if you need something."

"I'll be fine." Lucy pulled her face into a grimace as she added, "I have to call my mother and tell her what happened. It'll take all my skills of persuasion to keep her from flying up here to check on me in person."

"She's welcome to stay here."

"Thank you. I appreciate that. But the last

thing I need is for my mother to hover over me."

"Offer still stands." Approaching the settee, Sam bent to pet Renfield, who was sitting beside Lucy. "You watch over her," he told the bulldog, who regarded him solemnly.

"He is good company," Lucy said. "He's certainly quiet."

"Bulldogs aren't generally barkers." He paused and shot Renfield a chiding glance. "But there is the flatulence."

Renfield reacted to the comment with a look of extreme dignity, causing Lucy to laugh. She reached down to rub the dog's loose-skinned head as Sam left the house.

Although the morning wasn't yet over, the day was already hot, the sun burning through a slack canopy of clouds. Screen windows on both sides of the house let in stray breezes from the ocean.

Lucy relaxed on the sofa and let her gaze travel around the beautifully finished room, the gleaming black walnut floors, the Persian rug woven in cream and sage and amber, the meticulously restored cornice molding at the seams of the walls and ceiling.

Picking up her cell phone, she dialed her parents' number, and her mother answered.

No matter how Lucy tried to underplay the story, her mother sensed the truth, immediately launching into a state of excited worry.

"I'm coming. I'll be on the next plane."

"Mom, no. There's nothing you could do."

"That doesn't matter. I want to see you."

"You don't have to. I'm being well taken care of, I'm totally comfortable, and —"

"Who's taking care of you? Justine?"

"Actually, I'm staying with . . . a friend."

"Who?"

"His name is Sam Nolan."

After a perplexed silence, her mother said, "You've never mentioned him before. How long have you known him?"

"Not a long time, but —"

"You're staying in his apartment?"

"Not an apartment. He's got a house."

"Is he married?"

Lucy held the cell phone away from her face and looked at it in disbelief. Bringing it back to her mouth, she said, "Of course not. I don't go out with other people's boyfriends or husbands." Unable to resist, she added, "That's your other daughter."

"Lucy," her mother said on a note of gentle scolding. "Dad and I were planning to visit Alice next week — I'm going to change our flights so we can come out earlier."

"You don't have to. In fact, I'd really rather you not —"

"I want to meet this Sam person."

Lucy struggled to suppress a laugh at the way her mother had phrased it. "He's a perfectly nice guy. In fact, he's your dream son-in-law."

"You've gotten that serious with him?"

"No . . . God, no . . . I'm not even going out with him. I just meant he's the type of guy you've always wanted me to go out with. He owns a vineyard. He grows organic grapes and makes wine, and he's helping to raise his orphaned niece." As she spoke, Lucy looked out the windows behind the settee. She located Sam's strapping form amid a group of men working with spades. Deferring to the heat of the day, a couple of them had removed their shirts. Sam was fiddling with a gas-powered tiller, doing something with the start cord. He paused to draw a forearm across his sweaty brow.

"Is he divorced?" her mother asked.

"Never married."

"He sounds too perfect. What's wrong with him?"

"Commitment avoidant."

"Oh, they're all that way until you make

them see the light."

"This isn't your run-of-the-mill fear of commitment. It's a lifestyle choice."

"Are his parents still in the picture?"

"They've both passed away."

"Good, there'll be no competition on holidays."

"Mom!"

"I was joking," her mother protested.

"I wonder," Lucy said. Often with her mother, it seemed they were having two different conversations. Lucy suspected at least half of what she said had gone completely unnoticed. She continued to focus on Sam, who was pressing the primer button on the tiller to pump some gas into the motor. "You know, Mom, you're asking a lot more questions about the guy I'm staying with than you are about my injuries."

"Tell me what he looks like. Is he clean-shaven? Tall or short? How old is he?"

"He's —" Lucy broke off, her mind going blank as Sam stripped off his T-shirt, blotted his face and the back of his neck with it, and tossed it to the ground. He had an amazing body, lean and long, muscle stacked on muscle.

"What is it?" came her mother's voice. "Is everything all right?"

"Everything's fine," Lucy managed to say,

watching the tanned surface of Sam's back ripple as he bent to pull the start cord of the tiller repeatedly. Having no luck at getting the motor to turn over, he released the handle and talked with one of the crew, his posture loose-limbed, hands braced on lean denim-clad hips. "Sorry, lost my train of thought. I'm still on pain meds."

"We were talking about Sam," her mother prompted.

"Oh. Yes. He's . . . clean-cut. A little bit of a science geek." *With the body of a Greek god.*

"That sounds like a nice change from the last one."

"You mean Kevin, your future son-in-law?"

Her mother made a disgruntled sound. "That remains to be seen. It's one of the reasons I'm coming up to see Alice. I have the feeling the situation isn't as cut-and-dried as she claims."

"Why —" Lucy stopped as she heard a strange, unearthly baying. She sat up a little and glanced around the room. Renfield was nowhere to be seen. A metallic clank, like a saucepan or a colander being dropped, was followed by whimpering and another prolonged howl. "Uh-oh. Mom, I have to hang up. I think the dog's gotten into something."

"Call me back later. I haven't finished talking yet."

"Okay. Gotta go." Hanging up quickly, Lucy called Sam's number, straining for any glimpse of Renfield. The dog sounded like he was being butchered. She heard Sam's voice on the phone. "Lucy."

"Something's going on with Renfield. He's howling. I think he's in the kitchen, but I'm not sure."

"I'll be right there."

For the minute that it took Sam to high-tail it to the house, Lucy was tortured by her inability to do anything. She called Renfield's name, and the dog responded with a disembodied whine, the banging and snorting and howling coming closer, until finally he careened into the living room.

Somehow the dog had gotten his head stuck in a rusty cylinder that defied his efforts to shake it free. He was so frantic and miserable that Lucy pushed aside her ice packs and began to calculate how she could reach him without putting any weight on her splinted leg.

"Don't even think about moving off that sofa," Sam said as he strode into the living room. Amused exasperation filled his voice. "Renfield, how the hell did you get into that?"

"What is it?" Lucy asked anxiously.

"A smudge pot liner." Sam knelt on the floor and grabbed for the dog, who jerked and whimpered. "Easy, boy. Sit. *Sit.*" He pinned the stocky, wriggling body to the floor and began to pry the metallic tube off his head.

"What's a smudge pot?"

"They used to burn kerosene in them to keep orchards warm when a frost was settling in."

Renfield's head was covered with black soot and grime that accentuated the folds and wrinkles of his face. The dog lunged at Sam in a frenzy of gratitude.

"Easy, boy. Calm down." Sam petted and stroked the dog, trying to soothe him. "He must have gotten out the back door somehow. There's a junk pile we haven't gotten around to hauling off yet. All kinds of trouble for him to get into."

Lucy nodded, mesmerized by the sight of a shirtless Sam, his sun-burnished muscles gleaming with perspiration.

"I'll wash him outside," Sam said, scowling at the soot-covered bulldog. "If I'd had any say, I'd have gotten a nice golden or a Lab . . . a *useful* dog that would've chased pests out of the vineyard."

"You didn't choose Renfield for yourself?"

"Hell, no. He was a rescue case that Maggie was trying to pawn off on someone. And Mark had fallen so hard for her, he volunteered to take him."

"I think that's sweet."

Sam lifted his gaze heavenward. "Mark was a patsy for taking him. This dog doesn't do tricks. He can't keep up during a brisk walk. His vet bills rival the national debt, and he lies around the house in the places most guaranteed to pose a tripping hazard." But as he spoke, his hands were gentle on the dog's fur, smoothing his back, scratching his neck. Renfield closed his eyes and wheezed happily. "Come on, idiot. Let's go out the back way." Sam picked up the smudge pot liner and rose to his feet. He glanced at Lucy. "You'll be okay while I wash him?"

With an effort, Lucy tore her gaze from his half-clad form and switched on her electronic tablet. "Yes, I have everything I need."

"What are you reading?"

"A biography of Thomas Jefferson."

"I like Jefferson. He was a big patron of viticulture."

"Did he have a vineyard?"

"Yes, at Monticello. But he was more of an experimenter than a serious grape grower. He was trying to grow European vines — vinifera — which produced amazing wine in places like France or Italy. But the vinifera couldn't handle the weather, disease, and pests in the New World."

Clearly he was a man who loved what he did. To understand him fully, Lucy thought, you would have to learn about his work, why it meant so much to him, what the challenges were. "I wish I could walk through the vineyard with you," she said wistfully. "It looks beautiful from here."

"Tomorrow I'll take you outside to see something special."

"What is it?"

"A mysterious vine."

Lucy regarded him with a perplexed smile. "What makes it mysterious?"

"I found it on the property a couple of years ago, growing on an easement that was about to be plowed up for a road project. Transplanting a vine that size and age was a tricky proposition. So I asked Kevin to help me with it. We used tree spades to get as much of the root-ball as possible, and we moved it to the vineyard. It survived the transplant, but I'm still working to get it healthy."

"What kind of grapes does it produce?"

"That's the interesting part. I've got a guy

at the WSU land grant working on identifying it, and so far he hasn't been able to come up with anything. We've sent samples and pictures to a couple of ampelography experts in Washington and California — it's not on record. Most likely it's a wild hybrid that happened from natural cross-pollination."

"Is that rare?"

"Very."

"Do you think it will make a good wine?"

"Probably not," he said, and laughed.

"Then why have you gone to so much trouble?"

"Because you never know. The grapes might turn out to reveal some attributes of the wine that you never expected. Something that expresses this place more perfectly than anything you could have planned. You have to . . ."

As Sam paused, searching for the right phrase, Lucy said softly, "You have to take a leap of faith."

Sam gave her an arrested glance. "Yes."

Lucy understood all too well. There were times in life when you had to take a risk that might end in failure. Because otherwise you would be haunted by what you hadn't done . . . the paths you hadn't taken, the things you hadn't experienced.

After Sam had taken care of Renfield, he worked in the vineyard for an hour and went to check on Lucy, who had fallen asleep on the sofa. He stood in the doorway, his gaze tracing slowly along the length of her body. There was something extraordinary about Lucy, a delicate, almost mythical quality. Like a figure from a painting . . . Antiope, or Ophelia dreaming. Her dark hair trailed in ribbons across the pale green velvet, her skin as pale as night-blooming lilies. Dust motes glittered in a constellation in the sunlit air above her.

Sam was fascinated by Lucy's mixture of vulnerability and strength. He wanted to know her secrets, the things a woman would reveal only to a lover. And that was nothing short of alarming. He'd never had such thoughts before. But if it took the last ounce of decency he possessed, he would leave her alone.

Lucy stirred and yawned. Her eyes opened to regard him in momentary confusion, heavy lashes shadowing the drowsy depths of green. "I was dreaming," she said in a sleep-colored voice.

Sam went to her, unable to resist reaching

down to play with a lock of her hair. "What about?"

"I was here. Someone was showing me around . . . it was the house the way it used to be."

"Was I the one with you?"

"No. It was a man I've never met."

Sam smiled slightly, releasing the lock of hair. "I don't know if I like you hanging out with another guy in my house."

"He lived here a long time ago. His clothes were . . . old-fashioned."

"Did he say anything?"

"No. But he led me on a tour. The house was different. Darker. The furniture was antique, and there was fussy wallpaper everywhere. In this room, it was green-striped. And the ceiling was papered, and there was a square with a bird in it at each corner."

Sam stared at her alertly. There was no way Lucy could have known that when he and Alex had removed an ugly drop ceiling that had been installed in this room, they had found the original ceiling, papered exactly as Lucy had just described. "What else did he show you?"

"We went to the third-floor attic, the one with the slanted ceiling and the dormer windows. Children used to play in there.

And the stained-glass window that used to be at the second-floor landing . . . I told you about it yesterday, remember . . . ?"

"The tree and the moon."

"Yes." Lucy's gaze was earnest. "It was there. The same one I saw before. A design of a tree with bare branches, and the moon behind them. It was beautiful, but not what you would expect for a house like this. But it was right, somehow. Sam . . ." She grimaced as she leveraged herself to a sitting position. "Could I have a pencil and some paper?"

"Easy," he said, trying to help her. "Don't move too fast."

"I need to sketch it before I forget it."

"I'll find something." Sam went to a cabinet where they kept Holly's art materials. Retrieving some pencils and a spiral pad of art paper, he asked, "Will these do?"

Lucy nodded, reaching eagerly for the supplies.

For a half hour or so, Lucy worked on the sketch. When Sam brought a lunch tray to her, she showed the design to him. "It's not finished yet," she said. "But this is basically what I saw." The drawing was striking, the trunk and the branches of the tree spreading across the paper in a pattern like black lace. A moon appeared to be caught in the grasp of the upper branches.

"The tree would be done in lead?" Sam asked, studying the image, and Lucy nodded.

Imagining the picture as a stained-glass window for the front of the house, Sam felt a chill of rightness, of certainty too strong to be questioned. The house would never be complete until this was replaced.

"What would it take," he asked slowly, "for you to make this window? Exactly the way you saw it in the dream."

"I would do it for nothing," came Lucy's emphatic reply. "After the way you've taken care of me . . ."

Sam shook his head decisively. "This window's going to take some work. The design is intricate. What do you usually charge for something like that?"

"It depends on the type of glass, and how much detailing I would do . . . gilding and beveling, things like that. And that's not including the installation, especially since you would need it to be weather-sealed —"

"Ballpark guess."

Lucy gave a little grimace. "Three thousand dollars for everything. But I could skimp in some areas to bring down the cost —"

"No skimping. This is worth doing right."

Sam reached over and tucked a paper napkin at the top of Lucy's shirt. "What do you think about making this window at your own pace, and in return we'll lower the monthly rent for the Friday Harbor condo? That way it's fair for both sides."

Lucy hesitated, and Sam smiled. "You know you're going to say yes," he said. "You know that window has to be made. By you."

Sixteen

Over the next two days, Sam treated Lucy with implacable friendliness. In conversation, he steered away from personal matters, and whenever he came into physical contact with her, he was carefully impersonal. Understanding his decision to establish a safe distance between them, Lucy tried her best to accommodate him.

Sam took obvious enjoyment in his vineyard work, hand-tilling the soil, caring for the vines with a mixture of backbreaking effort and patience. As he explained the grape-growing process to Lucy, she began to understand more about the sophistication of *terroir,* the matching of the right grape varietal to the specific plot of land and its unique character. There was a difference, Sam had explained, between treating grape growing as a purely technical process, or having real communication with the land, a true give-and-take.

Living in proximity with the Nolans, Lucy saw that the three of them were a close and loving family unit. They had well-established routines and regular times for eating and sleeping, and it was clear that Holly's well-being was her uncles' primary concern. Although Mark was the father figure, Sam had his own place in Holly's affections. Every day after school the little girl chattered endlessly to him about her activities and her friends, and what had happened during recess that day, and she listed the contents of her friends' lunch bags in an effort to convince him to let her have some junk food. It both amused and touched Lucy to see how patiently Sam listened to Holly's concerns.

Lucy gathered from the way that Holly talked about Sam that he had infused their makeshift family with a sense of adventure. She told Lucy that Sam had taken her to explore the tidepools of False Bay, and to kayak on the west side of the island to see orca whales. It had been Sam's idea to take Holly and Mark to build a driftwood fort on Jackson's beach. They'd given each other pirate names — Captain Scurvy, Toothless McFilthy, and Gunpowder Gertie — and they had roasted hot dogs over a campfire.

After Holly came home from school, she

watched television with Lucy in the living room. Sam had gone upstairs to clear out a pile of debris from the attic renovation. While Lucy reclined on the green sofa with her leg propped up, she and Holly snacked on oatmeal cookies and apple juice.

"These are special," Lucy said, holding up one of the small Ruby Red antique juice glasses. "You can only get this color by adding gold chloride to the glass."

"Why are the sides bumpy?" Holly asked, inspecting her own juice glass.

"That's called a hobnail pattern, after the nails they used for shoes." Lucy smiled at the little girl's interest. "Do you know how to tell if the glass was made by hand? Just look at the bottom for a pontil mark — that's a little scar where the glassmaker's rod was attached. If you can't find one, it was made by machine."

"Do you know *everything* about glass?" Holly asked, and Lucy laughed.

"I know a lot, but I'm learning new things all the time."

"Can I watch you make something out of glass?"

"Of course. When I get better, you can visit my studio and we'll make something together. A little suncatcher, maybe."

"Yes, yes, I want to do that," Holly exclaimed.

"We can start right now — the first step in the process is to create a design. Do you have crayons and paper?"

Holly flew to her art cabinet, pulled out some supplies, and hurried back to Lucy. "Can I draw anything I want?"

"Anything. We might have to simplify it later, to make sure the pieces are the right shape and size for cutting . . . but for now, set your imagination free."

Holly knelt beside the coffee table and set out a pad of paper. Carefully she pushed aside an apothecary jar terrarium, filled with moss, button ferns, and white mini-orchids. "Did you always want to be a glass artist?" she asked, sorting through crayons.

"Ever since I was your age." Gently Lucy tugged the pink baseball cap from Holly's head and flipped it backward to make it easier for her to see. "What do you want to be when you grow up?"

"A ballerina or a zookeeper."

As she watched Holly concentrate on her drawing, her small hands gripping the crayons, Lucy was suffused with a feeling of satisfaction. How natural it was for children to express themselves through art. It occurred to Lucy that she could start an art class for children at her studio. Was there a way to honor her craft more than to share it with a child? She could start with just a few students, and see how it went.

Considering the idea, daydreaming, Lucy played with the empty Ruby Red juice glass, rubbing her thumb over the hobnail pattern. Without warning, her fingers turned hot, and the glass began to change shape in her hand. Startled, Lucy moved to set the glass down, but in the next instant it had disappeared, and a small, living form bolted away from her palm. With a loud buzz, it zipped across the room.

Holly let out a shriek and jumped onto the sofa, causing Lucy to flinch in pain. "What is it?"

Stunned, Lucy wrapped her arms around the girl. "It's okay, sweetie, it's just . . . it's a hummingbird."

Nothing like this had ever happened in front of someone before. How could she explain it to Holly? The tiny red bird batted against the closed windows in its efforts to escape, the impact of its delicate bones and beak making audible taps.

Gritting her teeth with effort, Lucy leaned to grip the window frame and tried to push it upward. "Holly, can you help me?"

Together they struggled with the window, but the frame was stuck. The hummingbird flew back and forth, striking the glass again.

Holly let out another cry. "I'll get Uncle Sam."

"Wait . . . Holly . . ." But the little girl had gone in a flash.

A cry from downstairs caused Sam to drop a garbage bag filled with debris. It was Holly. His hearing had become attuned so that he could instantly tell the differences among Holly's screams, whether they were happy, fearful, or angry. "It's like I know dolphin language," he had once told Mark.

This shriek was a startled one. Had something happened to Lucy? Sam went for the stairs, taking them two and three at a time.

"Uncle Sam!" he heard Holly shout. She met him at the bottom of the stairs, bouncing anxiously on her toes. "Come and help us!"

"What is it? Are you okay? Is Lucy —" As he followed into the living room, something buzzed by his ear, something like a bee the size of a golf ball. Sam barely restrained himself from swatting at it. Thankfully he hadn't, because as it went to a corner of the ceiling and batted against the wall, he saw that it was a hummingbird. It made tiny cheeping noises, its wings a blur.

Lucy was on the sofa, struggling with the

window.

"Stop," Sam said curtly, reaching her in three strides. "You're going to hurt yourself."

"He keeps slamming against the walls and windows," Lucy said breathlessly. "I can't open this stupid thing —"

"Humidity. It swells the wood frame." Sam pushed the window upward, leaving an open space for the hummingbird to fly through.

But the miniature bird hovered, darted, and batted against the wall. Sam wondered how they could guide it to the window without damaging a wing. At this rate it was going to die of stress or exhaustion.

"Let me have your hat, Holls," he said, taking the pink baseball cap off her head. As the hummingbird harrowed and hovered in the corner of the room, Sam gently used the cap to constrain it, until he felt the bird drop into the canvas pouch.

Holly gave a wordless exclamation.

Carefully Sam transferred the bird to the palm of his hand and went to the open window.

"Is he dead?" Holly asked anxiously, climbing onto the sofa beside Lucy.

Sam shook his head. "Just resting," he whispered.

Together the three of them watched and waited, while Sam extended his cupped hands beyond the sill. Slowly the bird recovered. Its heart, no bigger than a sunflower seed, spent heartbeats in music too fast and fragile to hear. The bird rose from Sam's hands and flickered away, disappearing into the vineyard.

"How did he get into the house?" Sam asked, looking from one of them to the other. "Did someone leave the door open?" With interest, he saw that Lucy's face had gone scrupulously blank.

"No," Holly said in excitement. "Lucy did it!"

"She did what?" Sam asked, not missing the way Lucy had blanched.

"She made it out of a juice glass," Holly exclaimed. "It was in her hand, and it turned into a bird. Right, Lucy?"

"I . . ." Visibly agitated, Lucy searched for words, her mouth opening and closing. "I'm not quite sure what happened," she finally managed to say.

"A bird flew out of your hand," Holly said helpfully. "And now your juice glass is gone." She picked up her own juice glass and thrust it forward. "Maybe you can do it again."

Lucy shrank back. "Thank you, no, I . . .

you should keep that, Holly."

She looked so thoroughly guilty and red-faced with worry that it actually gave weight to the crazy idea that had entered Sam's mind.

"I believe in magic," Lucy had once said to him.

And now he knew why.

It didn't matter that it defied logic. Sam's own experiences had taught him that the truth didn't always seem logical.

As he stared at her, he found himself trying to separate out a tangle of thoughts and emotions. For his entire adult life, he had kept his feelings organized in the way that some people kept their cutlery in a knife block, sharp edges concealed. But Lucy was making that impossible.

He had never told anyone about his own ability. There had never been a point. But in an astonishing turn of events, it had become a basis for connection with another human being. With Lucy.

"Nice trick," he said softly, and Lucy blanched and looked away from him.

"But it wasn't a trick," Holly protested. "It was real."

"Sometimes," Sam told his niece, "real things seem like magic, and magic seems real."

"Yes, but —"

"Holls, do me a favor and get Lucy's medicine bottle from the kitchen table. Also some water."

"Okay." Holly jumped off the sofa, causing Lucy to wince.

Grooves of pain and distress had appeared on Lucy's face. The exertions of the past few minutes had been too much for her.

"I'll replace the cold packs in a few minutes," Sam said.

Lucy nodded, practically vibrating with misery and worry. "Thank you."

Sam lowered to his haunches beside the sofa. He didn't ask for explanations, only let a long minute pass. In the silence, he took one of Lucy's hands, turned it palm-up and stroked the insides of the pale fingers until they were half curled like petals.

The color had leached from Lucy's face, except for the crimson band that crossed the tops of her cheeks and the bridge of her nose. "Whatever Holly said," she managed, "it isn't what —"

"I understand," Sam said.

"Yes, but I don't want you to think —"

"Lucy. Look at me." He waited until she brought her gaze to his. *I understand.*"

She shook her head in bewilderment.

Wanting to make things clear, but hardly

able to believe he was doing it, Sam extended his free hand to the terrarium on the coffee table. The miniature orchids, temperamental as usual, had started to droop and turn brown. As he let his palm hover over the vessel, the flowers and button ferns strained upward toward his touch, the petals regaining their creamy whiteness, the green plants reviving.

Silent and startled, Lucy moved her gaze from the terrarium to Sam's face. He saw the wonder in her eyes, the quick shimmer of unshed tears, the flush rising up her throat. Her fingers gripped his tightly.

"Since I was ten," Sam said in answer to her unspoken question. He felt exposed, could feel his heart beating uncomfortably. He had just shared something too personal, too intrinsic, and it alarmed him that he didn't regret it. He wasn't sure that he could stop himself from doing and saying even more in the irresistible urge to get closer to her.

"I was seven," Lucy whispered, a hesitant smile ghosting across her lips. "Some broken glass turned into fireflies."

He stared at her, fascinated. "You can't control it?"

She shook her head.

"Here's the medicine," Holly said brightly,

coming back into the room. She brought the prescription bottle and a large plastic cup of water.

"Thank you," Lucy murmured. After taking the medicine, she cleared her throat and said carefully, "Holly, I was wondering if we could keep it private, about how the hummingbird got into the room . . ."

"Oh, I already knew not to tell anyone," Holly assured her. "Most people don't believe in magic." She shook her head regretfully as if to say, too bad for them.

"Why a hummingbird?" Sam asked Lucy.

She had difficulty answering, seeming to struggle with the novelty of discussing something she had never dared put into words. "I'm not sure. I have to figure out what it means." After a pause, she said, "Don't stay in one place, maybe. Keep moving."

"The Coast Salish say the hummingbird appears in times of pain or sorrow."

"Why?"

Taking the medicine bottle from her, Sam replaced the cap as he replied in a neutral tone. "They say it means everything's going to get better."

"Holly, you're a corporate pirate," Sam said that night, delivering a handful of Monopoly money to his giggling niece. "I'm out, guys."

After a dinner of lasagna and salad, the four of them — Sam, Lucy, Mark, and Holly — had played board games in the living room. The atmosphere had been fun and easygoing, with no one behaving as if anything unusual had happened.

"You should always buy a railroad when you get a chance," Holly replied.

"Now you tell me." Sam gave Lucy, who was curled up in a corner of the sofa, a condemning glance. "I thought making you the banker would have gotten me a break."

"Sorry," Lucy replied with a grin. "Have to play by the rules. When it comes to money, the numbers don't lie."

"Which shows you know absolutely nothing about banking," Sam said.

"We haven't finished," Holly protested, seeing Mark dismantle the arrangement on the board. "I still haven't beaten everyone."

"It's bedtime."

Holly heaved a sigh. "When I'm a grown-up, I'll *never* go to bed."

"Ironically," Sam told her, "when you're a grown-up, going to bed is your favorite thing."

"We'll clean up the game," Lucy said to Mark with a smile. "You can take Holly upstairs now if you'd like."

The little girl leaned forward to give Sam butterfly kisses with her eyelashes, and they rubbed noses.

As Mark went upstairs with Holly, Lucy and Sam organized the game pieces and the various colors of paper currency.

"She's a sweetheart," Lucy said.

"We lucked out," Sam said. "Vick did a good job with her."

"So have you and Mark. Holly is obviously happy and well taken care of." Lucy wrapped a rubber band around the stack of accumulated money and handed it to him.

Sam closed the game box and gave Lucy a friendly, deliberate smile. "Want some wine?"

"That sounds nice."

"Let's drink it outside. There's a strawberry moon out."

"Strawberry moon? Why is it called that?"

"Full moon for June. Time to gather ripe strawberries. I would have assumed you'd heard the term from your dad."

"I grew up hearing a lot of scientific terminology, but not the fun stuff." Lucy grinned as she added, "I was so disappointed when my father told me that stardust was cosmic dirt — I imagined it was going to sparkle like pixie dust."

In a few minutes Sam had carried her out

to the front porch and lowered her into a wicker armchair with her leg propped on an ottoman. After handing her a glass of wine that tasted like berries and a hint of smoke, Sam sat in a chair beside hers. It was a clear night. You could see into the dark and infinite spaces between the stars.

"I like this," Lucy said, realizing that Sam had poured their wine into old-fashioned jam jars. "I remember drinking out of these when I used to visit my grandparents."

"In light of recent events," Sam said, "I decided not to trust you with our good glassware." He smiled at her expression.

As she averted her gaze from his, Lucy noticed that one of the Velcro straps on her splint wasn't perfectly aligned. Awkwardly she reached down to straighten it.

Without a word Sam came to help her.

"Thank you," Lucy said. "Sometimes I get kind of picky about wanting things to be lined up."

"I know. You also like the seam of your sock to run straight across your toes. And you don't like the foods on your plate to touch."

Lucy gave him a sheepish glance. "Is it that obvious that I'm obsessive-compulsive?"

"Not really."

"Yes it is. I used to drive Kevin crazy."

"I'm very tolerant of ritualistic behavior," Sam said. "It's actually an evolutionary advantage. For example, a dog's habit of turning circles on his bedding before lying down — that came from ancestors checking for snakes or dangerous creatures."

Lucy laughed. "I can't think of any benefits for my ritualistic behavior — it only serves to annoy people."

"If it helped to get rid of Kevin," Sam said, "I'd say it was a clear advantage." He sat back in his chair, contemplating her. "Does he know?" he asked eventually.

Understanding what he was referring to, Lucy shook her head. "No one does."

"Except me and Holly."

"I didn't mean for it to happen in front of her," Lucy said. "I'm sorry."

"Everything's fine."

"Sometimes if I feel something very strongly, and there's glass nearby . . ." Her voice faded, and she hitched her shoulders in an awkward shrug.

"Emotion causes it to happen," he said rather than asked.

"Yes. I was watching Holly color a picture, and I was thinking about teaching an art class for children. Showing them how to make things out of glass. And the idea made me feel incredibly . . . hopeful. Happy."

"Of course. When you have a passion for something, there's nothing better than sharing it."

Since that afternoon, something had altered between them. It was a good feeling, a safe feeling that Lucy wanted to savor. Letting it take hold, she looked at him. "Does emotion play a part in what you do? Your ability, I mean."

"It feels more like energy. Very subtle. And it's not there when I'm away from the island. When I was in California, I half convinced myself I'd imagined it. But then I came back here, and it was stronger than ever."

"How long did you live in California?"

"For a couple of years. I had a job as a winemaker's assistant."

"Were you alone? I mean . . . were you going out with anyone?"

"For a while I went out with the daughter of the guy who owned the vineyard. She was beautiful, smart, and she loved viticulture as much as I did." His thoughts had turned inward, his voice quietly reflective. "She wanted to get engaged. The idea of marrying her was almost tempting. I liked her family, loved the vineyard . . . it would have been easy."

"Why didn't you?"

"I didn't want to use her that way. And I knew it didn't have a chance in hell of lasting."

"How could you be sure? How can you know without trying?"

"I knew it the moment she and I started talking about making it permanent. She was certain that if we just went ahead and flew off to Vegas and did it, we would be fine. But to me it sounded like someone throwing a roll of paper towels and a can of frosting into an oven and saying, 'You know, I think there's a good chance this is going to turn into a chocolate cake.' "

Lucy couldn't help laughing. "But that just means she wasn't the right woman. It doesn't mean you couldn't have a good marriage with someone else."

"The risk-benefit ratio has never been worth it to me."

"Because you saw the worst side of love while growing up."

"Yeah."

"But according to the principle of balance in the universe, someone out there has to have the best side of love."

Considering that, Sam raised his jam jar in a negligent toast. "To the best side of it. Whatever that is."

As they clinked glasses and drank, Lucy reflected that there were probably many women who would regard Sam's views on marriage as a challenge, hoping to change his mind. She would never be that foolish. Even if she didn't agree with Sam's beliefs, she would respect his right to have them.

Past experience had taught her that when you loved a man, you had to take him "as is," knowing that although you might be able to influence some of his habits or his taste in neckties, you would never be able to change who he really was deep down. And if you were lucky, you might find a man who felt the same way about you.

That, she thought, was the best side of love.

SEVENTEEN

"Later this morning," came Sam's voice through the bathroom door, "you have a doctor's appointment. If he gives the go-ahead, you'll get the Aircast brace and crutches."

"I would love to be mobile again," Lucy said fervently, rinsing with the hot shower spray. "And I'm sure you would love not having to carry me everywhere."

"You're right. I can't imagine why I thought wrapping a half-naked woman in plastic and carrying her around would be any fun at all."

Lucy smiled and turned off the water. She removed the Hello Kitty shower cap that she'd borrowed from Holly, and wrapped a towel around herself. "You can come in now."

Sam entered the humid bathroom and came to help her. His manner was casual and matter-of-fact . . . but so far that morning, he hadn't quite been able to meet her gaze.

The previous night they had stayed out on the porch for a long time, eventually finishing the entire bottle of wine. Today, however, Sam was quiet and restrained. It was likely that he was getting tired of waiting on her hand and foot. Lucy decided that no matter what the doctor said later in the day, she would insist on getting crutches. Three days of putting Sam through so much trouble was enough.

Lucy stood, clutching the towel while balancing briefly on one foot. Carefully Sam hooked an arm beneath her knees, lifted her, and carried her into the bedroom. Setting her on the edge of the mattress with her legs dangling, he picked up a pair of small scissors and began to cut through the layers of plastic from her leg.

"You've done so much for me," Lucy said quietly. "I hope someday I can —"

"It's okay."

"I just want to tell you how much I —"

"I know. You're grateful. We don't have to go through this every time I help you out of the damn shower."

Blinking at his curt tone, Lucy said, "Sorry. I didn't realize ordinary politeness was going to annoy you."

"It's not ordinary politeness," Sam said, snipping through the last of the plastic, "when you're sitting there wet and mostly naked and staring at me with Kewpie doll eyes. Keep your thanks to yourself."

"Why are you so touchy? Do you have a hangover?"

He gave her a sardonic glance. "I don't get hangovers from two glasses of wine."

"It's having to do all this for me, isn't it? Anyone would be frustrated. I'm sorry. But I'll be out of here soon, and —"

"Lucy," he said with strained patience, "don't apologize. Don't try to figure anything out. Just . . . shut up for a couple of minutes."

"But I —" She broke off as she saw his expression. "Okay, I'm shutting up."

When the plastic was discarded, Sam paused at the sight of a bruise on the side of her knee. He traced the edge of the dark blotch, his touch so light it was nearly imperceptible. His head was bent, so Lucy couldn't see his expression. But his hands went to the mattress on either side of her hips, his fingers digging into the bedclothes. A deep tremor went through him, desire splintering through restraint.

Lucy didn't dare say a word. She stared fixedly at the top of his head, the span of his shoulders. Her ears were filled with the echoes of her heartbeat.

His head bent, the light sliding across the dark layers of his hair. The touch of his lips was soft and searing against the bruise, causing her to jerk in surprise. His mouth lingered, drifting to the inside of her thigh. His fingers tightened until he gripped the covers in handfuls. Lucy's breath caught as he leaned farther between her legs, the feel of his body heavy and sweet wherever it pressed.

Another kiss, higher, where the skin was thin and sensitive. Her skin turned hot and cold beneath the damp towel, sensation washing over her. Slowly his hands eased beneath the hem of the towel, the motion causing the white terry cloth to loosen and part. He moved higher, his palms sliding over her hips and stomach, his lips following in a path of excruciating sensation. Gasping, Lucy sank back bonelessly, her limbs turning weak. He pushed the sides of the towel open, the clean scent of her skin rising in a heated draft.

In a haze of excitement and confusion, Lucy turned her burning face to the side, her eyes closing to blot out everything but the intense pleasure of his touch. She wanted it so badly that nothing else mattered. He was making love to her, using his hands and mouth to draw her into a dark, sweet current of desire, and nothing had ever felt like this, a delight that seemed to dissolve her bones in liquid fire. His thumbs stroked her intimately, parting the humid flesh. A sob escaped her as she felt the heat of his breath, the pressure of his mouth opening against her. A stroke of his tongue, a gentle tug. He began to lick steadily, the rhythm teasing and luscious, until her body began to throb and clasp on emptiness. Helplessly she lifted against him with each silky flick and swirl, the sensation building to a flash point.

The metallic shrill of the doorbell cut through the brimming heat. Lucy froze, her nerves screaming in protest at the sound. Sam kept kissing and stroking her, so absorbed in the mindless sensuality of the moment that the noise hadn't registered. But the doorbell rang again, and Lucy gasped and pushed at his head.

With a guttural curse, Sam tore himself away from her. He fumbled for the towel and covered Lucy. Half sitting, half leaning against the edge of the mattress, he panted for breath. He was shaking in every limb.

"Probably one of my crew," she heard him mutter.

"Can you —"

"No."

He pushed away from the bed and went to the bathroom, and she heard the sound of water running. By the time Sam emerged, Lucy had managed to pull the covers over herself. His face was hard, his jaw set. "I'll be back in a minute."

Lucy bit her lip before asking, "Are you angry because of what you started, or because you didn't finish?"

Sam sent her a brooding glance. "Both," he said, and left the room.

As Sam went downstairs, the vicious ache of arousal was nothing compared to his scalding emotions. Anger, frustration, severe unease. He'd been so close, too damned close, to having sex with Lucy. He'd known it was wrong and he hadn't cared. Why had Lucy done nothing to stop him? If he didn't get control over the situation, over himself, he was going to make a serious mistake.

Reaching the front door, he opened it and was confronted by Lucy's sister, Alice. An incredulous scowl spread across his face. For one longing moment he let himself imagine the pleasure of booting her off his front porch.

Alice stared at him coldly, tottering on

impractical high heels. Her hazel eyes were large and heavily rimmed with glittery purple liner, startling in the narrow framework of her face. Her lips were lined and coated with hot pink. Even under the best of circumstances, Sam would have found her annoying. But having just been dragged out of bed with Lucy, with his body still screaming to go back and finish the job, Sam found it impossible to muster even the bare minimum of civility.

"We don't encourage people to drop by without calling first," he said.

"I'm here to see my sister."

"She's fine."

"I'd like to see for myself."

"She's resting." Sam stood with one hand braced on the doorjamb, blocking her way.

"I'm not leaving until you let her know that I'm here," Alice said.

"Lucy has a concussion." With no small amount of self-derision, he added, "She can't handle any kind of stress."

Her mouth compressed into a hyphen. "You think I would hurt her?"

"You've already hurt her," Sam said evenly. "It shouldn't be too hard to figure out that shacking up with Lucy's former boyfriend means you lose your place on the short list."

"It's not your place to judge me or my personal choices."

True. But considering the fact that Alice's affair with Kevin had led to a chain reaction that had ended in Lucy recuperating at Sam's house, he figured he had a say in the matter.

"As long as Lucy's under my roof," he said, "it's my job to look out for her. And your personal choices haven't struck me as being all that great for Lucy."

"I'm not leaving until I get to talk to her." Alice raised her voice and directed it into the entrance hall behind him. "Lucy? Can you hear me? *Lucy!*"

"I don't care if you stand on my porch caterwauling the rest of the day —" Sam broke off as he heard Lucy calling from upstairs. Giving Alice a baleful glance, Sam said, "I'm going to check on her. Stay there."

"Can I wait inside?" she dared to ask.

"No." He shut the door in her face.

By the time Sam returned to the bedroom, Lucy had dressed in a pair of khaki shorts and a T-shirt. She had heard enough of the commotion downstairs to know that Alice had dropped by without warning, and that Sam hadn't taken it well.

Still giddy with nerves, Lucy couldn't decide how to feel about what had just happened between them. Mostly she was dumbfounded by her reaction to him, the blood-hot pleasure that had obliterated every thought.

As Sam approached, she felt rampant color race over her skin. His gaze slid across her, and a frown notched between his brows. "How did you get those clothes?" he asked. "I left them on the dresser."

"I didn't put any weight on my leg," Lucy said. "It was just a step and a hop away from the bed, and then I just —"

"Damn it, Lucy. If that foot touches the floor again, I'm going to . . ." He paused, considering a variety of threats.

"Send me to bed without dinner?" Lucy suggested gravely. "Take away my cell phone?"

"How about a good old-fashioned smack on the ass?"

But she had seen the flash of concern in his eyes, and she knew what was behind his annoyance. She dared to give him a small smile. "Holly told me you don't believe in spanking."

As Sam stared at her, the tension eased from his shoulders, and the hard lines of his mouth softened. "I might make an exception for you."

Her smile lingered. "You're flirting with me again."

"No, I'm —" The front door rang impatiently. "Jesus," Sam muttered.

"I probably should see her," Lucy said apologetically. "Would you take me downstairs?"

"Why do you want to put yourself through that?"

"I can't avoid Alice forever. And Mom's coming out the day after tomorrow. It would make her happy if her daughters were at least back on speaking terms."

"It's too soon."

"I think so too," Lucy admitted. "But she's here, and I may as well get it over with."

Sam hesitated before bending to slide his arms beneath her.

The contact jolted through Lucy as if an electric current had opened between them. She tried to conceal her reaction, concentrating on keeping her breathing steady. But as she held on to his shoulders, she saw a flush rise from the neck of his shirt, and she knew that she wasn't the only one affected.

"Thank you," she said, as he turned sideways to take her through the doorway. "I know you'd rather just kick her out."

"I may kick her out anyway." Sam headed to the stairs. "I'm keeping an eye on you. At the first sign of trouble, she's gone."

Lucy frowned. "I don't want you standing over the two of us while we talk."

"I won't stand over you. But I'll be nearby in case you need backup."

"I won't need backup."

"Lucy, do you know what a concussion is?"

"Yes."

Sam continued as if he hadn't heard her. "It's when you hit your head so hard that your brain slams into your skull, killing off large numbers of neurons. It can cause sleep problems, depression, and memory loss, and those side effects are aggravated if you strain yourself in any way." He paused and added irritably, "And that includes sex."

"Did the doctor say that?"

"He didn't have to."

"I don't think sex would aggravate my concussion," Lucy said. "Unless we did it upside down or on a trampoline."

Although she'd meant to be funny, Sam didn't seem to be in the mood for humor.

"We're not doing it in any position," he said vehemently.

As Sam settled Lucy onto the sofa with her leg elevated, Renfield got up from his mat in the corner. He shambled over to them, his face split with a pugnacious canine grin. Lucy reached down to pet him, while Sam went to get Alice. Unceremoniously he ushered her sister into the living room.

Oddly, although Lucy was the one with the bandages and leg splint, Alice struck her as being far more vulnerable. The heavy makeup, the expression hemmed with strain, the movements constricted by her four-inch heels, all added to an appearance of bruised insecurity.

"Hi," Alice said.

"Hi." Lucy forced a shallow smile to her lips. "Make yourself comfortable."

As Lucy watched Alice lower herself carefully to the edge of a nearby chair, it seemed their history was all around them. Her relationship with Alice had been the most frustrating one of her life, filled with competition, jealousy, guilt, resentment. They had grown up having to battle for the limited resource of their parents' attention. Although Lucy had always hoped the conflict between them would ease as they got older, it was now worse than ever.

Noticing that Alice was staring at the dog, Lucy said, "This is Renfield."

The dog grunted and looked up at Lucy

with a string of drool hanging from his undershot jaw.

"Is something wrong with him?" Alice asked with distaste.

"It would be easier to tell you what's not wrong with him," Sam said. To Lucy, he added, "You have ten minutes. After that, your sister's leaving. You need to rest."

"Okay," Lucy said with a bland smile.

Alice wore an offended expression as she watched Sam leave the room. "Why is he so rude?"

"He's trying to look out for me," Lucy said in a low voice.

"What did you tell him about me?"

"Very little."

"I'm sure you've talked to him about how Kevin left you, and what you think I did to —"

"You're actually not the main subject of conversation around here," Lucy said, more sharply than she had intended.

Alice closed her mouth and looked affronted.

After a brittle silence, Lucy asked, "Did Mom ask you to check on me?"

"No. This was my idea. I still care about you, Lucy. I don't always behave in ways you'd like me to, but I am your sister."

Lucy bit back an acid comment. Realizing

that she had gone tense from head to toe, she tried to relax. A series of protesting twinges progressed along her spine.

Why in heaven's name was Alice there? Lucy wanted to believe that she was motivated by concern, or at least that there was some genuine sisterly feeling left between them. But apparently it was going to require more than a blood tie to reestablish a connection between them. Because the unfortunate truth was, if Alice weren't her sister, she was the kind of person Lucy wouldn't have anything to do with.

"How's it going with you and Kevin?" Lucy asked. "Are you still planning the wedding?"

"Yes. Mom and Dad are both coming out tomorrow to talk about wedding plans."

"So they are going to pay for it?"

"I think so."

"I thought they would," Lucy said darkly, before she could stop herself. No matter what they said to the contrary, her parents were never going to hold Alice accountable for anything.

"You don't think they should?" Alice asked.

"And you do?" Lucy countered.

"Of course I do. I'm their daughter." Alice's eyes turned hard. "There's something you need to understand, Lucy. I never planned to hurt you. Neither did Kevin. It was never about you. You were just . . ."

"Collateral damage?"

"I guess that's one way to put it."

"Neither of you bothered to think about anything beyond what you wanted right then."

"Well, love is like that," Alice replied with no trace of guilt.

"Is it?" Settling deeper into the corner of the sofa, Lucy wrapped her arms around herself. "Did you ever think that when Kevin realized he wanted to end his relationship with me, you might have seemed like the easiest way out?"

"No," Alice shot back. "I had the incredible ego to think that maybe he actually fell in love with me, and that — impossible as this may be to believe — someone might actually prefer me over you."

Lucy held up a staying hand and tried to think over a rush of anger. A fight was brewing, and she knew she couldn't handle it. The stress of simply being near Alice had been enough to set off a headache that wrapped around her forehead. "Let's not go there. Let's try to figure out how we go on from here."

"What is there to figure out? I'm getting

married. We're all moving on. So should you."

"It's a little more complicated than that," Lucy said. "This isn't soap opera land, where people conveniently forget the past and everything magically turns out okay." As she saw Alice stiffen, Lucy remembered too late that she'd lost her job writing for *What the Heart Knows*. "Sorry," she muttered. "I didn't mean to remind you of that."

"Right," Alice said sourly.

They were both quiet for a moment. "Are you looking for a new job?" Lucy dared to ask.

"That's my business. You don't have to worry about it."

"I'm not worried, I just . . ." Lucy let out a frustrated breath. "A conversation with you is a minefield."

"Not everything is my fault. I can't help it if Kevin wanted me more than he wanted you. He was going to leave you anyway. What was I supposed to do? I just wanted to be happy."

Did Alice truly not understand the pitfalls of trying to be happy at someone else's expense? And did she have any goals beyond that? Ironically, Alice had never looked *less* content than she did now. The problem with chasing after happiness was that it wasn't a destination you could reach. It was something that happened along the way. And what Alice was doing now — grabbing at every available pleasure, throwing aside every scruple so she could do whatever she wanted . . . that was practically a guarantee that she would end up miserable.

But all Lucy said was, "I want you to be happy too."

Alice made a little snorting sound of disbelief. Which Lucy didn't blame her for, since she knew that Alice didn't understand what she'd meant.

The mantel clock measured out a generous half minute before Alice spoke. "I'm going to invite you to the wedding. It's up to you whether or not you want to come. If you want a relationship with me, that's up to you too. I'd like for things to go back to normal. I'm sorry for everything that's happened to you, but none of it's my fault and I'm not going to spend the rest of my life paying for it."

This, Lucy realized, was what her sister had come to say.

Alice stood. "I have to go now. By the way, Mom and Dad want to meet Sam. They want to take you out to dinner tomorrow night, or have something brought in."

"Oh, great," Lucy said wearily. "Sam will

love that." Leaning her head back against the sofa, she asked, "Do you want him to show you out? I'll call for him."

"Don't bother," Alice said, her heels clacking loudly on the wood floor.

Lucy was still and silent for a few minutes. Gradually she became aware that Sam was standing beside her, his face unreadable.

"How much did you hear?" she asked dully.

"Enough to know that she's a narcissistic bitch."

"She's miserable," Lucy muttered.

"She got what she wanted."

"She always does. But it never makes her happy." Sighing, Lucy rubbed the sore back of her neck. "My parents are coming tomorrow."

"I heard."

"You don't have to go to dinner with us. They can pick me up and take me somewhere, and you can finally have some privacy."

"I'll go with you. I want to."

"That's more than I can say. I'm pretty sure they're going to pressure me into making up with Alice, and they'll want me to attend the wedding. If I do go, it'll be awful. If I don't, I'll look like the jealous, bitter older sister. As usual, there's no winning in my family. Except for Alice. She gets to win."

"Not forever," Sam said. "And not if winning means marrying Pearson. It's a match made in hell."

"I agree." Lucy leaned her head against the back of the sofa, contemplating Sam. A bittersweet smile curved her lips. "I need to get back to my glasswork. It's the only thing that will help me to stop thinking about Alice and Kevin and my parents."

"What can I do?" Sam asked quietly.

Lucy found herself looking up into his blue-green eyes and thinking that in the neatly organized inventory of all her plans and hopes, Sam Nolan didn't fit at all. He was a complication she hadn't counted on.

But despite Sam's self-admitted flaws, he was an honest, caring man. God knew she'd had too few of those in her life. The problem was that *forever* did not apply to a relationship with a man like Sam. He'd been nothing but clear about that.

Instead of focusing on what she couldn't have with him . . . maybe she should try to discover what was possible. She'd never had a relationship based on friendship and pleasure without the entanglement of emotions. Could she do that? What would she gain from it?

A chance to feel alive, and let go. A chance to have some pure, unadulterated fun before she went on with the next part of her life.

Making the decision, Lucy looked at him resolutely. He had asked what he could do for her, and she had the answer.

"Have sex with me," she said.

EIGHTEEN

Sam stared at her for so long, and with such a flabbergasted expression, that Lucy began to feel somewhat indignant.

"You look like you just swallowed one of Renfield's heartworm pills," she said.

Tearing his gaze away, Sam raked a hand through his hair, leaving some of the dark brown locks standing on end. He began to pace around the room, each step infused with agitation. "Today's not a good day to joke about that stuff."

"Dog medication?"

"Sex." He said the word as if it was a profanity.

"I wasn't joking."

"We can't have sex."

"Why not?"

"You know the reasons."

"Those reasons don't apply now," Lucy said earnestly. "Because I've thought about it, and . . . please stop moving around. Will you sit next to me?"

Warily Sam approached and sat on the coffee table, facing her. Bracing his forearms on his spread knees, he gave her a level stare.

"I know your rules," Lucy said. "No commitment. No jealousy. No future. The only things we exchange are body fluids, not feelings."

"Yeah," Sam said. "Those are the rules. And I'm not doing any of that with you."

Lucy frowned. "You told me not long ago that if I wanted to have revenge sex, you would do it with me."

"I had no intention of going through with it. You're not the kind of woman who can do friends-with-benefits."

"I am, too."

"You're so *not,* Lucy." Sam stood and began to pace again. "At the beginning you'll say you're fine with casual sex. But that won't last for long."

"What if I *promise* not to get serious?"

"You will anyway."

"Why are you so sure?"

"Because my kind of relationship only works when both people are equally shallow. I'm great at shallow. But you would throw the whole thing off balance."

"Sam. I've had bad luck with relationships. Believe me, there is no man on earth

I couldn't live without, including you. But this morning when we were upstairs together . . . it was the best feeling I've had in a long time. And if I'm willing to try things your way, I don't see why you should have a problem with it."

Sam had stopped in the middle of the room. He stared at her with baffled annoyance, having clearly run out of arguments.

"No," he eventually said.

Her brows lifted. "Is that a definitive no, or an I'm-thinking-about-it no?"

"It's a no-way-in-hell no."

"But you'll still have dinner with my parents and me tomorrow?"

"Yeah, I can do that."

Lucy shook her head, dumbfounded. "You'll have dinner with me and my parents, but you won't have sex with me?"

"I have to eat," he said.

"There's a simple rule for managing stairs on crutches," Sam said later in the day, staying close behind Lucy as she approached the front steps of the house. "Up with the good, down with the bad. When you're going up, always lead with the healthy leg. When you're going down, lead with the bad leg and the crutches."

They had just returned from the doctor's

office, where Lucy had been fitted with an Aircast brace. Having never needed to use crutches before, Lucy was discovering they were much more difficult than she had assumed.

"Try not to put any weight on your right leg," Sam said, watching Lucy's wobbly progress along the path. "Just swing it through and take a hop with your left."

"How do you know so much about it?" Lucy asked, puffing with effort.

"I fractured an ankle when I was sixteen. Sports injury."

"Football?"

"Bird-watching."

Lucy chuckled. "Bird-watching is not a sport."

"I was twenty feet up a Douglas fir, trying to get a view of a marbled murrelet. An endangered species that nests in old-growth forests. Naturally I was climbing without rigging. I caught sight of the murrelet chick and got so excited I slipped and fell, hitting just about every branch on the way down."

"Poor thing," Lucy said. "But I bet you thought it was worth it."

"Of course it was." He watched as she hopped forward on the crutches. "I'll carry you the rest of the way. You can practice later."

"No, I can do the stairs. It's a relief to be moving around again. This means I can go to my studio tomorrow."

"Tomorrow or the next day," Sam said. "Don't push too hard, or you'll reinjure that leg."

Lucy's smile turned quizzical. His mood was difficult to interpret. Ever since her proposition, he'd been back to treating her with the impersonal friendliness of the first two days at Rainshadow Road. But it wasn't precisely the same. At certain moments she had caught him glancing at her in a way that was both preoccupied and intimate, and she knew somehow that he was thinking about what had happened — or almost happened — between them that morning. And he was thinking about her claim that she would be fine with a no-strings affair. She knew that even though he hadn't believed her, he wanted to.

By the time Lucy had made it into the house, she was sweaty and tired, but triumphant. She accompanied Sam to the kitchen, where Holly was having an after-school snack and Mark sat on the floor with Renfield.

"You're upright," Mark said, glancing at Lucy with a brief smile. "Congratulations."

"Thanks," she said with a laugh. "It's

good to be moving around again."

"Lucy!" Holly hurried over to admire the crutches. "Those are cool! Can I try them?"

"They're not for playing, sweetheart," Sam said, bending to kiss his niece. He helped Lucy onto a stool at the wooden worktable, and leaned the crutches next to her. He glanced at Mark, who had pinned Renfield to the floor and was attempting to open his mouth while wearing a pair of heavy-duty gardening gloves. "What are you doing with the dog?"

"I'm trying to give him his third antiseizure pill."

"He's only supposed to have one."

"What I meant was, we're on the third attempt." Mark scowled at the stubborn bulldog. "He chewed up the first one and sneezed the powder into my face. The second time I pried his mouth open with a dessert spoon and shoved the pill in. He managed to spit out the pill and eat the spoon."

"He didn't really eat the spoon, though," Holly said. "He coughed it up before it went down."

Shaking his head, Sam went to the refrigerator, took out a piece of cheese, and handed it to Mark. "Hide the pill in this."

"He's lactose intolerant," Mark said. "It

311

gives him gas."

"Trust me," Sam replied, "no one will notice."

Looking skeptical, Mark shoved the capsule into the cube of cheese, and offered it to Renfield.

The bulldog gobbled down the cheese and plodded out of the kitchen.

"Guess what?" Holly asked Lucy, crouching on the floor to inspect her Aircast brace. "Dad and Maggie are getting married in two months. And I'm going on the honeymoon with them!"

"You finally set the date?" Sam asked Mark.

"We're doing it in mid-August." Mark went to the sink to wash his hands. "Maggie wants to get married on a ferry."

"You're kidding," Sam said.

"Nope." Mark blotted his hands. Turning around, he told Lucy, "A significant portion of our courtship occurred on the Washington State ferry system. It forced Maggie to sit with me until she finally realized how magnetically attractive I was."

"Must have been a long ride," Sam said, and ducked a fake jab Mark threw at him. Laughing, he added, "I can't believe they'll let you have a wedding ceremony on one of those tubs."

"Believe it or not, we wouldn't be the first. But the ceremony won't be on an active ferry — there's a retired antique one on Lake Union, with a great view of the city and the Space Needle."

"That's romantic," Lucy said.

"I'm going to be the maid of honor," Holly said, "and Uncle Sam's going to be the best man."

"I am?" Sam asked.

"Who else has such ample story material for the reception speech?" Mark asked. He grinned at his brother. "Will you be my best man, Sam? After all we've been through, there's not even a close second. I actually almost like you."

"I'll do it," Sam said. "But only if you promise to take the dog when you move out."

"Deal." They exchanged a brief, back-slapping hug.

As evening approached, Mark and Holly left to pick up Maggie from work and take her out to dinner. "Have fun," Mark said as he and Holly walked out hand in hand. "Don't wait up for us, we're going to be out late."

"Par-tay!" Holly exclaimed before the door closed.

Lucy and Sam were left alone. Sam kept

staring in the direction his brother had gone in, absorbed in some private reflection. Then he glanced at Lucy, and something changed in his face. The silence turned electric.

Sitting on a stool at the kitchen worktable, Lucy asked casually, "What are we having for dinner?"

"Steak, potatoes, and salad."

"That sounds great. Let me help. Can I chop vegetables for the salad?"

Sam brought a cutting board, a chef's knife, and raw vegetables and greens. As Lucy chopped cucumber and yellow bell peppers, Sam opened a bottle of wine and poured two glasses.

"No jam jar?" Lucy asked with a faux-wistful expression as Sam gave her a crystal stem filled with dark, glittering Cabernet.

"Not for this wine." He clinked his glass with hers and made a toast. "To Mark and Maggie."

"Do you think Alex will mind that you're going to be the best man?" Lucy asked.

"Not at all. They don't typically have much to do with each other."

"Is that because of the age difference?"

"Maybe in part. But it's really more of a personality issue. Mark's the typical older brother. When he gets worried about some-

314

one, he gets bossy and overbearing, which sends Alex up the wall."

"What do you say to them when they argue?"

"When I'm not running for cover, you mean?" Sam asked dryly. "I tell Mark that he's not going to change Alex or stop him from drinking. That's up to Alex. And I've told Alex that at some point, I'm going to drag his ass to rehab. Not the kind of rehab with celebrities and spa treatments. The kind with an electrified fence, where they give you a scary roommate and make you clean your own toilet."

"Do you think it would ever get to that point? Where you could convince him to . . . get help somewhere?"

Sam shook his head. "I think Alex will stay functional enough to avoid ever having to deal with it." He studied the depths of his wineglass, swirled the deep garnet liquid. "He won't admit it, but he's angry at the whole damn world because our family was such a screw job."

"But you don't seem to feel that way," Lucy said quietly. "Angry at the world, I mean."

Sam shrugged, his gaze turning inward. "I had it a little easier than he did. There was this old couple who lived a couple of houses away from us. They were my escape. They had no kids of their own, and I used to go hang out at their house." He smiled reminiscently. "Fred would let me take apart an old alarm clock and put it back together again, or show me how to replace the kitchen sink drain pipes. Mary was a teacher. She gave me books to read, helped me with homework sometimes."

"Are either of them still alive?"

"No, both gone. Mary left me some money to use as part of the down payment for this place. She loved the idea of the vineyard. She used to make blackberry wine in a gallon jug. Godawful sweet stuff." Sam fell silent, his expression hazed with memories.

Lucy realized that he was trying to make connections for her, explain himself in a way that wasn't easy. He wasn't the kind of man who made excuses or apologized for who he was. But on some level he wanted her to understand the person who had been formed by the bitter implosion of his parents' relationship.

"On my twelfth birthday," Sam said after a while, "I came home after school and Vick had taken Alex somewhere, and Mark had disappeared. My mother was passed out on the sofa. Dad was drinking something straight from the bottle. Around dinnertime I started to get hungry, but there was nothing to eat. I went to look for Dad, and finally found him sitting in his car in the driveway, shouting some crap about suicide. So I went to Fred and Mary's house, and stayed for about three days."

"They must have meant a lot to you."

"They saved my life."

"Did you ever tell them that?"

"No. They knew." Recalling himself to the present, Sam leveled a wary glance at Lucy. She knew that he'd told her more than he had meant to, and he wasn't certain why, and he regretted it. "Back in a minute," he said, and went to set the steaks on an outside grill at the back of the house.

As the steaks cooked on the grill, and a pan of red potatoes roasted in the oven, Lucy told Sam about her parents, and the recent discovery that her father had been married once before he'd married her mother.

"Are you going to ask him about it?"

"I'm curious," Lucy admitted, "but I'm not sure I want to hear the answers. I know that he loves Mom. But I don't want him to tell me that he loved someone else more than her." She traced her fingers over the scarred surface of the worktable. "Dad's always been distant from the rest of us. Reserved. I think his first wife kept a piece of his heart that he couldn't give to anyone else after she died. I think he was permanently damaged, but Mom wanted him anyway."

"Must be hard to compete with someone's memory," Sam said.

"Yes. Poor Mom." Lucy grimaced. "I'm sorry you'll have to meet them. It's not fair to you. Waiting on me hand and foot, then having to suffer through a visit from my parents."

"No problem."

"You'll probably like Dad. He tells physics jokes that no one ever gets."

"Like what?"

"Like, 'Why did the chicken cross the road? Because a chicken at rest tends to stay at rest. Chickens in motion tend to cross the road.'" Lucy rolled her eyes as he laughed. "I knew you'd think it was funny. Where do you think we should go for dinner?"

"Duck Soup," Sam said. It was one of the best restaurants on the island, a vine-covered inn featuring local produce and items from its own kitchen garden, and freshly caught seafood. A whimsical portrait of Groucho Marx hung in the entrance foyer.

"I love that place," Lucy said. "But Kevin and I had dinner with them there once before."

"Why does that matter?"

Lucy shrugged, not quite certain why she'd mentioned it.

Sam looked at her steadily. "I'm not worried about being compared to Kevin."

Lucy felt her color rise. "I wasn't thinking that," she said irritably.

After pouring more wine, Sam lifted his glass and said, "Time wounds all heels."

Lucy brought herself to smile, recognizing the quote by Groucho Marx. "I'll drink to that," she said, and raised her own glass.

Over dinner they discussed movies, discovering a shared liking for old black-and-white films. When Lucy confessed that she had never seen *The Philadelphia Story* with Cary Grant and Katharine Hepburn, Sam insisted that she had to watch it. "It's a classic screwball comedy. You can't say you like old movies without having seen it."

"It's too bad we can't watch it tonight," Lucy said.

"Why can't we?"

"Do you have it on DVD?"

"No, but I can download it."

"But that'll take forever."

Sam looked smug. "I've got a download accelerator that maximizes data delivery by initiating several simultaneous connections from multiple servers. Five minutes, tops."

"At times you hide your inner geek so well," Lucy marveled. "And then it just appears like a bolt of lightning."

After dinner they went to the living room to watch the movie. Lucy was immediately taken with the story of the prickly, cold-natured heiress, her debonair ex-husband, and the cynical newspaper reporter played by Jimmy Stewart. The dialogue was filled with elegant quicksilver humor, every pause and reaction perfectly timed.

As the black-and-white images flickered on the screen, Lucy leaned into Sam's side, half expecting him to object. The relaxed evening together, the tentative confidences, had created a feeling of intimacy that Sam might not want to encourage. But he put his arm around her, and let her head rest against his shoulder. She sighed, relishing the solid warmth of him next to her, the anchoring weight of his arm. As awareness of him gathered in a slow simmer, it was difficult not to touch him, reach for him.

"You're not watching the movie," Sam said.

"Neither are you."

"What are you thinking about?"

In the silence, the movie dialogue floated like champagne froth.

"It can't be anything like love, could it?"

"No, no, it can't be."

"Would it be inconvenient?"

"Terribly."

"I was thinking," Lucy said, "that I've never tried a relationship where no one makes any promises. I like that rule. Because if you don't make promises, you can't break them."

"There's another rule I didn't tell you about." Sam's voice was guarded. His breath stirred the hair on top of her head.

"What is it?"

"Know when to stop. When either of us says it's time to break it off, the other agrees. No arguments, no discussion."

Lucy was silent, her stomach leaping as he altered his position on the sofa.

Sam turned to face her, his head silhouetted against a background of flickering ghost-images. The low sound of his voice undercut the muted flurry of words and images from the screen behind him. "Of all the people I've never wanted to hurt, Lucy . . . you're at the top of the list."

"I think you're the first man who's ever

worried about that." Lucy dared to reach out and touch the side of his face, her fingers shaping gently against his cheek. She felt the subtle flex in his jaw, the forceful beat of his pulse against her fingertips. "Let's take a chance," she whispered. "You won't hurt me, Sam. I won't let you."

Taking his time, Sam reached for the controller, fumbled with it, and hit the mute button. The movie continued, light and shadow without sound. His mouth found hers in a long, fluent kiss, exchanging heat for heat, taste for taste. One of his hands went to the nape of her neck, massaging blindly. The excitement deepened into something dark and nameless, a feeling that rose in a slow tide from her toes to the top of her head. It was more than desire . . . it was a craving so absolute that she would have done anything to satisfy it.

Sam took the hem of her shirt and tugged it upward, stripping the knit fabric away from her. His fingers stroked along the elastic straps of her bra, easing them down her shoulders before moving to the clasp at the back. A shiver ran through her as she felt him work at the tiny hooks. Tossing the garment aside, Sam drew his hands along the sides of her rib cage, sliding upward to cup her naked breasts. He bent over her.

With diabolical slowness, he took the tip of her breast in his mouth and held it with his teeth, and stroked with his tongue. She had to bite her lips to keep from begging him to take her right then. He began to tug gently, repeatedly, licking between each pull.

Moaning, Lucy clutched at the back of his T-shirt, trying to tear it off, needing the feel of his skin against her. He paused to strip away the garment, and eased her back until she was stretched out on the sofa. Her injured leg was propped up, her other dangling wantonly to the side.

Lowering over her, Sam sealed his mouth against hers, his kisses rough and voluptuous and sweet. She couldn't find herself in the sudden blaze of sensation, couldn't control anything. She answered him, letting herself be caught like a falling star, burning from the inside out.

Dimly she heard him murmur that they should stop for a second, they needed to use some kind of protection. She gasped out a few words to make him understand that it wasn't necessary, she was on the pill to regulate her cycle, and he said he was still going to take her upstairs because their first time shouldn't be on the sofa. But they kept kissing compulsively, ravenously, and Sam reached down to open her shorts. He yanked them over her hips, taking her underwear with them, the air cool against the blaze of her skin.

Lucy had gone weak with need, wanting him to touch her, kiss her, do *anything,* but the panties and shorts had caught on the Aircast brace, and he had paused to untangle them. "Leave them," she said breathlessly. "Don't stop." She gave him a red-faced scowl as he persisted in trying to unloop the underwear elastic from the brace clasp. *"Sam —"*

Her impatience drew a muffled laugh from him. He reached for her, sliding his arm beneath her neck. His mouth came to hers in a searching kiss, licking deep, pausing to tug at her upper lip and then her lower one. "Is this what you want?" he asked, his hand sliding between her shaking thighs. He teased her aching flesh open, caressing with light, voluble circles until she'd gone utterly wet. Her head fell back over his arm, and he kissed her throat and breathed hotly against her skin as he let his fingers enter her.

She writhed and hitched upward awkwardly, her leg encumbered by the brace. He murmured softly against her ear . . . be still, let him do it, don't strain . . . but she couldn't help lifting into the pleasure.

Gasping, she pulled him closer in a desperate wordless plea for more, her hands groping over the hard-muscled surface of his back. His skin was smooth and tough and silky, the slope of his shoulder so enticing that she dug the crescent of her teeth lightly into the sturdy muscle, a love-bite that made him shudder.

He reached between them to fumble with the fastening of his jeans. She couldn't move, could only wait helplessly as he pressed into her with a low, heavy slide. She felt herself tighten, relax, tighten again. He went deeper. Inarticulate sounds rose in her throat. There weren't words for what she needed, for what was happening to her. His hand withdrew and slid up to her breast, damp fingertips clamping gently on the hard peak.

Through the thunder of her heartbeat, she heard him whisper for her to take him, let him inside. As she strained and clung to him, she felt his hand sliding beneath her bottom to angle her higher. He thrust again, the slippery-hot friction making her cry out as if in pain.

Sam froze, looking down at her, his eyes unearthly blue in the shadows. "Did I hurt you?" he whispered.

"No. No . . ." Flooded with desire, steaming, Lucy gripped his hips, urging him more tightly against her. "Please don't stop."

Sam began a deliberate rhythm, making her squirm and arch as if she were on a torture rack.

She rocked upward in silent demand, but there was no altering his slow and relentless pace. The tension coiled, her inner muscles clenching against the delicious invading hardness. His thrusts canted deeper, and she moaned every time he drove inward. It was all too much, the big, driving body over hers, the teasing brush of his chest hair against her nipples, the strong hand urging her hips upward into every measured lunge. She felt the pleasure break into ecstatic spasms. Sam caught her sobs with his mouth, and pushed deep, letting her shuddering body work him, drain him.

For a while, neither of them moved or spoke, only breathed in labored gusts.

Circling her arms around his neck, she kissed his jaw, his chin, the corner of his mouth. "Sam," she said drowsily, her voice thick with satisfaction. "Thank you."

"Yes." He sounded dazed.

"That was amazing."

"Yes."

Close to his ear, she added, "And just to make you feel safe . . . I don't love you."

Judging from the rustle of laughter in his chest, that had been the right thing to say. Sam leaned over her, his lips grazing her smiling mouth. "I don't love you too."

When Sam was able to move, he gathered up their discarded clothes and took Lucy upstairs. They lay together on the wide bed, conversation temporarily banked like coals beneath a layer of cool ash.

Sam felt a thrill of unease, as if his body knew he'd made a mistake even though his brain kept coming up with all the reasons why he hadn't. Lucy was a grown woman, able to make her own decisions. He hadn't misled her, hadn't presented himself in any light other than what he was. She seemed happy with the situation, and God knew he was satisfied, replete, in a way he'd never known before.

Maybe that was the problem. It had been too good. It had been *different*. The question of why it was like this with Lucy was something he should think about. Later.

The outline of her body in the semidarkness was slightly blurred like the penumbra of shadow in a painting. Moonlight from the window brought a faint luminosity to her skin, as if she was a magical creature from a fairy tale. Sam gazed at her in fascination, running his hand along her hip and flank.

"What happens at the end?" Lucy whispered.

"The end of what?"

"The movie. Which guy does Katharine Hepburn marry?"

"I'm not going to spoil it for you."

"I like spoilers."

Sam played with her hair, letting rivers of dark silk spill through his fingers. "Tell me what you think happens."

"I think she ends up with Jimmy Stewart."

"Why?"

"Well, she and Cary Grant were married once and they got divorced. So it's doomed."

Sam smiled at her prosaic tone. "What a little cynic."

"Marrying someone for the second time never works. Look at Liz Taylor and Richard Burton. Or Melanie Griffith and Don Johnson. And *you* can't call *me* a cynic — you don't even believe in marrying someone the first time."

"I believe in it for some people." He continued to sift his fingers through her hair. "But it's more romantic not to get married."

Lucy lifted up on an elbow, looking down at him. "Why do you think that?"

"Without marriage, you're only together for the good times. The best part of the relationship. And then when it goes bad, you cut loose and move on. No ugly memories, no soul-killing divorce."

Lucy was silent, considering. "There's a flaw in your reasoning."

"What is it?"

"I don't know. I haven't figured it out yet."

Sam smiled and pulled her beneath him. Bending over her breast, he licked at the stiffening peak and used his thumb to rub in the moisture. Her skin was like pale silk, impossibly smooth against his fingertips. The textures of her body fascinated him, everything soft and yielding and sleek. And the scent of her — flowery, cottony, with the erotic hints of salt and musk — aroused a hot clamor in his blood. He moved over her, dragging his mouth in a slow path along her body, savoring the taste of her. As he moved lower, her limbs trembled beneath his hands. He felt her hands caress his hair, the back of his neck, the touch of her cool fingers making him instantly hard. He followed the feminine scent to where it was deeper, more enticing, and Lucy made an agitated sound, her legs spreading easily.

She whimpered as he nuzzled into the softness between her thighs, licking into the silk and heat, the flavor of her erotic and drugging. He toyed with her, stroking, sucking lightly, until she pushed herself at him with a sob. Catching every throb and pulse, he urged her through sensation into softness, until she was relaxed and still beneath him.

Rising, he covered her with his body and sank into the luscious wet depths, thrusting slowly to savor the feel of her. Her nails slid over his back, a delicate electrifying clawing that provoked him into heavier, deeper drives. The release surged without warning, full-bodied and severe, spreading over every inch of skin from his scalp to the soles of his feet.

Winded and stunned, Sam collapsed to his side when it was over. Lucy snuggled next to him. He closed his eyes, struggling to moderate his breathing. His limbs felt unbelievably heavy. He had known pleasure before, but never with this intensity, this profusion. Exhaustion settled over him, and he wanted nothing more than to sleep. Just like this . . . in his own bed . . . with Lucy beside him.

But that last thought snapped his eyes open.

He never slept with someone after having sex, which was one of the reasons he preferred it to happen at the woman's place rather than his. Far easier to be the one to leave. On a couple of occasions in the past, Sam had actually gone so far as to load a protesting woman into his car and take her home. The idea of spending an entire night with a woman had always filled him with an aversion bordering on panic.

Forcing himself to leave the bed, he went to take a shower. After putting on a robe, he brought a hot washcloth to the bed and took care of Lucy, and drew the covers up to her shoulders. "I'll see you in the morning," he murmured, pressing a brief kiss to her lips.

"Where are you going?"

"The roll-away bed."

"Stay with me." Lucy flipped back a corner of the bedclothes invitingly.

Sam shook his head. "I might hurt your leg . . . roll on it or something . . ."

"Are you kidding?" A sleepy smile curved her lips. "This brace is indestructible. You could drive your truck over it."

Sam took a long moment to reply, alarmed by his own desire to actually climb back into bed with her. "I like to sleep alone."

"Oh." Lucy's voice was deliberately casual. "You never spend the night with a woman."

"No."

"That's absolutely fine," she said.

"Good." Sam cleared his throat, feeling inept. Oafish. "You know it's nothing personal, right?"

Her gentle laugh curled through the air. "Good night, Sam. I had a great time. Thank you."

Sam thought it was probably the first time a woman had ever thanked him for having sex with her. "The pleasure was all mine." And he went to the other room with the same uneasiness he'd felt before.

Something had changed inside him, and God help him, he didn't want to know what it was.

NINETEEN

Lucy's mother, of course, was instantly smitten with Sam. Her father's reaction was more guarded, at least initially. However, during dinner at Duck Soup, they found common ground when Sam asked about the robotic space probe that her father had helped to design. Comprehending the generous helping of geekiness that lurked under Sam's exterior, Lucy's usually reticent father started chattering like a magpie.

". . . so what we expected," Phillip was saying, "was that the comets would consist of a combination of presolar particles, and ice that had formed at the edge of the solar system at absolute zero." He paused. "If you're not familiar with the term, absolute zero is —"

"The null point of any thermodynamic temperature scale," Sam said.

"That's right." Her father practically beamed at him. "Contrary to our assumptions, most of the comet's rocky matter had been formed inside the solar system at extreme high temperatures. So comets are formed in conditions of severe heat *and* ice."

"Fascinating," Sam said, and it was obvious that he actually meant it.

As the men continued to talk, Lucy's mother leaned close to whisper to her. "He is *wonderful*. So good-looking and charming, and your father *loves* him. You have to hold on to this one, sweetheart."

"There's nothing to hold on to," Lucy whispered back. "I told you. He's a lifelong bachelor."

It was obvious that her mother relished the challenge. "You can change his mind. A man like him shouldn't stay single. It would be a crime."

"I'm not going to torture a perfectly nice man by trying to change him."

"Lucy," came her mother's impatient whisper, "what do you think marriage is *for?*"

After dinner they went to the house at Rainshadow for coffee. That hadn't been the original plan, but after hearing Sam's description of the vineyard and the renovated Victorian house, Lucy's mother had all but demanded to see it. Mark and Holly were away for the weekend, having gone with Maggie to visit her parents in Bellingham. Obligingly Sam asked Cherise if she wanted the twenty-five-cent tour.

"I'll stay in the kitchen and make some coffee," Lucy said. "Mom, don't interrogate Sam while he's showing you the house."

Her mother gave her a look of wide-eyed surprise. "I never interrogate anyone."

"You should probably know that I only take preapproved questions," Sam said. "But for you, Cherise, I'll allow some latitude."

Her mother giggled.

"I'll help Lucy with the coffee," her father said. "Discussions of home renovation are lost on me — I don't know a pediment from a pergola."

After Lucy ran a cupful of beans through the electric grinder, she measured the coffee into the machine, while her father filled a pitcher at the sink. "So what do you think of Sam?" Lucy asked.

"I like him. A smart fellow. He appears to be healthy and self-supporting, and he laughed at my Heisenberg joke. I can't help but wonder why a man with such a good brain would waste it on tending a vineyard."

"It's not a waste."

"Thousands of people all over the world make wine. There's no point in coming up with yet another one, when there are already so many being produced."

"That's like saying no one should produce any more art, because we already have so much out there."

"Art — or wine — doesn't benefit people the way science does."

"Sam would say the opposite." She watched her father pour water into the coffeemaker.

The appliance clicked and steamed as it began to percolate.

"A more significant question," her father remarked, "is what you think of him."

"I like him too. But there's no chance of the relationship getting serious. He and I both have future plans that don't include each other."

Her father shrugged. "If you enjoy his company, there's no harm in spending time with him."

They were quiet for a moment, listening to the placid sputter of the coffeemaker.

"You're going to see Alice and Kevin tomorrow?" Lucy asked.

Her father nodded, his smile turning grim. "You know that that marriage — if it happens — doesn't have a snowball's chance in hell."

"You can't be a hundred percent certain,"

Lucy said, even though she privately agreed. "People surprise you."

"Yes, they do," he admitted. "At my age, however, not often. Where are the coffee mugs?"

Together they opened a couple of cabinets until they found them.

"Your mother and I have been talking recently," Phillip said, and stunned her by adding, "I gather she's told you that I'd been married once before."

"Yes," Lucy managed to say. "That was kind of a shocker."

"All this business with you and Alice and Kevin has stirred up some issues your mother and I haven't faced in quite a while."

"Is that bad?" Lucy asked gingerly.

"I don't know. I've never been convinced that everything in a relationship needs to be talked about. Some things can't be fixed by a conversation."

"I'm guessing these issues have to do with . . . her?" For some reason the words "your first wife" were too jarring for Lucy to say.

"Yes. I love your mother. I would never make comparisons. The other relationship was . . ." A pause, fraught with a kind of pensive strain she had never seen from him before. "It was in its own category."

"What was her name?" Lucy asked softly.

His lips parted as if to answer, but he shook his head and stayed silent.

What kind of woman had she had been, Lucy wondered, that decades after her death, he couldn't speak her name?

"That intensity of emotion . . ." he said after a while, as if to himself. "That sense of two people being so right for each other, they're halves of a whole. It was . . . extraordinary."

"So you don't regret it," Lucy said.

"I do regret it." Her father looked at her directly, his eyes glittering. His voice was thick as he added, "Better not to know. But that's just me. Other people might say that it's worth any price to have just a few moments of what I had." Turning away, he began to pour the coffee.

Stunned into silence by the rare display of emotion, Lucy hobbled to get spoons from the flatware drawer. Had he been a more tactile man, she would have gone to embrace him. However, his buttoned-up civility had always been a suit of armor, repelling gestures of affection.

Now she understood something about her father that she never had before — his calmness, his endless composure, had nothing to do with peace.

■ ■ ■ ■

After the Marinns had returned to California, Lucy's mother called to tell her that the day they had spent with Alice and Kevin had gone as well as could have been expected. According to Cherise, the pair had been subdued. Kevin had been especially quiet. "But I did get the feeling," her mother said, "that they've both made up their minds to go through with it, no matter what. I think Kevin's being pushed by his parents — they seem very intent on getting him married."

Lucy smiled ruefully. Kevin's parents were an older couple who had spoiled their only son and had subsequently been dismayed by his immaturity and self-centeredness. But it was too late for them to wonder what might have been, what they should have done differently. Perhaps they thought that marriage would be good for him, make him more of an adult.

"We went out to dinner," Cherise said, "and everyone was on their best behavior."

"Even Dad?" Lucy asked wryly.

"Even Dad. The only awkward moment came when Kevin asked me about you."

"He did?" Lucy felt a startled jab in her

stomach. "In front of everyone?"

"Yes. He wanted to know about your leg, and how you were feeling, and then he asked how involved you were with Sam."

"My God. I bet Alice wanted to kill him."

"It wasn't good timing on his part," her mother said.

"What did you tell him?"

"The truth — that you look well, and happy, and you seem to be getting very close to Sam. And I couldn't be any more pleased about it."

"Mom. I've already told you why there's no chance for me to have a serious relationship with Sam. So please don't get your hopes up for something that's impossible."

"Don't say 'it's impossible,'" her mother said with annoying sanguinity, "about something that you're already doing."

Two days after her parents' visit, Lucy moved into the condo at Friday Harbor. To her surprise, Sam had objected to her leaving Rainshadow so soon, insisting that she needed more time to rest and heal. "Besides," he'd said, "I don't think you've gotten the hang of those crutches yet."

"I've totally gotten the hang of them," Lucy said. "I can even do tricks with them. You should see my freestyle moves."

"All those stairs. All that walking. And you can't drive yet. How are you going to get groceries?"

"I've got a whole list of numbers from the Hog Heaven congregation."

"I don't want you to hang out with a bunch of bikers."

"I won't be hanging out with them," Lucy said, amused. "They're just going to lend me a hand every now and then."

Although it was clear that Sam would have liked to argue further, he muttered, "It's your life."

Lucy gave him an impish grin. "Don't worry," she said. "I'll let you come over for a quickie every now and then."

He scowled at her. "That's great. Because sexual convenience was my main concern."

Although Lucy was rather sorry to leave the house at Rainshadow, she felt it was better for both of them. Another few days of proximity, and she was fairly certain that Sam would have started to feel claustrophobic. And most important, Lucy was happy to be able to return to her studio.

She missed her glass desperately, could almost feel it calling to her.

On her first morning back at Swing on a Star, Lucy was filled with creative fire. She set out to produce a cartoon, or a full-sized design, of the tree window for the Rain-shadow Vineyard house. Using a combination of hand sketching and computer software, she detailed the cut lines and numbering sections for color shading. When it was finished to her satisfaction, she would make three copies of the pattern, one for reference, one to cut apart with shears, and one on which to assemble the window. Then the meticulous process of glass scoring and breaking would begin, accompanied by reshaping and grinding the edges of pieces as needed.

Lucy was still working on the cartoon when Sam came to the studio at lunchtime. He brought in two crisp white paper bags from the Market Chef, both of which looked satisfyingly weighty. "Sandwiches," he said.

"I didn't expect you," Lucy exclaimed. A teasing grin spread across her face. "You just can't stay away from me."

Sam glanced at the pile of sketches on the table. "Is this preferable to the life of leisure you had with me?"

Lucy laughed. "Well, being waited on hand and foot was very nice . . . but it's good to be productive again."

Sam set the bags on the worktable and came around to view the cartoon. He stared intently at the design. "It's beautiful."

"It's going to be stunning," Lucy said. "You have no idea what the glass will add."

The corners of his mouth quirked. "Knowing you, I'll be prepared for anything." After studying the design for a minute, he said, "I brought you a housewarming present. I thought you'd probably want to keep it here."

"You didn't have to get me a present."

"You won't be able to use it for a while."

"Where is it?"

"Sit still. I'll bring it in."

Lucy waited with an expectant grin as Sam went outside. Her eyes widened as he wheeled in a bicycle with a huge bow adorning the center of the handlebars. "I don't believe it. Oh, Sam. You are the sweetest, sweetest —" She broke off with a crow of delight as she looked at the fabulous vintage restored bike, painted a rich forest green with crisp white ballooner fenders.

"It's a 1954 Ladies Schwinn Hornet," Sam said, rolling it over to her.

Lucy ran her fingers over the rich patina, the thick black wall tires, the white leather seat. "It's perfect," she said, surprised to discover that her voice was scratchy and her eyes were blurring. Because a present like this could only have come from someone who understood her, who *got* her. And it was a sign that Sam truly felt something for her, whether or not he'd intended it that way. She was surprised by the realization of how much that meant to her, how much she had wanted him to care for her on some level.

"Thank you. I . . ." She stood and threw her arms around him, and pressed her face against his shoulder.

"It's nothing." Sam patted her back uncomfortably. "No need to get all girly."

Feeling how tense he'd gotten, understanding the reason why, Lucy said in a muffled voice, "It is incredibly sweet, and probably the nicest thing anyone's ever given me." She forced a laugh and leaned up to kiss his cheek. "Relax. I still don't love you."

"Thank God." He grinned at her, relaxing visibly.

For the next two months, Lucy occupied herself with her work. Sam often dropped by on the pretext of checking on her, but his visits usually resulted in the two of them having dinner together. Although there had been countless romantic interludes at the condo afterward, sex was not something that Sam demanded or automatically expected. He seemed to enjoy talking with her, just being with her, whether or not they ended up sleeping together. One afternoon he brought Holly to Lucy's studio, and Lucy helped her to make a simple sun-catcher with glass and copper foil. On another day they took Holly to the sculpture park, where Sam was quickly surrounded by at least a half-dozen children, all of them giggling wildly as he led them in attempts to pose like statues.

Lucy found Sam's behavior more than a little perplexing. For a man who was so determined to avoid emotional involvement, his actions were those of a man who desired closeness. Their discussions frequently strayed into personal territory, as they shared their thoughts and childhood memories. The more Lucy gleaned about the Nolans' background, the more compassion she felt for Sam. Children of alcoholics often grew up to be suspicious of intense emotion. They usually tried to isolate themselves, to defend against being hurt or manipulated, or worst of all, abandoned. As a result, intimacy was the most dangerous thing of all, something to be avoided at all cost. And yet Sam was drawing closer, gradually learning to trust her without seeming to be aware of it.

You're more than you think you are, Lucy

longed to tell him. It wasn't impossible to believe that Sam might someday reach the point of being able to love someone and be loved in return. On the other hand, that kind of momentous change, of self-realization, might take a very long time. Perhaps a lifetime. Or it might never happen at all. The woman who pinned all of her hopes on Sam would almost certainly end up with a broken heart.

And only to herself, Lucy acknowledged that she was dangerously close to becoming that woman. It would be so easy to let herself love Sam. She was so irresistibly drawn to him, so happy when they were together, that she understood there was a fast-approaching time limit for their relationship. If she waited too long to break it off, she would be seriously hurt. Far more hurt, in fact, than she had been by Kevin.

In the meantime, she resolved to enjoy every moment she could with Sam. Stolen moments, filled with the bittersweet knowledge that happiness was as ephemeral as moonlight.

Although Lucy wasn't in direct contact with Alice, her mother had kept her informed about the progressing wedding plans. The ceremony would be held at the Our Lady of

Good Voyage chapel at Roche Harbor, on the west side of the island. The tiny white chapel, more than a century old, was poised on the shoreline overlooking the harbor. Afterward a reception would be held in the courtyard of McMillin's, a historic waterfront restaurant.

It galled Lucy that even though her mother was lukewarm about Kevin, she was becoming enthused about the wedding itself. Once again, it seemed, Alice could do whatever she wanted and get away with it.

On the day the invitation arrived, Lucy put it on the corner of the kitchen counter and felt bitter and annoyed every time she looked at it.

When Sam arrived to have dinner with her, he noticed the sealed envelope right away.

"What's that?"

Lucy made a face. "The wedding invitation."

"Aren't you going to open it?"

"I'm hoping that if I procrastinate and ignore it, it will somehow disappear." She busied herself at the sink, rinsing lettuce leaves in a colander.

Sam approached her. He settled his hands at her hips and pulled her back against him. And he waited patiently, a steady presence

347

behind her. Ducking his head, he brushed his lips against the edge of her ear.

Lucy turned off the water and blotted her hands on a nearby dishtowel. "I don't know if I can go," she said in a surly tone. "I don't want to. But I have to. I can't see an alternative."

Sam turned her to face him, putting his hands on either side of the counter. "Do you expect it's going to hurt, to see Kevin walk Alice down the aisle?"

"A little. But not because of Kevin. It's all about my sister. I'm still furious about how she betrayed me and how they both lied to me, and now my parents have gone right back into the old pattern and they're paying for everything, which means Alice's never going to change, she is never going to learn —"

"Breathe," Sam reminded her.

Lucy inhaled deeply and let out an explosive sigh. "As much as I hate the idea of going to that wedding, I can't sit at home while it's going on. It'll look like I still have feelings for Kevin, or that I'm jealous or something."

"Want me to take you somewhere?" Sam asked.

Her forehead wrinkled in confusion. "You mean . . . while they're getting married?"

"I'll take you to a nice little resort in Mexico. You can't get too worked up about their wedding day when you're relaxing on a white sand beach, drinking mojitos."

She looked up at him with wide eyes. "You would do that for me?"

Sam smiled. "I'd get something out of it too. Starting with the sight of you in a bikini. Tell me where you want to go. Los Cabos? Baja? Or maybe Belize or Costa Rica —"

"Sam." Lucy patted his chest in an anxious little flutter. "Thank you. I appreciate the offer more than I can say. But there wouldn't be enough mojitos to blank out the fact that it's their wedding day. I'm going to have to go. I don't suppose you —" She broke off, unable to bring herself to ask him.

"You've agreed to be my plus one at Mark and Maggie's wedding," Sam said. "It's only fair if I go with you to your sister's."

"Thank you."

"Don't mention it."

"No . . . really," she said earnestly. "I already feel better, knowing you'll be with me." As soon as the words left her lips, she wanted to take them back, fearing she had revealed too much. Any indication that she needed Sam, depended on him emotionally, would drive him away.

But he took her head in his hands and kissed her. His palm traveled along her spine before settling low on her hips, pressing her against him. Her eyes widened as she felt the pressure of his arousal thickening against her. By now Sam knew far too much about her, where she was most sensitive, what excited her. He kissed her until her eyes closed and she leaned heavily against him, her heart racing. Slow, searing kisses, draining her strength and filling her with sensation.

Lucy turned her face away just enough to breathe, "Upstairs." And he lifted her in his arms.

The following weekend Mark and Maggie were married on the retired ferry in Seattle. The day was warm and beautiful, the waters of Lake Union a glittering shade of sapphire blue. A feeling of serenity pervaded the wedding. There were no signs of nerves or uncertainty, no tension or fuss, nothing but a wholehearted happiness that emanated from both the bride and groom.

Maggie was beautiful in a knee-length slip dress made of textured ivory silk, the V-neck and the straps edged with delicately translucent cream chiffon. She wore her hair in a simple updo adorned with a cluster of white roses. Holly was dressed in a similar cream-colored dress, the skirt puffed out with a tulle underlay. It touched Lucy when, as Mark and Maggie stood with the justice of the peace for the vows, they gestured for Holly to stand with them. After Mark kissed the bride, he bent to kiss Holly as well.

A spectacular buffet was served inside the ferry: a cornucopia of fruit, a selection of brightly colored salads and pasta and rice, fresh Pacific seafood, brioche loaded with cheese, bacon, and chutney, and rows of tarts and vegetable roulades. Instead of the traditional wedding cake, a tower of tiny individual cakes was arranged on Plexiglas tiers. A live jazz quartet played "Embraceable You."

"I'm sorry this wedding didn't happen after Alice's instead of before," Lucy told Sam.

"Why?"

"Because everyone is so happy, and Mark and Maggie are so obviously in love. It's going to make my sister's wedding look even worse by comparison."

Sam laughed and gave her a glass of champagne. He was breathtakingly handsome in a dark suit and a patterned tie, although he wore the clothes with the collar-tugging impatience of a man who didn't like to be bound up in formal clothing. "Offer of a Mexican getaway still stands," he told her.

"Don't tempt me."

After the guests had loaded their plates at the buffet and the tables were filled, Sam stepped forward to make the toast. Mark stood with his arms around both Maggie and Holly.

"If it weren't for public transportation," Sam said, "my brother wouldn't be getting married today. He and Maggie fell in love along the ferry route from Bellingham to Anacortes . . . which brings to mind the old saying that life is a journey. Some people have a natural sense of direction. You could put them in the middle of a foreign country and they could find their way around. My brother is not one of those people." Sam paused as some of the guests started laughing, and his older brother gave him a mock-warning glance. "So when Mark by some miracle manages to end up where he was supposed to be, it's a nice surprise for everyone, including Mark." More laughter from the crowd. "Somehow, even with all the roadblocks and detours and one-way streets, Mark managed to find his way to Maggie." Sam raised his glass. "To Mark and Maggie's journey together. And to Holly, who is loved more than any girl in the whole wide world."

Everyone clapped and hooted, and the band started playing a slow, romantic version of "Fly Me to the Moon." Mark took Maggie in his arms, and the two of them took a turn around the dance floor.

"That was perfect," Lucy whispered to Sam.

"Thanks." He smiled at her. "Don't go anywhere. I'll be right back."

Giving his empty champagne glass to a passing waitress, Sam went to Holly and led her to the dance floor, twirling her, dancing with her feet standing on his, then catching her up in his arms and turning a slow circle.

Lucy's smile turned pensive and distracted as she watched them. In the back of her mind, she was worrying over an e-mail she had received from Alan Spellman, her former professor, that very morning. She hadn't mentioned it to anyone, feeling troubled and conflicted when she should have been nothing but thrilled.

Alan had written that the committee at the Mitchell Art Center had elected to offer her the year-long artist-in-residence grant. He had congratulated her effusively. All she needed to do was sign a document agreeing to the terms and conditions of the grant, and then the official public announcement would be made. *"I couldn't be more pleased,"* he had written. *"You and Mitchell Art Center are a perfect match."*

Lucy had been mildly amused by that phrase. It wasn't lost on her that after all her failed relationships, her perfect match had turned out to be an art program. She was going to spend a year in New York. She would have national recognition. Working with other artists, experimenting with new techniques, giving occasional "design performances" in the art center's public glass lab. She would have her own featured exhibition at the end of the residency. It was the kind of opportunity Lucy had always dreamed of. And nothing stood in her way.

Except Sam.

She had made no promises. Neither had he. The entire point of the arrangement was that either of them could break it off and leave without a backward glance. An offer like the one from Mitchell Art Center wouldn't come her way often, if ever again. And she knew that Sam would never want her to make such a sacrifice on his behalf.

Why, then, was she filled with such melancholy?

Because she wanted more time with Sam. Because their relationship, even with its limitations, had meant a lot to her.

Too much.

Lucy's thoughts returned to the present as she watched Maggie's father claim a dance with his daughter, while Mark went to cut in on Sam and Holly. More couples joined them, dancing to the sweetly yearning music.

Sam returned to Lucy and wordlessly extended his hand.

"I can't dance," Lucy protested with a laugh, gesturing to the Aircast brace on her leg.

A slow smile curved his lips. "We'll fake it."

She went into Sam's arms. She breathed in the scent of him, tanned male skin and cedary sweetness, mingled with the hints of summer wool and starched cotton. Since Lucy couldn't dance in the brace, they merely swayed from side to side, their heads close together.

A tumult gathered inside her, longing tangled with low-level panic. Once she left him, she realized, she could never come back. It would hurt too much, seeing him with other women, watching the path of his future diverge from hers . . . and remembering the summer when they had been lovers. They had come so close to making a rare and wondrous connection, something beyond the physical. But ultimately all their inner defenses had remained intractable. They had remained separate, never reaching the true intimacy that Lucy had always craved. And yet this might be the closest she would ever get.

"Better not to know," her father had said. God help her, she was beginning to understand what he meant.

"What is it?" Sam whispered.

She summoned a quick smile. "Nothing."

But Sam wasn't deceived. "What are you worrying about?"

"My . . . my leg's a little sore," she lied.

His arms tightened around her. "Let's go sit somewhere for a while," he said, and led her from the dance floor.

The next morning, Lucy woke up later than usual, rich sunlight pouring through the bedroom of her condo. With a long, shivering stretch and a yawn, she turned onto her side, and blinked with surprise at the sight of Sam sleeping beside her.

Combing through her recollections of the previous night, she remembered Sam bringing her back home. She had been cheerfully tipsy after one too many glasses of champagne. He had undressed her and put her to bed, and had laughed quietly as she had tried to seduce him.

"It's late, Lucy. You need to sleep."

"You want me," she had crooned. "You do. I can tell." She had loosened the knot of his silk tie, and had used it to pull his head down to hers. After a smoldering kiss, she had succeeded in drawing the tie free of his collar, and she had given it to him triumphantly. "Do something wicked," she said. "Tie me up with this. I dare you." She lifted her good leg and wrapped it around him. "Unless you're too tired."

"I would be dead before I was too tired for that," Sam had informed her, and he'd kept her busy well into the night.

Apparently after those pleasurable exertions, the temptation of sleep had overridden Sam's rule about never staying all night with a woman.

Lucy let her gaze travel over the long, powerful limbs, the sleek expanse of his back and shoulders, the tempting disarray of his hair. His face looked younger in sleep, his mouth relaxed, the thick crescents of his lashes flickering infinitesimally as dream images chased through his mind. Seeing the faint notch gather between his brows, Lucy

357

couldn't stop herself from reaching out to smooth it with a gentle fingertip.

Sam awakened with a quiet sound, disoriented and drowsy. "Lucy," he said in a sleep-roughened voice, reflexively reaching out to gather her close. She snuggled against him, nuzzling into the light mat of hair on his chest.

But in the next moment, she felt the jolt of alarm that went through him.

"What . . . where . . ." Sam's head shot up, and his breath stopped as he recognized his surroundings. "Jesus," she heard him mutter. He sprang out of bed as if it had just burst into flames.

"What's the matter?" Lucy asked, startled by his reaction.

Sam stared at her with an expression of near-horror that she found distinctly unflattering. "I never went home last night. I slept here."

"It's okay. Renfield's at the kennel. Holly is with Mark and Maggie. Nothing to worry about."

But Sam had started to snatch up his discarded clothes. "Why did you let me fall asleep?"

"I fell asleep too," Lucy said defensively. "And I wouldn't have woken you up anyway — you were exhausted, and I didn't mind sharing the bed, so —"

"*I* mind," Sam said forcefully. "I don't do this. I don't stay until morning."

"What are you, a vampire? It's no big deal, Sam. It means nothing."

But he wasn't listening to her. He took his clothes into the bathroom, and in a minute she heard the shower running.

". . . and then he just took off," Lucy said to Justine and Zoë later that morning, "like a scalded dog. He barely said a word to me on the way out. I couldn't tell whether he was pissed off or scared shitless, or both. Probably both."

After Sam had left, Lucy had gone to the inn to see her friends. The three of them sat in the kitchen with mugs of coffee. Lucy wasn't the only one with problems. Zoë's usual sunny disposition was dampened with worry about her grandmother, who was having health problems. Justine had just broken up with Duane, and although she was trying to be nonchalant, it was clear that the situation was difficult for her.

When Lucy had asked what had caused the rift between them, Justine had said evasively, "I, er . . . accidentally scared him."

"How? Did you have to take a pregnancy test or something?"

"God, no." Justine waved her hand in an impatient gesture. "I don't want to talk about my problems. Your problems are way more interesting."

After telling them about Sam's behavior, Lucy leaned her chin in her hand and asked with a scowl, "Why would someone freak out over spending one night in a bed? Why is it that Sam has no problem having sex with me, but the idea of literally *sleeping* with me sends him into a tailspin?"

"Think about what a bed is," Justine said. "The place where you sleep is where you are most vulnerable. You're helpless. You're unconscious. So when two people sleep in one bed in that ultimate state of vulnerability, it's an enormous act of trust. It's a different kind of closeness than sex — but just as powerful."

"And Sam won't let himself be close to anyone," Lucy said, swallowing against the needling pain in her throat. "It's too dangerous for him. Because he and his brothers and sister were hurt repeatedly by the people who were supposed to love them the most."

Justine nodded. "Our parents teach us how to have relationships. They show us how it's done. Kind of hard to rewire yourself after that."

"Maybe you could talk to Sam," Zoë suggested, laying her hand on Lucy's tense arm. "Sometimes if you bring something out into the open —"

"No. I promised myself I wouldn't try to change him or fix him. Sam's responsible for his own problems. And I'm responsible for mine." Lucy wasn't aware of the tears that had slid down her cheeks until Justine handed her a napkin. Sniffling, sighing, she blew her nose and told them about having been awarded the art center grant.

"You're going to take it, right?" Justine asked.

"Yes. I'm leaving a few days after Alice's wedding."

"When are you going to tell Sam?"

"Not until the last minute. I want to make the most of the time we have left. And when I tell him, he'll say I should go, and that he'll miss me . . . but inside he'll be incredibly relieved. Because he can feel it too, this . . . *thing* that's happening to our relationship. We're becoming involved. And it has to stop before it goes too far."

"Why?" Zoë asked softly.

"Because Sam and I both know that he'll hurt me. He'll never be able to say 'I love you' and surrender his heart to someone." She blew her nose again. "That last step is a doozy. It leads to a place he has no intention of going."

"I'm sorry, Lucy," Justine muttered. "I never would have encouraged you to get together with Sam if I'd known it would make you unhappy. I thought you needed some fun."

"It has been fun," Lucy said earnestly, wiping her eyes.

"I can see that," Justine said, and Lucy gave a watery giggle.

As Lucy worked in her studio later that afternoon, she was interrupted by a knock at the door. Setting aside her glass-cutting tools, she reached up to tighten her ponytail as she went to see the visitor.

Sam stood there with a mixed bouquet of flowers, including orange roses, yellow lilies, pink asters, and gerbera daisies.

Lucy's gaze went from his inscrutable face to the vivid bouquet. "Guilt flowers?" she asked, trying to bite back a smile.

"Also guilt candy." Sam gave her a rectangular satin box, weighted with what had to be at least two pounds of premium chocolate. "Along with a sincere apology." Encouraged by her expression, he continued. "It wasn't your fault that I slept with you. And after thinking about it, I've realized I wasn't actually harmed by the experience.

I'm actually glad it happened, because it was the only way I could ever have found out how beautiful you are in the morning."

Lucy laughed, a tide of pink rising over her face. "You give great apologies, Sam."

"Can I take you out to dinner?"

"I would like that. But . . ."

"But?"

"I've been doing some thinking. And I was wondering if we could just have the friendship without the 'benefits.' At least for a few days."

"Of course," Sam said, his gaze searching. Quietly he added, "Can I ask why?"

Lucy went to set the flowers and chocolate on a table. "I just have a few things I'm trying to work out. I need a little personal space. If that changes your mind about dinner, I understand."

For some reason that seemed to annoy him. "No, it does not change my mind about dinner. I" — he paused, casting about for the right words — "want you for more than just sex."

Lucy smiled as she returned to him, a warm and unforced smile that seemed to bemuse him. "Thank you."

They stood facing each other, not quite touching. Lucy suspected they were both grappling with the puzzling contradiction that something was wrong between them, and something was equally right.

Sam stared down at her intently, his gaze causing the hairs on the back of her neck to lift. His features were austere, still, except for the twitch of a muscle in his cheek. The silence became acute, and Lucy fidgeted as she tried to think of a way to break it.

"I want to hold you," Sam said, his voice low.

Flustered, aware of her light blush deepening to crimson, Lucy gave a nervous catch of laughter. But Sam wasn't smiling.

They had shared the most intimate sexual acts possible, had seen each other in every possible stage of dress and undress . . . but at this moment, the simple matter of a casual embrace was positively unnerving. She stepped forward. His arms went around her slowly, as if any sudden move might frighten her. They drew together in cautious increments, curves molding against hard places, limbs fitting just so, her head finding its natural resting spot on his shoulder.

Relaxing fully, Lucy felt every breath, thought, heartbeat adjust to his, a current opening between them. If it was possible for love to be expressed purely between bodies, not in a sexual union but in something equally true and whole, then it was this.

Here. Now.

She lost track of time, standing there with him. In fact, it seemed as if they had slipped outside of time altogether, lost in each other, in this mysterious quintessence they had become together. But eventually Sam pulled away and said something about picking her up at dinnertime. Lucy nodded blindly, gripping the door frame to keep herself upright. Sam left without looking back, walking along the path with the slightly overdone caution of a man who wasn't quite certain on his feet.

When Lucy called Alan Spellman to tell him that she would accept the art center grant, she asked him to delay the announcement until the end of August. By that time, Alice and Kevin would be married, and Lucy would have finished all of her current projects.

She set aside a portion of each day to work on the stained-glass window for the house at Rainshadow Vineyard. It was a complicated and ambitious piece, demanding all her technical skills. Lucy was possessed by the urgency to get every detail right. All her feelings for Sam seemed to pour into the glass as she cut and arranged the pieces in a visual poem. The colors were all natural shades of earth, tree, sky, and moon, glass fused and layered to give it a three-dimensional quality.

After the glass had been shaped, Lucy stretched the lead came using a vise and pliers. She assembled the window carefully, inserting glass pieces into lead channels, then cutting and fitting the lead around them. Once all the interior leading was completed, she would use the U-shaped perimeter came to finish all the outside edges. Next would come the soldering, and the application of cement for waterproofing.

As the window took shape on her worktable, Lucy was aware of a peculiar warmth in the glass, a glow that had nothing to do with heat transferred from soldered metal. One evening as Lucy was closing up shop, she happened to glance at the unfinished window, lying flat on the worktable. The glass glowed with its own incandescence.

Her relationship with Sam had remained platonic since the night he'd slept with her at the condo. Platonic, but not asexual. Sam had done his utmost to seduce her, with sweltering kisses and passionate interludes that made them both feverish with unsatisfied desire. But Lucy was afraid of the very real possibility that if she were to have sex with him now, she would blurt out how much she loved him. The words were there, in her mind, on her lips, most of the time, desperate to be said. Only her sense of self-preservation gave her the strength to refuse Sam. And although he had received her refusals with good grace at first, he was obviously finding it more difficult to stop now.

"When?" Sam had asked after their last session, his breath hot against her mouth, a dangerous flare of heat in his eyes.

"I don't know," Lucy had said weakly, shivering as his hands stroked her back and hips. "Not until I can be sure of myself."

"Let me have you," he had whispered, resting his forehead on hers. "Let me make love to you all night. I want to wake up with you again. Just tell me what you need, Lucy, and I'll do it."

Make love. He had never called it that before. The two words had clamped around her heart like a vise. This was the torture of loving Sam — that he was willing to get so close, but not quite close enough.

And since the thing that she needed most — for him to love her — was impossible, she refused him once again.

Lucy finished the window two days before

Alice's wedding. People had started to arrive from out of town, most of them staying in cottages at the Roche Harbor resort, or taking rooms in the Hotel de Haro. Lucy's parents had arrived that morning, and had spent the day with Alice and the wedding coordinator. Tomorrow Lucy would have lunch with them, but tonight she was going to have dinner with Sam. And she would tell him that she was leaving Friday Harbor.

Her thoughts were interrupted by a knock at the studio door. "Come in," she called. "It's unlocked."

To her surprise, it was Kevin.

Her former boyfriend gave her a vaguely sheepish grin. "Luce. Got a couple of minutes?"

Lucy's heart sank. She hoped this would not be an attempt to make peace, to discuss their shared past and smooth things over so that his wedding day with Alice was untarnished. It was entirely unnecessary. Lucy was over him, thank God, and she was willing to let bygones be bygones. The last thing she wanted to do was to autopsy their past.

"I've got a couple of minutes," she said cautiously, "but I'm kind of busy. And I'm sure you must be even busier with all the wedding stuff going on."

"Actually, there's not all that much for

the groom to do. I just show up when and where they tell me to." Kevin was as handsome as ever, but there was an odd look about him. He had the blank, bemused expression of a man who had just stumbled on the sidewalk and turned to see what invisible object had tripped him up.

As he approached, Lucy found herself pulling spare pieces of paper over her tree window, feeling the need to shield it from his view. She went to the side of the worktable and leaned against it.

"Your brace is off," Kevin remarked. "How's the leg?"

"Great," she said lightly. "I just have to be a little careful with it. No high-impact stuff for a while."

He stopped a little closer to her than she was comfortable with, but she didn't want to back away.

Contemplating him, Lucy wondered how a man she had once been so close to could now seem like a stranger. She had been so certain that she had been in love with him . . . and it had been a good approximation, just as silk flowers could look very much like real ones, or cubic zirconium could sparkle just like diamonds. But their version of love had been a form of playacting. All their love-words and cozy rituals had been a way to cover up the emptiness beneath. She hoped that he had found a deeper, more genuine relationship with Alice. But she doubted it. And that actually made her feel sorry for him.

"How are you?" she asked.

Something in her tone caused Kevin's shoulders to lower. He sighed deeply. "It's like being caught up in a tornado. The color of the flowers, the guest favors with personalized ribbons, the photographer and videographer and all that crap . . . this thing is way more complicated and crazy than it should be. I mean, it's just a wedding."

Lucy brought herself to smile at him. "It'll be over soon. Then you can relax."

Kevin began to pace around the studio, which was familiar territory to him. He had been in there countless times when they had lived together. He had even helped to install the vertical storage racks for the glass. But Lucy felt uneasy as he intruded farther into her studio. Kevin didn't belong there anymore. He no longer had the right to wander through her workplace in such a cavalier way.

"The weirdest part of all of it," he said, inspecting a shelf of finished lampshades, "is that the closer the wedding gets, the more I find myself trying to figure out what happened with us."

Lucy blinked. "You mean . . . you and me?"

"Yes."

"What happened was that you cheated on me."

"I know. But I need to figure out why."

"It doesn't matter why. It's over. You're getting married the day after tomorrow."

"I think if you'd just given me a little more space," Kevin said, "I would never have gone to Alice. I think the relationship with her started as my way of showing you that I needed more room."

Her eyes widened. "Kevin, I really don't want to go there."

He came back to her, standing even closer than before. "I felt like there was something missing between you and me," he said, "and I thought I would find it with Alice. But lately I've realized . . . I had it with you all along. I just didn't see it."

"Don't," Lucy said. "I mean it, Kevin. There's no point."

"I thought you and I were too settled, and life was getting boring. I thought I wanted excitement. I was an idiot, Luce. I was happy with you, and I threw it away. I miss what we had. I —"

"Are you crazy?" she demanded. "You're

having second thoughts about the wedding? *Now,* after all the plans have been made and the out-of-town guests are arriving?"

"I don't love Alice enough to marry her. It's a mistake."

"You made promises to her. You can't back out! Do you get some kind of sadistic thrill out of making women fall in love with you and then dumping them?"

"I've been pushed into this. No one's asked me what I wanted. Don't I get to decide what makes me happy?"

"My God, Kevin. That sounds like something Alice said to me. 'I just want to be happy.' Both of you think happiness is this *thing* you have to chase after, like a child with a shiny toy. It won't happen until you start finding ways to take care of other people instead of ways to please yourself. You need to leave, Kevin. You need to live up to the commitment you've already made to Alice. Take some responsibility. *Then* you might have a shot at being happy."

Judging from Kevin's scowl, he found her advice condescending. There was a mean, raw edge to his tone. "What makes you the fucking expert? You, who's going out with that D-class poser, Sam Nolan. Mr. Wine Expert who comes from a family of trailer-trash drunks and is going to end up just like them —"

"You have to leave now," Lucy said, going to her worktable, putting it between them. In the spectrum of self-pity to rage, he had swung from one extreme to the other.

"I talked him into going out with you. It was a *setup,* Luce . . . I was the one who did it. He owed me a favor. I showed him your picture on my cell phone, and asked him to take you out. It was Alice's idea." Now Kevin was smiling as if at a macabre joke. "To stop you from acting like the victim. Once you were going out with someone, once you moved on, it would get your parents off our case."

"Is that what you came here to tell me?" Lucy shook her head. "I already know that, Kevin. Sam told me about it at the beginning." She reached down to the worktable until her fingers encountered the soothing flat coolness of glass.

"But why did you —"

"It doesn't matter. If you're trying to cause problems between me and Sam, there's no point. I'm leaving the island right after the wedding. I'm going to New York."

Kevin's eyes widened. "Why?"

"I've got an art scholarship. I'm going to start a new life."

As Kevin took in the news, a bright flare

of excitement appeared in his eyes, and his color rose. "I'll go with you."

Lucy stared at him blankly.

"Nothing's keeping me here," he said. "I can move my business — I can do landscaping anywhere. God, Lucy, this is the answer! I know I hurt you, I know I fucked up, but I'll make it up to you. I swear it. We'll start a new life together. We'll leave all this shit behind."

"You are insane," Lucy said, so astonished by his behavior that she could hardly find words. "You're . . . Kevin, you're getting married to my sister —"

"I don't love her. I love you. I never stopped loving you. And I know you feel the same way about me, it hasn't been that long. It was so good between us. I'll make you remember, you have to —" He came to her and gripped her arms.

"Kevin, stop it!"

"I slept with Alice, and you slept with Sam, so we're even. All in the past. Lucy, listen to me —"

"Let go." In the midst of her outrage, she was intensely aware of the glass all around them, panes of glass, shards of it, beads and tiles and frit. And she understood in a fraction of a second that with the force of her will, she could shape it into whatever she

wanted. An image appeared in her mind, and she focused on it.

Kevin gripped her closer, breathing harshly. "It's me, Lucy. It's *me*. I want you back. I want you —"

He broke off with a muffled curse, and Lucy was released with startling suddenness.

A bone-chilling squeak rent the air as a small dark shape darted and flapped around Kevin's head. A bat. "What the *hell* —" Kevin lifted his arms and flailed at the aggressive winged creature. "Where did that come from?"

Lucy looked at her soldering table. Two of the corner pieces she hadn't yet affixed to the rest of the window, cuts of black obsidian glass, curled and wriggled. "Go on," she said, and instantly they flew from the table, another pair of bats joining the attack against Kevin.

The trio of bats sliced through the air with serrated wings, diving until they had driven Kevin to the door. Stumbling and swearing, he went outside. Two of the bats followed him. The third flew to the corner of the room and dropped to the floor, scuttling across the cement surface.

Taking a deep breath, Lucy went to the window and opened it. The sun was low, rolling toward twilight, the air weighted with the lingering heat of the day.

"Thank you," Lucy said, standing back from the window. "There you go." After a moment the bat took flight, slipping through the open window, disappearing into the sky.

TWENTY

"You're going to have to clear out soon," Sam said, lowering to his haunches and watching as Alex worked underneath a tiny staircase that led from the second floor to the central cupola of the house. Alex had scraped and cleaned every crevice beneath the rickety staircase, and was now in the midst of pounding shims into the edges of all the treads and risers. By the time his brother was finished, the staircase would be solid enough to support an elephant.

"Why's that?" Alex asked, pausing in his hammering.

"Lucy's coming over for dinner."

"Give me ten minutes, I'll be finished with this."

"Thanks." Sam contemplated his brother with a frown, wondering what to say to him, how to help him.

Alex was behaving strangely these days, slinking around like a nervous cat. Sam and

Mark had both hoped that getting through the divorce would have provided some kind of relief to Alex, but instead he was going downhill. He was thin and haggard-looking, with dark circles draped under his eyes like funeral swags. It was a testament to Alex's genetic blessings that, even emaciated and exhausted, he was still strikingly handsome. At Mark's wedding he had stayed in the corner, drinking, and women still hadn't been able to leave him alone.

"Al," Sam said, "you're not getting into bad shit, are you?"

The hammering stopped again. "I'm not doing drugs, if that's what you're asking."

"You look like hell."

"I'm fine. Never been better."

Sam gave him a dubious glance. "Good to hear."

At the sound of the doorbell, Sam went downstairs to see who it was.

He opened the front door to discover that Lucy had arrived early. Instantly he knew that something was wrong — she looked the way someone did when a death had occurred. "Lucy?" He reached for her automatically, and she swayed back. Recoiling from him.

Sam was mystified, staring at her alertly.

Lucy's mouth looked dry and ravaged, as

if she'd been biting it. And then she forced herself to smile. "I have something to tell you. Please don't interrupt, or I won't be able to get through it. It's great news, actually."

Sam was so distracted by Lucy's counterfeit cheerfulness, and the obvious misery beneath, that it was hard to take in what she was telling him. Something about an artist grant or program . . . something about an art center in New York. The Mitchell Art Center. She was going to accept. It was a prestigious grant — the kind of opportunity she had worked for her entire life. It would last a year. She probably wouldn't come back to the island afterward.

Then she fell silent and looked at him, waiting for his response.

Sam groped for words. "That's great news," he managed. "Congratulations."

Lucy nodded, wearing a smile that looked like it had been tacked on with pins. He stepped forward to embrace her, and she let him for just a moment, but all her muscles were knotted and stiff. It was like putting his arms around a cold marble statue.

"I couldn't turn it down," she said against his shoulder. "A chance like this . . ."

"Yeah." Sam let go of her. "You should do it. Definitely."

He continued to stare at her, trying to wrap his brain around the fact that Lucy was leaving him. Lucy was leaving. The phrase filled him with a numb, blank sensation that he guessed was relief.

Yes. It was time. Their relationship had started to get tricky. Always best to cut things off when they were still good.

"If you need me to help you put your stuff in storage —" he began.

"No, everything's under control." Lucy's eyes had turned wet even though she was still smiling. She stunned him by saying, "It's easier if I don't see you or talk to you from now on. I need a clean break."

"Alice's wedding —"

"I don't think there'll be a wedding. Which is good, for Alice's sake. Marriage is hard enough for people who actually love each other. I don't think she and Kevin had a chance. I don't think —" She broke off and let out a shivering breath.

As Lucy stood there with tears glittering in her eyes, Sam was gripped by an unfamiliar feeling, the worst feeling he'd had in his adult life. Sharper than fear, more painful than grief, emptier than loneliness. It was what he imagined an ice pick in the chest might feel like.

"I don't love you," Lucy said with a wobbly smile. At his silence, she said, "Tell me you feel the same way."

Their familiar ritual. Sam had to clear his throat before he could bring himself to speak. "I don't love you too."

Lucy continued to smile and gave a satisfied nod. "I kept my promise. No one's been hurt. Good-bye, Sam." She turned and went down the front steps, favoring her right leg.

Sam stood on the front porch, watching as Lucy drove away. Equal parts of panic and angry wonderment engulfed him.

What the hell had just happened?

Slowly he made his way back inside the house. Alex was sitting at the bottom of the main staircase, patting Renfield, who was at his feet.

"What's going on?" Alex asked.

Sam sat beside him and told him everything, hearing his own voice as if it came from outside himself. "Not sure what to do now," he said gruffly.

"Forget her and move on," Alec said prosaically. "That's what you always do, right?"

"Yeah. But it never feels like this." Sam dragged his hand through his hair until it stood in wild tufts. He felt physically ill, nauseous. Like his veins were filled with poison. He ached in every muscle. "I think

I'm coming down with something."

"Maybe you need a drink."

"If I start that right now," Sam said roughly, "I may never stop. So do me a favor and don't say that again."

A short silence followed. "Since you're already in a shitty mood," Alex ventured, "I have something to tell you."

"What?" Sam asked irritably.

"I need to move in with you next week."

"What?" Sam asked again, in an entirely different tone.

"Just for a couple of months. I'm low on cash, and Darcy got the house as part of the settlement. She wants me out of there while she tries to sell it."

"Christ," Sam muttered. "I just got rid of Mark."

Alex gave him a disquieting glance, a troubling shadow in his eyes. "I have to stay here, Sam. I don't think it'll be long. I can't explain the reason why." He hesitated, and managed to say the word he'd used only a handful of times in his entire life. "Please."

Sam nodded, chilled by the thought that the last time he'd seen that exact look in someone's eyes, the pupils black as midnight, the wide staring bleakness of a lost soul, was when he'd seen his father just before he died.

■ ■ ■ ■

Unable to sleep, Lucy worked in her studio for most of the night, finishing the stained-glass window. She wasn't aware of the passing hours, only noticed that the sky was lightening and the early-morning bustle of Friday Harbor was beginning. The tree window was gleaming and flat and still, but every time she put her fingertips to it, she felt a subtle vitality coming off the glass.

Feeling drained but resolute, Lucy walked to her condo and took a long shower. It was the day before Alice's wedding. Tonight the rehearsal dinner would take place. She wondered if Kevin had talked to Alice or broken up with her, or had kept silent about his second thoughts.

Lucy was actually too tired to care one way or the other. She wrapped her wet hair in a turban, put on some comfortably aged flannel pants and a thin stretchy tank top, and crawled into bed.

Just as she was beginning to sink into a deep sleep, the phone rang.

Lucy groped for the phone. "Hello?"

"Lucy." It was her mother's brittle voice. "Are you still asleep? I hoped Alice was with you."

"Why would she be with me?" Lucy asked around a yawn, rubbing her sore eyes.

"No one knows where she is. I got a call from her just a little while ago. Kevin's gone."

"Gone," Lucy repeated hazily.

"He took the first flight out this morning. That asshole changed the plane tickets that we bought for their honeymoon — he's going to West Palm by himself. Alice was in hysterics. She's not at their house, and she won't answer her phone. I don't know where she is, or even how to start looking for her. Some of the out-of-town guests are already here, and more are getting in today. It's too late to cancel the flowers or the food. That little bastard — why did he have to wait until the last minute to do this? But the important thing is Alice. I don't want her to do something . . . dramatic."

Painfully Lucy sat up and staggered out of bed. "I'll find her."

"Do you need Dad to come with you? He's dying for something to do."

"No, no . . . I'll handle it by myself. I'll call you when I find out something."

After she hung up, Lucy pulled her hair into a ponytail, dressed in jeans and a T-shirt, and fumbled with the coffee machine until she managed to produce a pot of inky black liquid. It was too strong — she hadn't measured properly. Even a heavy dose of half-and-half didn't lighten the color. She grimaced and drank it like medicine.

Picking up the phone, she dialed Alice's number, preparing to leave a message. She was almost startled when Alice answered.

"Hi."

Lucy opened and closed her mouth, wanting to say ten different things at once. She finally settled with an abrupt, "Where are you?"

"The McMillin mausoleum." Alice's voice was raw.

"Stay there."

"Don't bring anyone."

"I won't. Just stay there."

"All right."

"Promise me."

"I promise."

The mausoleum, named Afterglow Vista, was one of the most beautiful spots on the island. It was located in the woods north of Roche Harbor. The founder of a hugely successful lime and cement company, John McMillin, had designed the monument himself. It was a massive columned structure, Masonic in its heavy use of symbolism. Towering pillars circled a stone table and seven stone chairs. One of the columns had deliberately been left unfinished, beside the empty space where an eighth chair should have been positioned. According to local rumor, visiting spirits from nearby graves had been seen sitting at the table after midnight.

Unfortunately for Lucy, the forested trail leading to Afterglow Vista was approximately a half-mile long. She walked gingerly, hoping she wasn't doing any damage to her recently healed tendons. After passing through a little graveyard with many of the headstones surrounded by tiny fences, she saw the mausoleum.

Alice was sitting on the winding steps, dressed in jeans and a Henley shirt. She cradled a mound of foamy white fabric — some kind of tulle or chiffon — in her lap.

Lucy didn't want to feel sorry for her sister. But Alice's face was wretched, and she looked all of about twelve years old.

Hobbling to her — Lucy's leg was beginning to hurt — she sat beside Alice on the chilled stone steps. The forest was quiet but not at all silent, the air filled with rustling of leaves, chitters of small birds, flaps of wings, droning of insects.

"What is that?" Lucy asked after a while,

looking at the white fabric on Alice's lap.

"Veil." Alice showed her the pearl-studded headband the tulle was attached to.

"It's pretty."

Alice turned to her, sniffling, and gripped the sleeve of Lucy's shirt with both hands as a small child might. "Kevin doesn't love me," she whispered.

"He doesn't love anyone," Lucy said, putting an arm around her.

Another pained whisper. "You think I deserve this."

"No."

"You hate me."

"No." Lucy turned enough to put her forehead against her sister's.

"I'm fucked up."

"You'll be fine."

"I don't know why I did it. Any of it. I shouldn't have taken him away from you."

"You couldn't have. If he'd really been mine, no one could have."

"I'm so sad. So s-sorry."

"It's okay."

Alice was quiet for a long time, her tears seeping through the fabric of Lucy's sleeve. "I couldn't do anything. Mom and Dad . . . they never let me try anything. I felt useless. Like a failure."

"You mean when we were growing up."

Alice nodded. "And then I got used to having everything done for me. If something got hard, I gave up and someone always finished it for me."

Lucy realized that every time she and her parents had stepped in to take care of Alice, they had given her the message that she couldn't do it for herself.

"I've always been jealous of you," Alice continued, "because you could do anything you wanted. You're not afraid of things. You don't need anyone to take care of you."

"Alice," Lucy said, "you don't need Mom and Dad's permission to take charge of your own life. Find something you want to do, and don't give up on it. You can start tomorrow."

"And then I'll fall flat on my face," Alice said dully.

"Yes. And after you fall, you'll pick yourself up off the ground, and stand on your own two feet without anyone helping you . . . and that's when you'll know you can take care of yourself."

"Oh, bite me," Alice said, and Lucy smiled and hugged her.

Twenty-One

Everyone on the island, including Sam's vineyard crew, had heard about the cancellation of Kevin and Alice's wedding, and all the subsequent fallout. Everyone was talking about it. The only reason Sam had listened to the gossip was in hopes of catching any little crumb of information about Lucy. But her name was seldom mentioned. He'd heard that the Marinns had gone ahead and given the rehearsal dinner, and the next day they had held the reception that had been planned for after the wedding. There had been music and food and drinking. Sam had also heard that the Marinns were considering suing Kevin for at least part of the expenses, including the plane ticket he'd used to go on his self-bestowed vacation.

It had been three days since Lucy had visited Rainshadow. Mark, Maggie, and Holly had just come back from the honeymoon, and Sam and Alex had helped to move them into their new place, a remodeled three-bedroom farmhouse with a pond.

When Sam couldn't stand it any longer, he called Lucy and left a short message, asking if he could talk to her. She didn't return the call.

Sam was at wit's end. He couldn't eat or sleep. Not thinking about Lucy took more energy than thinking about her.

Mark had talked to him at length about the situation. "This Mitchell Art Center thing sounds like a big deal."

"It's as prestigious as hell."

"So you don't want to ask her to turn it down."

"No. I'd never want Lucy to make that kind of sacrifice. In fact, I'm glad she's going. It's good for both of us."

Mark had given him a sardonic glance. "How exactly is it good for you?"

"I don't do commitment."

"Why?"

"Because I *can't*," Sam had snapped. "I'm not like you."

"You're exactly like me, idiot. Trying like hell to avoid a repeat of what we went through growing up. Do you think it was easy for me, admitting that I was in love with Maggie? Asking her to marry me?"

"No."

"Well, it was." Mark smiled at Sam's baffled expression. "Find the right person, Sam, and the most difficult thing in the world becomes the easiest thing in the world. I had the same problems as you. No escape from that, in the Nolan family. But I'll tell you this — there's no way I could let Maggie go without at least telling her I loved her. And once I did that . . . I had no choice but to hold my breath, and take the leap."

Approximately eighty-five and a half hours after Sam had last seen Lucy — not that he was counting — a delivery was made to the house at Rainshadow Vineyard. A couple of guys with a pickup truck carefully unloaded a large flat object and brought it up the front steps. Coming in from the vineyard, Sam reached the house just as the men drove off. Alex was in the entrance hall, staring down at the partially uncrated object.

It was the tree window.

"Is there a note with it?" Sam asked.

"Nope."

"Did the delivery guys say anything?"

"Only that it was going to be a bitch to install." Alex lowered to his haunches, looking at the window. "Look at this thing. I expected something kind of flowery and Victorian. Not this."

The window was strong and bold and delicate, layers of glass fused in natural colors and variegated textures. The tree trunk and branches, made of lead, had been incorporated into the window in a way Sam had never seen before. The moon seemed to glow as if from its own light source.

Alex stood and reached for the phone in his back pocket. "I'm going to call some of my guys to help me put the window in. Today if possible."

"I don't know," Sam said.

"About what?"

"I don't know if I want to install it."

Alex responded with an impatient scowl. "Don't give me that crap. This window *has* to go into this house. The place needs it. There was one just like it a long time ago."

Sam gave him a quizzical glance. "How do you know that?"

Alex's face went expressionless. "I just meant that it seems right for the place." He walked away, dialing his phone. "I'll take care of it."

Thanks to the accuracy of Lucy's measurements, Alex and his workmen were able to fit the stained-glass window against the existing panel, and seal the edges with clear silicone caulking. By late afternoon, the majority of the installation had been completed. After the silicone had had twenty-four hours to cure, they would finish the window with wood trim around the edges.

"Just installed the window," Sam texted Lucy. *"You should come see it."*

No reply.

Usually Sam was slow to emerge from sleep, but this morning his eyes flipped open and he sat bolt upright. He felt annoyed, uneasy, like he was about to jump out of his skin. Trudging into the bathroom, he shaved and took a shower. A routine check in the mirror revealed a taut, bitter expression that didn't seem to belong to him, but was oddly familiar. Then he realized it was the expression Alex usually wore.

He dressed in jeans and a black T-shirt, and headed down to the kitchen for coffee and breakfast. On the way, however, he saw the stained-glass window at the second-floor landing, and he went still.

The window had changed. The glass sky was now flushed with pink and apricot dawn, the dark branches covered with luxuriant green leaves. The restrained hues of the window had given way to radiant color. Brilliant colors had infused the glass, the sight entering his eyes like visual music, reaching a place in him where deepest instinct resided. It was more than beauty, the effect of this window. It was a form of truth that he couldn't deny. Truth that broke apart his defenses, and left him blinking as if he'd just come from a dark room into sunlight.

Slowly Sam went outside into the quiet vineyard, to see what kind of magic Lucy had made for him. The air was perfumed from growing things, and salted by the ocean. To Sam's heightened senses, the vines were greener than usual, the soil richer. Before his eyes, the sky turned a shade of blue so radiant that he had to squint against the sting of tears. The land was idealized as a painter might have conceived it, except that it was real, art you could walk through and touch and taste.

Something was at work in the vineyard . . . some force of nature or enchantment, a wordless language that summoned the vines in a canticle of respiration.

Dreamlike, Sam wandered to the transplanted vine that no one had been able to identify. He felt its energy before he even touched it, the trunk and vines thrumming, flourishing with life. He sensed how deeply the rootstock had delved into the ground, anchoring the plant until nothing could have moved it. Passing his hands across the leaves, he felt them whispering to him, felt the vine's secret being absorbed into his skin. Picking one of the blue-black grapes, Sam put it between his teeth and bit down. The flavor was deep and complex, evoking the bittersweet shallows of the past, then rolling into the rich dark mystery of things still just beyond his reach.

Hearing the sounds of an approaching car, he turned to see Alex's BMW proceeding along the drive. Alex never came to the house this early. Slowing, Alex rolled down the car window and asked, "Want a lift?"

In a trance, Sam shook his head and motioned for him to go on. He couldn't explain what had happened, couldn't begin to find words . . . and Alex would discover it soon enough.

By the time Sam made it back to the house, Alex had already reached the second-floor landing.

Sam went upstairs and found his brother staring fixedly at the window. There was no wonder in his face, only the baffled tension of a man who related to the world on his own visceral and literal terms. Alex wanted an explanation when there clearly was none.

Or at least none that he would accept.

"What did you do to it?" Alex asked.

"Nothing."

"How did —"

"I don't know."

They both gazed at the stained glass, which had continued to alter as Sam had walked outside . . . the burnt-ash moon had disappeared, and the glass sky had turned gold and blue, intoxicated with sun. The leaves were even more profuse, emeralds embedded in spindrifts that nearly obscured the branches.

"What does it mean?" Alex wondered aloud.

Emotion made visible, Lucy had once said about her stained glass.

This, Sam thought, was love made visible. All of it. The vineyard, the house, the window, the vine.

The realization was so simple that many people would dismiss it as being beneath more sophisticated minds. Only those with some remnant potential for wonder would understand. Love was the secret behind everything . . . love was what made vineyards grow and filled the spaces between the stars, and fixed the ground beneath his feet. It didn't matter if you acknowledged it or not. You couldn't stop the motion of the earth or hold back the ocean tides, or break the pull of the moon. You couldn't stop the rain or pull a shade over the sun. And one human heart was no less a force than any of the rest.

The past had always surrounded him like the bars of a prison cell, and he'd never understood that he'd had the power to walk out at any time. He'd not only suffered the consequences of his parents' sins, he had voluntarily carried them with him. But why should he spend the rest of his life being weighted down by fears, hurts, secrets, when if he *just let go,* he would be free to reach for what he wanted most? He could have Lucy. He could love her madly, joyfully, without limit.

All he had to do was hold his breath and take the leap.

Without a word to his brother, Sam bounded downstairs and grabbed the keys to his truck.

Both the condo and Lucy's studio were ominously still and dark, the way a place looked when it would be vacant for a long time.

A cold feeling settled into Sam's chest and at the back of his neck. The urgency that had driven him to town had gathered in a desperate knot that constricted his heart.

Lucy couldn't have left already. It was too soon.

On impulse Sam went to Artist's Point, looking for Justine. As he entered the inn, comforting breakfast smells wafted around him, hot flour-dusted biscuits, pastries, applewood-smoked bacon, fried eggs.

Justine was in the dining room, carrying a stack of used plates and flatware. She smiled when she saw him. "Hi, Sam."

"Can I talk to you a minute?"

"Sure." After carrying the plates to the kitchen, Justine returned and went with him to a corner of the reception area. "How's it going?"

Sam shook his head impatiently. "I'm looking for Lucy. She wasn't at the condo or the studio. I was wondering if you had any idea where she was."

"She's gone to New York," Justine said.

"It's too soon," Sam said tersely. "It wasn't supposed to be until tomorrow."

"I know, but her professor called, and they wanted her there for a meeting and some big party —"

"When did she leave?"

"I just dropped her off at the airport a little while ago. She's taking the eight o'clock flight."

Sam yanked out his phone and looked at the time. Seven-fifty. "Thanks."

"Sam, it's too late for you to —"

But he was out of the inn before Justine could finish.

Leaping into the truck, he drove toward the airport and called Lucy on his cell phone. The call went to an automatic voice mail box. Swearing, Sam pulled over to the side of the road and texted her.

don't leave

He pulled the truck back onto the road and floored it, while the words ran through his mind in a constant loop.

Don't leave. Don't leave.

The Roy Franklin Airport, named after the World War II fighter pilot who had founded it, was located on the west side of Friday Harbor. Both scheduled and chartered flights took off from the airport's single runway. Passengers and visitors who were obliged to wait for one reason or another could usually be found in Ernie's café, a blue-painted coffee shop right next to the airfield.

Sam parked beside the terminal and went to the door in ground-eating strides. But before he had even made it inside, the snarl of a Cessna turbine engine filled the air. Shading his eyes, Sam looked up at the yellow and white nine-passenger plane, climbing high and fast on its way to Seattle.

Lucy was gone.

It hurt more than he'd expected to watch the plane carrying her away from him. It hurt in a way that made him want to go to some dark corner and not think or talk or move.

Making his way to the terminal building, Sam propped himself beside the doorway. He tried to straighten out his thoughts, tried to think of what to do next. His eyes were burning. He closed them for a moment, letting the fluids soothe away the sting.

The terminal door opened, followed by the rattle of suitcase wheels. Through a blur, he saw the small form of a woman, and his heart stopped. He said her name on a breath.

Lucy turned to face him.

For a moment Sam thought she was a figment of his imagination, conjured from the magnitude of his need to see her. In the past few minutes, he'd gone through lifetimes.

Reaching her in three strides, Sam hauled her against him, the impact spinning them both. Before Lucy could say a word, he covered her mouth with his, devouring every word and breath until the suitcase handle dropped from her fingers and clattered to the pavement.

Her mouth yielded and clung to his, her arms lifting around his neck. She fit against him as if she'd been made for him, so perfectly close, and still separate from him. He wanted to pull her inside himself, to make them one being. He kissed her harder, almost savagely, until she turned her face away with a gasp. Her fingers came to his nape, stroking as if to soothe him.

Sam took her face in hands that weren't quite steady. Her cheeks were fever-colored, her eyes hazed with bewilderment. "Why aren't you on the plane?" he asked hoarsely.

Lucy blinked. "You . . . you texted me."

"And that was enough?" Sliding his arms around her, Sam asked huskily, "You got off the plane because of two words?"

She looked at him in a way no one ever had before, her eyes lit with brilliant tenderness. "They were the right two words."

"I love you," Sam said, and set his mouth against hers, and broke off the kiss because he had to say it again. "I love you."

Lucy's trembling fingers came to his lips, caressing them gently. "Are you sure? How do you know it's not just about sex?"

"It is about sex . . . sex with your mind, sex with your soul, sex with the color of your eyes, the smell of your skin. I want to sleep in your bed. I want you to be the first thing I see every morning and the last thing I see at night. I love you the way I never thought I could love anyone."

Her eyes flooded. "I love you too, Sam. I didn't want to leave you, but —"

"Wait. Let me say this first . . . I'll wait for you. There's no choice for me. I can wait forever. You don't have to give up New York. I'll do whatever's necessary to make it work. Long-distance phone calls, cyber-whatever. I want you to have your dream. I don't want you to give it up or have less of a life because of me."

She smiled through her tears. "But you're part of my dream."

Sam wrapped his arms around her, and rested his cheek on her hair. "It doesn't matter where you go now," he murmured. "No matter what, we're together. A binary star can have a distant orbit, but it's still held together by gravity."

Lucy's chuckle was muffled in his shirt. "Geek love talk."

"Get used to it," he told her, stealing a hard kiss. He glanced at the terminal. "You want to go in and reschedule your flight?"

Lucy shook her head decisively. "I'm staying here. I'm going to turn down the art grant. I can do my glasswork here just as easily as I can there."

"No you're not. You're going to New York, to become the artist you were meant to be. And I'm going to spend a fortune in plane tickets to see you as often as possible. And at the end of the year, you'll come back here and marry me."

Lucy looked up at him with round eyes. "Marry you," she said faintly.

"The formal proposal comes later," Sam said. "I just wanted you to be aware of my honorable intentions."

"But . . . you don't believe in marriage . . ."

"I changed my mind. I figured out the flaw in my reasoning. I told you it was more romantic not to get married, because then you just stay with each other for the good times. But I was wrong. It only means something when you stay during the bad times. For better or worse."

Lucy pulled his head down for another kiss. It was a kiss about trust and surrender . . . a kiss about wine and stars and magic . . . a kiss about waking up safe in a lover's arms as the morning climbed past the flight of eagles and the sun unraveled silver ribbons across False Bay.

"We'll talk about New York later," Lucy said when their lips had parted. "I'm still not sure I'm going. I'm not even sure that I need to, now. Art can happen anywhere." Her eyes sparkled as if she were pondering some secret knowledge. "But right now . . . would you take me to Rainshadow Road?"

For an answer, Sam picked up her suitcase and put his arm around her as they walked to the truck. "Something happened to that window you made for me," he told her after a moment. "The vineyard is changing. Everything is changing."

Lucy smiled, seeming not at all surprised. "Tell me."

"You have to see it for yourself."

And he took her home, on the first of many roads they would travel together.

Epilogue

A hummingbird's heart couldn't have beat any faster than Lucy's as the taxi turned onto False Bay Drive and headed toward Rainshadow Road.

During the past year she had made the journey between New York and Friday Harbor countless times, and Sam had traveled to see her just as often. But this trip, unlike all the others, wouldn't end in good-bye.

Lucy had returned to the island two days earlier than she had originally planned. After a year of living apart, she couldn't stay away from Sam any longer.

They had mastered the art of the long-distance relationship. They had lived by the calendar, scheduling calls and plane flights. They had sent cards, texted, e-mailed, and Skyped. "Do you think we'll talk this much when we're actually together in person?" Lucy had asked, and Sam's reply had been a distinctly lecherous "No."

If there was such a thing as changing together while living apart, Lucy thought they had done it. And the effort required in maintaining a long-distance relationship had made her realize that too many people took the time they spent with someone they loved for granted. Every precious minute together was something they had earned.

During her time as the Mitchell Art Center's artist in residence, Lucy had joined other artists to create conceptual works with techniques such as vitreous painting — applying a mixture of ground glass and pigment to the glass — or layering mixed-media pieces with glass fragments. Her main work, of course, was with stained-glass windows, using natural motifs and experimenting with ways to manipulate color with light and refraction. A respected art critic had written that Lucy's stained-glass work was a "revelation of light, animating glass images with exhilarating color and tangible energy." Near the end of her tenure, Lucy had been offered commissions to create stained-glass windows for public buildings and churches, and she had even received a request to design theater sets and costumes for a production of the Pacific Northwest Ballet.

In the meantime, Sam's vineyard had flourished to the point that he had reached his target yield of two tons of grapes per acre at least a year earlier than he had expected. The fruit quality, he had told Lucy, promised to be even better than he could have hoped for. Later in the summer, Rainshadow Vineyard would hold its first on-site bottling process.

"Nice place," the taxi driver commented as they turned onto Rainshadow Road and approached the vineyard lit with orange and gold.

"Yes, it is," Lucy murmured, drinking in the sight of the sunset-colored house, the gables and balustrades gilded with light, the shrub roses and white hydrangeas spilling over with profusions of blossoms. And the vineyard rows, lush with fruit. The air rushing through the car windows was sweet and cool, ocean breezes filtering through healthy young vines.

Although Lucy could have asked Justine or Zoë to pick her up at the airport, she hadn't wanted to spend time talking with anyone — she wanted to see Sam as soon as possible.

Of course, she thought with a self-deprecating grin, since Sam wasn't expecting her, he might not have been home.

However, as they pulled up to the house, she saw Sam's familiar form as he walked back from the vineyard with a couple of his crew. A smile tugged at her lips as Sam saw the taxi and went still.

By the time the vehicle stopped, Sam had already reached it and wrenched open the door. Before Lucy could say a word he had pulled her from the taxi. He was sweaty from working outside, all testosterone and masculine heat as his mouth covered hers in a devouring kiss. In the past few weeks he had put on a few pounds of new muscle, and his tan was so deep that his blue-green eyes were startlingly vivid by contrast.

"You're early," Sam said, kissing her cheeks and chin and the tip of her nose.

"You're scratchy," Lucy replied with a breathless laugh, setting her palm against his bristly face.

"I was going to get cleaned up for you," Sam said.

"I'll help you shower." Standing on her toes, Lucy said near his ear, "I'll even take care of your hard-to-reach places."

Sam let go of her just long enough to pay the cabdriver. In another few minutes, he had said good-bye to his grinning crew and informed them not to show up before noon the next day.

After carrying Lucy's suitcase into the house, Sam took her hand in his and led her upstairs. "Any particular reason you're here two days early?"

"I managed to wind things up and pack a little faster than I'd expected. And then when I called the airline about changing my flight, they waived the change fee because I told them it was an emergency."

"What emergency?"

"I told them my boyfriend had promised to propose to me as soon as I reached Friday Harbor."

"That's not an emergency," he said.

"An emergency is an occasion requiring immediate action," she informed him.

Sam paused at the second landing and kissed her again.

"So are you going to?" Lucy persisted.

"Propose to you?" His lips curved against hers. "Not before I take a shower."

In the early hours of the morning Lucy awakened with her head nestled against a hard masculine shoulder, her nose tickled by the light mat of hair on his chest. Sam's warm hands drifted over her, raising goose-flesh.

"Lucy," he whispered, "I don't think I can let you leave me again. You'll have to take me with you."

"I'm not leaving," she whispered back. Her palm slid to the center of his chest, the morning light catching the sparkle of an engagement ring and causing brilliant flecks to dance on the wall. "I know where I belong."

As she rested against Sam, his heartbeat strong and steady beneath her hand, she felt as if they were a pair of far-flung stars, caught in each other's orbit by a force stronger than luck or fate or even love. There was no word for it, this feeling . . . but there should have been.

As Lucy lay there steeped in happiness, pondering nameless wonders, the panes of a nearby window slowly pulled from their wooden framing, their edges curling, the glass turning luminous blue.

And if any passersby had happened to glance in the direction of the bay at that early hour, they would have seen a stream of butterflies dancing into the sky, from the white Victorian house at the end of Rain-shadow Road.

DISCUSSION QUESTIONS

1. How can adult siblings move past the old conflicts of their shared childhood? Is there anything parents can do to help prevent rivalry between their children, or is it inevitable?

2. Is there any acceptable way for someone to have a relationship with one person and then have a relationship with that person's sibling? What about two best friends? What about two acquaintances? Where would you draw the line?

3. Justine advises Lucy to "lower her standards" in order to find a decent guy to go out with. Do you know anyone whose standards are too high? Is there any merit in "settling" for someone?

4. According to Sam, "sex is the canary in

the coal mine" of a relationship — do you agree?

5. Sam and Mark are both concerned about their brother Alex's drinking. How would you handle it if you felt that a close friend or sibling was drinking too much?

6. Are there any benefits to a "no strings attached" relationship, or is it always a bad idea?

7. Lucy's parents, Phillip and Cherise Marinn, have experienced a strain in their marriage because the memory of his first wife is still between them. What is the difference between "moving on" and "letting go" for a widow or widower?

8. Lucy tells Kevin that he and Alice seem to believe "happiness is this thing you have to chase after, like a child with a shiny toy." What is true happiness, and how do you achieve it?

9. Many women struggle with choices between career and personal life. Have you ever given up a career opportunity for the sake of a personal relationship or a family member? Did you regret your

choice, or was it worth it?

10. Do you feel that every person in this novel got what he or she deserved? Why, or why not?

11. What would you love to see happen in subsequent Friday Harbor novels?

ABOUT THE AUTHOR

Lisa Kleypas is the award-winning author of 21 novels. Her books are published in fourteen languages and are bestsellers all over the world. She lives in Washington State with her husband and two children.

The employees of Thorndike Press hope you have enjoyed this Large Print book. All our Thorndike, Wheeler, and Kennebec Large Print titles are designed for easy reading, and all our books are made to last. Other Thorndike Press Large Print books are available at your library, through selected bookstores, or directly from us.

For information about titles, please call:
(800) 223-1244

or visit our Web site at:
http://gale.cengage.com/thorndike

To share your comments, please write:
Publisher
Thorndike Press
10 Water St., Suite 310
Waterville, ME 04901